M000209051

THE SWORD

& SHIELD

EMMA KHOURY

All rights reserved. No part of this book may be reproduced, stored in a retrieval system or transmitted in any form or by any means without the prior written permission of the publishers, except by a reviewer who may quote brief passages in a review to be printed in a newspaper, magazine or journal.

9781935355991

Second printing

This is a work of fiction. Names, characters, businesses, places, events, and incidents are either the products of the author's imagination or used in a fictitious manner. Any resemblance to actual persons, living or dead, or actual events is purely coincidental.

The Sword and Shield is printed in Andalus

Thank you to everyone who has supported and encouraged me throughout my journey.

THE SWORD
& SHIELD

CONTENTS

1

RAINY DAYS

If the rain continued much longer, Ezra was going to kill the client himself and write this job off as a wash. Alacia, a large country by the sea, had accrued a great deal of fame for its persistent, annual rainy season. Ezra wiped cold droplets of water from his brow, the scarf atop his head doing nothing to prevent the water as it was already sopping wet. His whole body cramped from his prolonged position surveilling from the roof, his clothing thoroughly soaked. After three weeks of long-range, outdoor surveillance, two hours sleep a night, and weather that could drown a mermaid, he was more than ready to go home for some chamomile tea and a long, well-deserved nap.

Ezra perked up a bit, hearing the jingle of bells that accompanied booby traps going off at the edge of the forest. Another round of assassins. Hopefully, the last group if his client's information could be trusted. It would have been so much easier to go after the man actually hiring them, but no.

Politics.

He hated that word.

Would that the client had only let him kill the man in charge, Ezra could have been done and on to another job. Possibly finished with another job by now. But there were supposedly important reasons that his plan wasn't viable. Stupid reasons, no doubt. The lord he had been hired to protect tried to explain it to him, but Ezra stopped listening after a while. Life could be so much simpler if people didn't let social niceties weigh them down.

Another set of bells rang in the distance. He crawled to a more defensible place on the roof. Based on where the bells were sounding, two people were dead. Or, at the very least, out of commission for the time being. Four dark figures emerged from the tree line, hardly visible given the rain and their dark clothing. But he saw them. The group moved in a 'V' formation, running in tandem. Through the gloom, he saw that their faces were covered.

Ezra sighed, pulled his longbow up, and loosed the first bolt. It caught the first assassin in the stomach, knocking him back. No one stopped, a smart decision irrelevant as it may be. He shot the next in the neck—easier with a closer target. The force of it tore right through, nearly decapitating the figure, and kept going, sticking in the ground several meters away. The other two had taken cover behind trees that bordered the garden. He had been unable to place traps on the actual property due to the fact that the client and his family were still there. It had made the job more complicated, but not impossible.

Not that it mattered. He stood, shaking the stiffness out of his frozen limbs. The end result would be the same.

Ezra jumped down, swinging from a branch to slow his descent, to land between the two assassins.

"I am going to give you the warning I gave all the others who made it this far," he announced. "My name is Ezra Toth. If you've heard of me, you'll know I'm being generous when I offer retreat. Leave now and tell your boss to break contract on this hit."

He waited, hoping. So many of the men he had killed had been people he'd known. Those who passed through the Sword and Shield were a close-knit circle, despite the inevitability of incidents such as this. The others had declined his offer because they were like him. Their reputation rested on their contract. Were they to back away, they'd have to leave the city to find work. No one would hire them here. Which is why the two remaining assassins now circled him.

Daggers in hand, he waited, his pulse quick but steady. The first rushed in, letting anger over his fallen friends cloud his judgment. Ezra kicked him square in the stomach, his reach exceeding that of the man's blades. The attacker nearly dropped, lurching back, winded. In the time it took him to recover Ezra appeared at his side, slicing up his femoral artery in a practiced swipe. The man collapsed, screaming. He turned on the remaining man. Ezra could only imagine at the state of his appearance, his face covered in the blood of the assassin's fallen comrade.

To the boy's credit, he didn't run away or give in to fear or frustration. From his size and fighting style, he was clearly young, with all the potential in the world.

That made it so much worse. He had a rule about killing children.

Ezra granted him a quick death. Drawing his sword, he sliced the boy's head off. The body fell to the ground before the head rolled away. He cleaned his blades on the wet grass before tucking them away, keeping the sword at the ready in case there were more. But after a sweep of the property, he felt satisfied that tonight's batch of assassins had been dispatched.

He dragged them out of sight of the house. The lord had small ones who certainly didn't need to see such carnage. The rain would take care of the rest. The two killed with his bow were together. The one with the stomach wound had crawled to the other, dying next to him. He passed them and walked into the forest.

The first to die, a woman by the size of her, had tripped the wire that let loose a swinging log covered in the spikes upon which she was now impaled. He brought her down and re-set the trap. Close by, Ezra stepped carefully around the edges of a pit. It had been meant to capture, not kill, but it appeared as though the man had fallen wrong and snapped his neck. Pulling a length of rope from his coat that he kept for purposes such as these, Ezra lowered a noose around the man's ankle, yanked to tighten, and hoisted him up.

Once all six bodies were on the edge of the property line he made for the servant's entrance and knocked. At this time of night, it would only be opened by one of the lord's overpaid and under-worked guards. The man cringed at the sight of him but asked that he wait. Sir Pierce, the Lord's Captain of Arms, appeared minutes later.

"None of our lookouts reported anything happening," Pierce said it as more of a question than a statement.

"They may not have seen anything," Ezra replied, "but the six corpses waiting on your pleasure would argue that something did, in fact, happen. Any word as to how much longer this is to carry on?"

Sir Pierce's eye's narrowed, though not at Ezra. More likely his thoughts had turned to the less-than-watchful watch and their punishments. Ezra did not envy those guards.

"I planned on waiting to tell you this morning—rightly so it seems—but now I no longer believe your services to be necessary. The traitor responsible for these attacks has been arrested and dragged to the castle last night to await trial," Sir Pierce said.

"It's likely he had standing orders to make one last attempt in the event of his capture," Ezra mused.

Sir Pierce nodded in agreement.

"That is what I thought as well. It is why I waited to tell you. In any case, we are grateful for the work you have done. You have gone far beyond what we anticipated for you." He pulled a slip of paper from his jacket. "You are the first in your—ahem—your trade that I have ever paid with a Bill of Deposit. Most ask for gold. In any case, it is twice your remaining fee for your trouble."

Ezra checked the amount. It had been signed and was just waiting for deposit at the Treasury.

"The way I see it," Ezra explained, "there's no point in carrying gold to the bank when I can simply do this." He folded the slip up, placing it in an inner pocket. "Please let me know if I can ever be of service in the future."

"Let us hope that is not necessary, Mr. Toth," The old knight said.

Ezra grinned at him before heading out into the rain. He had walked no more than a minute before doubling back towards the forest. It would seriously impede his chances of future work, or a referral at the very least if a member of the lord's household set off one of his many traps.

2

AN UNEXPECTED DETOUR

By the time he reached the capital, the sun had begun to peak over the horizon. For the millionth time, Ezra asked himself why he didn't have a horse. His body ached from weeks of constant vigilance, combined with a lack of sleep. And for the millionth time, he reminded himself that a horse, a Clydesdale if he didn't want it to collapse under his weight, would not be happy in his three-room apartment.

Ezra passed bakers with their newly baked loaves, the smell simply mouthwatering after weeks of hardtack and dried meats. He bought a steaming long roll from a terrified baker and inhaled it on his way to the Treasury. They were just opening their doors when he arrived.

The Treasury, a building that regulated all the wealth of the capital of Olaesta, stood as a testament to Olacian architecture. A fortress of great magnificence. After an incident several decades ago, it had been separated from the Royal Treasury and now served only the people. Its sparkling white stone in the new sun suddenly made Ezra aware of his filth. He dipped the end of his sleeve into a nearby fountain and wiped at his face while he walked up the steps.

Inside, only one clerk stood at the ready, the rest likely preparing the accounts for the day. Ezra approached him and fished out the slip.

It had a bit of dirt and a smear of blood on it, but the words were clear. He handed it to the very reluctant man, who stamped it, wrote down the transfer in his ledger, and went searching for Ezra's account book. The Wall of Accounts was not sorted alphabetically or by any organizational system with which he was familiar. The intent behind the convoluted system was to detract thieves from easily finding a specific person's books. However the Treasurer's Guild did it, the man came back quickly with Ezra's book in hand, copied the additional amount from the slip to the book, and added it, entering the new amount.

"Are you making any additional deposits or withdrawals today, sir?" the man asked, his voice wavering. Ezra did a quick calculation, thinking of the supplies he'd need.

"I'll take thirty gold crowns out today. Half of that in silver dinars. Thanks for reminding me."

The clerk stared for a moment before bending down to unlock the drawer. He filled the pouch and handed it over.

"Anything else today, sir?" The clerk managed, looking everywhere but directly at him.

"No. That will be all, thank you." Ezra wondered if the man would be all right as he left. But that wasn't his problem. Ezra walked out, his squelching boots echoing in the near-empty corridor.

Outside, the sky had brightened significantly, and people were out and about, starting their day. The street was alive with the aroma of vendors selling all sorts of loaves of bread, pies, and meats. Not even the toll of the bells, signaling a call to prayer, halted the merchants setting up their carts.

The rich could afford to stop and pray but the gods were understanding of those who were unable to put pause of everything for worship. The poor were just as good, if not better than the nobles at visiting the temples, though. They just did it on their own time.

Ezra wanted to go straight home, but not even the gods would be unable to protect him if he didn't stop to visit Granny and Marya first. He sighed, turning left towards the textiles district. Ezra thought he might choke from the overwhelming dye fumes as he rushed through. The laundresses were already well underway, parcels of freshly washed, folded clothes were being stacked out for their owners to collect and they had already begun washing today's load. It was best to avoid this way around noon as they had all their hanging out on lines, stretching between buildings that crossed over the street. At least he knew rainwater was clean.

Soft clicking could be heard, which meant looms were already hard at work. And next to them stood the only stall that mattered in this chaotic alley.

Granny Kelva and her granddaughter Marya were seamstresses. They sold beautiful handkerchiefs, and scarves and did custom work on anything brought to them. It was before Ezra's time, but he had heard tales that Granny once wielded an incredible reputation as one of the best craftsman in the land. She had clearly passed that on to her granddaughter though.

Marya was a beautiful girl. With the pale skin and white-blonde hair of her homeland, she was a veritable snowflake in the mud that covered everything in the Borough. Her hair, long enough to reach her waist when it hung loose, was currently tied up in an intricate braid. Small wisps had escaped from the confines of the braid and swayed to and fro in the breeze. Her fingers, long and thin, darted quickly over a blue dress that she was busy embroidering. Her own dress radiated an autumn orange, with red vines trimming the hem and cuffs of her dress.

Embroidery covered everything she owned. From the most formal of gowns to the well-worn clothes she wore when training, beautiful stitching embellished everything she wore.

Marya frequently received requests from noble ladies and her skill kept the business running. Even now he saw Granny haggling with a woman while Marya worked behind the counter. Granny snorted, perhaps at the lowball offer the woman was trying to sneak by her, causing Marya to glance up and see him.

"Ezra!" she screamed. Granny clutched at her chest in surprise and leaned on the counter while the customer only stared at the girl who flung herself at a filthy, menacing figure. He dodged her and she skidded to a halt.

"Don't even try it," Ezra scolded. "One hug from me and you'll need to bathe and change your clothes."

Marya pouted, looking more like the child he'd rescued long ago than the young woman before him.

"Weeks without a word and you say, 'Don't get your dress dirty?' What kind of greeting is that?"

"I wanted to go straight to bed, then bathe, then see you. But I decided to stop by on the way home. I guess I'll just go…" He turned to leave.

"Wait-wait-wait!" She grabbed his arm and pulled him to sit down on the stool by the stall.

"You smell like shit," she commented, giving him a once over. Marya might have been a respectable lady had she not spent so much of her youth following him around. That and having a grandmother who swore like a sailor. In Old Ruskin, but still, shit smells the same no matter the country.

"How bad?" He wiped at his face, bits of dried mud he'd missed flecking off. "I went to the Treasury this morning and—"

"You went to Treasury looking like that? Koja ne odgojila kozu?" Granny Kelva muttered under her breath. He let her pull him in front of the full-length mirror and understood the stares, more than usual, that he had been getting.

Ezra cut an intimidating figure any day. He stood at six and a half feet, weighing fifteen stone of lean muscle, and carried a general demeanor which he had been told implied he was in a killing mood. Something that was simply not true as he thought of himself as a relatively laid back individual. His brown hair hung past his shoulders, pulled back to stay out of his face, but long enough to cover his neck and some shoulder. Green-blue eyes stood out against tan skin and his usually short and scruffy facial hair had grown out after weeks without maintenance. But whatever drew a person's eye to him first, his scars ultimately held their gaze. Not mutilating or disfiguring. But plentiful to say the least.

The scars covered him like bark covers a tree. Less so on his face, but the rest of his body was covered with white, pink, and brown faded lines. Things that would have, should have, healed on a normal person. They never quite did on him. Nor his mother for that matter. Not that it mattered to her. She had long since died. The immediate problem did not have anything to do with his height, bulk or even his scars at the moment though. His clothes and hair were crusted with blood and mud. Some of it still on his neck, face and hands, and the rest coating his clothes. Were he not known in this city they would likely have called for the City Guard by now.

Granny clicked her tongue in disgust and handed him a wet rag. He cleaned himself up as best he could rather than risking her continued ire.

"You fine, yes? Go and come back when you rested. You scaring away my customers." Her grasp of the Olacian language was tenuous at best, but she always managed to get her point across.

"I love you too, Granny." He smiled, folding the rag and tossing it on the pile of dirty linens.

"Bah!" She scoffed, failing to hide a smile. "You go with him!" she said to Marya, pushing her after him.

When they were out of sight Ezra handed her some coin. "Buy Granny something sweet. She seems tired."

Marya took it, learning long ago not to protest when he gave money. It would get to them one way or another. Their business brought in sufficient profit, but sometimes a little boost never hurt.

"Are you really all right, though? That's a lot of blood and you were gone longer than you said." He ruffled her hair, and she smiled.

"I'm really all right. The blood's not mine. I would have written if I'd been able. It just turns out the other guy was more determined than the client anticipated."

Marya was the sister he'd never had, and he knew she worried about him. She also stood as one of the few women he knew strong enough to see him covered in blood and not be terrified. Which may or may not be a good thing. Sometimes he was afraid he'd skewed her perceptions of what normal should look like. But she was certainly safer for knowing him. Not just from his protection, but from the training he had given her. Not even the Gods could help any boy who tried to force her.

The street on which he lived was populated predominately by people like him. Knives for hire. Thieves. Muscle. If you had money and needed a job done, the man lived here. Some would argue that it was not safe for Marya to be there. Especially alone when she returned to her stall. But everyone knew she was under his protection. And they knew horrible things awaited the person who touched her. Ezra smiled to himself. He used to favor anonymity, but a reputation was fairly useful.

"You're doing it again." Marya shook him.

"Doing what?"

"Your 'murder smile' – Cut it out." Ezra mushed his face out of shape until she started laughing.

"Better?"

"You're an idiot." She giggled. "Have you been taking your medicine, by the way?"

He turned his eyes upward, palms up like he had seen the priests do.

"Yes. I have paid penance for my sins by drinking rat piss twice a day."

She punched him in the shoulder.

"I'm serious."

The scars weren't the only thing he and his mother had shared. Perhaps they were a side effect of the condition, but Ezra had been sickly as a child. Back then, he'd occasionally teetered on the edge of death but usually was just weak and frail. The tonic he drank kept him healthy. Exercise did the rest.

"Ezra…"

Ezra heard the fear in her voice. And when he faced her, he saw it in her expression. She pointed. He followed her finger towards the entrance to his apartment. And to the men standing in front of it.

•   •   •   •   •

Ezra was more open about his life than most people in his profession. He even used his real name, though some insisted 'Ezra' was a stupid name for an assassin. After they stopped bleeding they reconsidered.

But he never told clients where he lived. The residents of the slum were aware of the location if only to better avoid him and so did Marya, Ian, and a few other select individuals because they were the only people he really trusted.

The fact that men were waiting for him meant that they had been following him, without his knowledge. A difficult thing to do. Keeping an eye on the men, he gripped Marya by the shoulders.

"Listen to me carefully. Go home. Don't run. Walk. Don't look back. I'll come to you when it's safe. Don't come back here until then. Don't answer the door for anyone asking about me. Now, go!" He pushed her away, and she walked, calmly but with purpose, and did not look back.

Ezra turned his full attention to the men. As impressive as it was that they had found him, their observational skills left something to be desired. Somehow, they had yet to see him, though his head poked above the throng. He ducked down and moved with the flow of people, allowing it to take him out of the street and onto the steps of the building next door.

He vaulted from one porch to the other, landing softly behind the men. Two wore armor, burdensome and unnecessary. The other dressed in lighter, protective leathers. Much like his own, though less advanced and considerably cleaner.

"Can I help you?" All three drew their swords in panic, swinging them at the place where Ezra's voice had been. But by then, he had moved to the front steps of his building, in full view of the street. Hopefully, if they had plans of killing him, a mass of witnesses might deter them.

"Did we have an appointment?" Ezra called, raising his voice, drawing them in the right direction. No one pointed their swords his way, though they remained out. It was then that he noticed the crest on the hilt of the leather-clad man. He was a knight. The other two wore chest plates bearing the royal crest.

"Are you Ezra Toth?" the knight inquired. His face pursed in a sour manner, like he smelled something unpleasant. Unsure whether that was because the knight was unpleasant or because his neighbor,

Hugh, was high as a kite and didn't bathe unless forced, Ezra decided not to comment.

"That depends," Ezra joked. "Is he under arrest?"

Tragically, they all seemed to suffer from a lack of humor.

"You have been summoned to the palace. And you are not under arrest." The knight added as an afterthought.

"Why?" Ezra asked.

"Why what?"

"Why am I being summoned?" Ezra spoke slowly.

The knight's nostrils flared.

"It does not matter why. Your presence has been requested and we are here to escort you." The knight's tone was even and clipped, the frustration leaking through. It was a game Ezra liked to call 'Poke the Bear'.

"What if I don't want to go? You said 'requested'. That sounds like I have a choice and I've got to tell you, I'm exhausted. I'm sure you can tell just by looking at me I am not at my best." Ezra raised his arms to better show off his swamp monster form. The knight's fingers tightened around his still unsheathed sword.

"Quite." he agreed, "However, we are willing to overlook your current appearance for the sake of urgency. The carriage is waiting around the corner."

"Not in this neighborhood, it's not." Ezra muttered, thinking quickly. Important people knew they were here. So, witnesses or no, he couldn't kill them as the palace would just send more men of a less courteous variety. He always had the option of just telling them to go away but again, it sounded like they might return. Revisiting and then once more dismissing murder he accepted the fact that he couldn't kill them unless he wanted to flee the city. Something that involved a great deal of excess work.

He decided to acquiesce.

"How long will this take?" He cast one last longing glance at his door and the bed that waited within before turning his attention to the men.

"We will return you to your home by the end of day at the latest. This should not take long. If you would follow us?" The knight turned to leave.

"Uh, just a tick," Ezra interrupted.

The knight froze and turned around slowly as though he did not trust himself with quick movements.

"Yes?" he ground out.

"Nothing against you. Any of you. But I can't be seen in your company, illustrious as it may be. Reputation and all. Meet you at the carriage?"

Before the knight could shoot him down, Ezra jumped down the front steps and ran into the alley between the buildings. He waited in the dark until they had gone and then dug through his bag until he found his cloak. The cloak represented one of Kelva's best ideas. Though crafted by Marya, Granny was the real genius behind it. The hooded cloak swept the ground when he wore it, with inner pockets and sewn-in pins for lock picking. The best feature though was its double lining. If he wore it one way, the black-brown cloth made him near invisible in the darkness. And when turned inside out, the cloak was a dark tan, with lighter shades of tan mixed in. He slipped it on, hood up, and walked through the market without a second glance.

Only one place existed in the Borough where they could have safely left the carriage, and it was the inn where, ironically, most out of town mercs stayed. But no one stole from the inn. It wouldn't do to steal a horse only to find out it belonged to a psychopath.

Ezra had a favored shortcut for his trips to the inn. Sadly, that involved him doing a bit of climbing so, rubbing his hands together, he ran at the wall and dug them into the crevasses between the brick. After falling the first time he'd done this, he'd gone and carved foot and hand holds into the mortar. Now it took next to no effort to scale the building and heave himself onto the roof.

From there he could see the three heading exactly where he thought they would, and he followed. He jumped across rooftop after rooftop, making sure he gained enough speed before there was no more roof on which to jump. He landed into an ever-present, conveniently placed mountain of hay. From the lack of shouting, no one had seen him, this time. The only sound came from an alarmed Puppy, the cow, named so for her big puppy dog eyes. Ezra gave her a loving head scratch before heaving himself up, brushing hay off his already filthy clothes.

Ezra bought several meat pies and an apple as he walked, stuffing them into his mud free bag. The carriage sat just outside the entrance to the inn and he had made it at the same time as his potential employer.

He followed the knight inside the carriage and pulled the door closed behind them. The knight, who had been staring at a miniature, snapped the locket shut and reached for his weapon. Ezra forced the knight's sword back into its scabbard, while he used the other to throw back his hood.

"You're far too easy to startle for a man of your position. Perhaps you should consider working on that?"

The knight ignored him, muttering a string of profanity under his breath before shouting to the guards that they could leave.

"Who's that portrait of? Your sister?"

The knight's nose flared, clearly a tell the man had for his anger. Ezra sensed he would see it often.

"Maybe we got off on the wrong foot," Ezra continued, knowing he would fall asleep if they kept silent.

"You know I am Ezra Toth. I'm a law-abiding citizen who pays his taxes. You are a knight by the name of?" It wasn't surprising that he had only just asked for the man's name. He usually forgot to request such information until someone else asked him, to which he would reply that he didn't know.

"I am Sir Joseph Burtness II. You may address me as Sir Joseph, or Lord Burtness if you prefer."

"It's nice to meet you, Joe," Ezra tried to say, his speech somewhat muffled by one of Mother Dharma's meat pies.

Joe's face scrunched up in disgust and they spent the remainder of the ride in companionable silence, broken on and off by Ezra's munching and occasional humming. The noise of the city increased as they reached its center. Dirt roads gave way to cobblestones which were, in Ezra's opinion, far worse. Had he known the ride would be like this he may have reconsidered going.

He just couldn't get comfortable. The carriage felt all the smaller for the curtains which let light in but gave no real indication of the outside view. His head kept bumping against the roof and his knees were starting to cramp from a lack of room. By no means was Joe a dwarf, but he certainly seemed to be having an easier time of it.

They stopped for a moment and Ezra made for the door but Joe stopped him, listening. The guards talked to someone who laughed, and they started moving again. Ezra couldn't help groaning. Now the sounds of the city were all but gone. They must be inside the castle walls.

Suddenly, the carriage transitioned from cobblestone back to dirt. He shot the knight a questioning look but Joe only shook his head, taking a quick peek out the window. Finally, after the longest ride of his life, the carriage stopped, and the door opened.

Ezra ducked through the small doorway and stretched. Each joint crackled in relief. Taking in his surroundings, though, he felt less than relieved. He was, in fact, revisiting the possible, arrest theory he had joked about initially. They were not at the main gate. Nor at a common side door. Or even a servant's entrance. Guards were lighting torches while Joe waited at the entrance of an old, vine-covered tunnel.

"Umm, no."

"What is it this time?" Joe fumed, rounding on him with wide eyes and even wider nostrils.

Ezra wondered faintly about turning this character trait into a drinking game before he realized he was getting distracted.

"Here's the deal," Ezra began. "I have this thing against going down dark, old tunnels with people I just met for reasons they won't explain to meet with a person whose identity has yet to be revealed. It's irrational, I know, but I'm told many people are likewise afflicted by such unreasonable fears." Ezra folded his arms and leaned back, knives palmed in case things became difficult. He no longer had witnesses, and no one saw them leave together.

Joe rubbed his temple and closed his eyes. When Ezra did this, he was usually asking the gods for patience. Or a broadsword. More likely the former in this case, though Ezra wouldn't put it past him.

"I am bringing you to see a friend of mine. A man I have served with and for since we were both young. He needs your help on a matter of great urgency and secrecy. If you would be so kind as to follow me, I guarantee no harm will come to you."

Ezra could see he had inadvertently reached the stage in 'Poke the Bear' where, with one more nudge, he'd likely be mauled.

And frankly, he was curious.

"Lead on, then." He took a torch and followed Joe into the darkness.

3

THE OFFER

Though damp and smelly, the tunnel was far larger than he'd anticipated. There was something refreshing about not to having to duck down, as was often the case with these underground passages. They were simply not built with an Ezra-friendly mentality. This tunnel, however, was broad and tall. Equal in both breadth and height, Ezra was able to just brush his fingers against the ceiling. Unfortunately, the hand came away slimy, forcing him to wipe said hands on his increasingly disgusting clothes.

"How many people know about this tunnel?" His voice echoed in the dark.

"Fewer than you'd think. They were forgotten for a generation and only recently rediscovered by a very bored pair of children." Ezra could hear the smile in Joe's voice.

"So you, my potential employer, those guards, and the rats," he said, noting the familiar sound of scurrying inside the walls and just beyond the torchlight.

The knight neither confirmed nor denied Ezra's assessment, continuing onward. A few minutes of winding later the path ended in a set of steep, uneven steps. Ezra lifted his torch but was unable to see the end of the path in the darkness.

"I hate you right now. Just so you know," Ezra commented, but Joe continued to ignore him and began to climb. Ezra followed suit. Of all the days for this to happen, why did it have to be today? His mind and body were exhausted. But he had done worse, feeling worse. He ascended, eyes closed in a half sleep, until he bumped into the knight.

"We're here."

They weren't at the top of the stairs, but rather, a platform in front of a wall. The steps continued onwards and upwards, into the gloom. Joe pulled a key from around his neck and slipped it into a keyhole that Ezra would never have seen had he not been looking right at it. The lock clicked and the stone wall parted slightly, revealing a door that had not been there before. Ezra promised himself he'd go back to examine it when he had more time.

"Quiet," Joe hissed. As if Ezra's silent footfalls were the problem when compared to the knight's clunky steps. Joe pushed him through and closed the door behind them.

Once he'd blinked away the sudden light, Ezra found himself facing a room divider. His mind automatically said paper, but on closer inspection, he realized it was a finely woven silk. Looking back at the door, he saw that a tapestry hung over the passageway. Ezra opened his mouth to speak but Joe silenced him with a look.

"I am alone, Joseph. It is safe to come out." The voice came from within the room. Joe led the way and Ezra followed.

As a boy, he had spent time with his uncle in the Eastern Lands. There, and on his travels back to Olacia, he had visited the homes of royalty and nobility, which was how he knew he was in the presence of royalty now. Their chambers always held a certain opulence that bordered on the unnecessary.

Ezra stood in the bedroom of a large suite. Large in that the bedroom equaled his entire apartment in size. The massive canopy bed hardly took up a fourth of the space. But beyond the double doors, he saw a sitting room and a dining room beyond that. Without a doubt the suite also included a washroom with its own bathtub, to be filled with hot water by servants. All of it furnished in such a way that begged his inner pickpocket to grab something. Ezra stuffed twitching fingers in his coat and directed his attention to the reason he had been hijacked from his home.

A man stood by the picture window. He was younger than Ezra. Perhaps twenty-two years of age. Though his eyes seemed older. They were tired. Looking at him it was obvious who he was. His hooded, thin Zouszian eyes and blue-black hair marked him.

"I can see you know who I am," Crown Prince Christophe said. "And it is a pleasure to meet you, Mr. Toth. I apologize for the unconventional circumstances that brought about our introduction." He reached out and Ezra found himself clasping arms with the future king.

"Ezra, please. Mr. Toth was my uncle." Ezra gave the briefest of nods to the prince after sensing the knight's eye's burning into the back of his head.

"Ezra, then. Please sit, we have much to discuss." The prince sat down at a small, window-side table and gestured to the chair across him. Normally Ezra preferred to stand, as it allowed him to be able to jump to action more readily in the event of an attack. But, after all this, they weren't going to kill him now. Especially since, with a mere flick of his wrist, the heir to the throne could be dead. The chair was plush velvet with gold inlay in the wood, and would likely never be the same after he sat in it. But it was very comfortable.

"Tea? Wine? Perhaps something to eat? I understand you have just returned from a rather strenuous job." The prince waved to the knight, who stood and left out a side door. Ezra didn't ask how the prince knew that, any more than he knew where his home was. Joseph re-appeared with food and drink and Ezra didn't hesitate to tuck in.

"I assume you need someone killed, then?" Ezra asked, making sure he emptied his mouth before speaking this time. "Surely you don't need my protection, surrounded as you are by loyal knights and the Palace Guard."

Christophe and Joe exchanged a dark gaze.

"Mr. To—Ezra, I need your word that what is said now does not leave this room. It is a matter of the greatest secrecy."

The prince's face was grave but all Ezra could do was snort and then subsequently choke on his tea.

"I'm sorry. No offense meant, your highness," Ezra apologized, coughing crumbs and tea into his sleeve. "But if the secret carriage to the secret tunnel to meet with the secret client did not indicate to me the nature of this endeavor, Joe made sure to emphasize that this was a matter of the utmost secrecy. I think I've got the idea." He caught the prince mouthing 'Joe?' to the knight who only shook his head.

"But to put your mind at ease, I don't divulge my client's confidences. Not for any price. Now, why am I here?" Ezra leaned back and waited expectantly. The prince took a deep breath.

"The reason you are here is because I cannot be sure who to trust. My younger brother has his eyes on the throne. I fear he has our father's support. And an attempt has already been made on my life."

"Oh please no," Ezra groaned, leaning back in his chair. "I hate family shit. It's messy. It's always messy. Not just because of the blood. And there will be. There always is. But because of the *blood.* Emotions get in the way and it just stinks. No one wins." He stretched out and down, with every intention of sliding to the floor and turning into a puddle with the ability to drain away from this dreadful meeting.

"Any chance you want me to kill him?" Ezra asked hopefully, perking up.

"Because otherwise," he continued, "I may be protecting you for the rest of your life, depending on Prince Daniel's persistence. I've done long jobs before, but I believe that might be a bit beyond me." He remembered his impatience on the latest job that had only spanned three weeks and then contemplated how long it would take cabin fever to set in before he committed treason. Joe bristled beside him but said nothing.

"Don't worry," Christophe said. "I have no intention of asking you to shadow me forever." Remnants of the prince's smile still lingered over his last words in a way that made Ezra think the prince still believed they might not be true.

"Father is dying," the prince continued. "That is what, I believe, spurred my brother to action. As soon as my father passes and I take the throne, I will have the power to manage him."

Not for the first time, Ezra found himself thankful he was an only child. And that he had been born in the slums. It seemed that the richer you were, the more people wanted you dead.

"Why does your father want to kill you? I get your brother. He wants the throne. But what did you do to piss off your dad?" Ezra didn't just want to know. Motive was key in any job as it helped in preparing for possible attacks. He needed to know the king's ultimate endgame. Why he wanted his son dead.

The silence stretched on so long, Ezra thought Christophe wasn't going to answer.

"Because I am my mother's son," he finally replied, voice tense. "Any other questions?"

His answer made a sad amount of sense. Christophe's mother was the late Queen Jeongseon. Formally Princess Ahn Jeongseon, a princess from the country of Zouszian, she had been sent as part of a delegation to arrange peace talks. The primary item of negotiation being her marriage to the then Crown Prince, now King. It was a nation-wide tragedy and enduring source of gossip when she died in childbirth. But he re-married, almost immediately, to a duchess who bore him another son. Daniel. Perhaps he resented Christophe for taking the late Queen away from him? Or maybe he'd hated her, and Christophe served as a reminder of something he wanted to forget? Every woman, bar rat, and bard had their theory. This was why he usually declined messy family cases. But, as that was all Christophe was going to say, Ezra decided to change the subject.

"Not to be insensitive," as Ezra usually was, "I just wanted to clarify 'dying'. Is the King on his deathbed now, feeling poorly, or dying in the sense that he is old and death is coming for us all?"

Christophe stared at him and Joe tilted his head skyward as if the Gods might be so kind as to reach down and save him from Ezra's presence.

"You are not what I expected," Christophe admitted

"And what did you expect?" Ezra certainly knew what the prince was talking about. To those with whom he was not friendly, Ezra had a hard time hiding his proverbial fangs. Or his 'murder face' as Marya had called it. That combined with the happy way he talked about disembowelment caused people to give him a wide berth.

"Um—" The prince stalled, realizing the corner he had backed himself into.

"It's fine. Nothing I haven't heard before. Now you were going to tell me the degree to which your father is dying?"

Joe was now openly gaping at Ezra.

"The physicians say months, perhaps a year if the latest treatment takes, and that would be a miracle—"

"For your brother maybe," Ezra muttered. "Sorry," he apologized, realizing he had interrupted. Joe had begun to shift in his chair every few seconds, clearly anxious to show Ezra exactly how he felt about the lack of respect being shown towards the prince.

"Most likely four to six months," the prince continued, ignoring the interruption.

"I would retain your protective services until such a time as I am on the throne and have devised a way to deal with my brother. You would be well compensated and have my life long favor should you ever need it." The prince stated this in a rehearsed monotone that implied he had written this down and read it out several times.

Ezra did the calculations in his head. Overall, he'd likely make less than if he did several, smaller jobs over that span of time, but the favor of the future King was something else. One could never have too many powerful friends.

"I'll need some time to rest and gather supplies. Today's Monday?" He ticked off the things he needed, the time it would take to get them and subtracted a day for sleep. "I can start on Saturday. And I always take half my pay up front, the rest upon completion of the contract."

Joe scoffed at this, having reached his limit.

"Hang on, how do we know that you won't take the money and run," the knight complained.

But any other protestations were cut short by the knife Ezra held at the knight's throat. Ezra didn't remember pulling it from his sleeve or resting it against Joe's artery for that matter. Occasionally, when someone insulted him, he had a habit, built from years of necessity as a child, to react.

"That was very rude, don't you think?" Ezra's arm screamed in protest from a pulled muscle but he could have held it there all day. "You invite me into the Crown Prince's presence, armed for that matter, and then you question my honor? How is that smart?"

Ezra was not proud to say this was a bit of a sore subject with him.

Despite his less than wholesome career path, he had always thought of himself as a man with a code. And the constant questioning of that by his employers, until he had built his standing as a man of his word, had left him a bit touchy when it came to his reputation. Something difficult to establish and even harder to maintain considering the people he associated with and the people he worked for.

As a child, he'd sat at his mother's bedside and listened to her lecture on the freedom of choice. And the soul. And how the gods would one day judge him for not just his actions but for the reasoning behind them. Yes, he killed people. But never for pleasure. Never for revenge or personal vendetta. And when he made a promise, he kept it. Because, above all, that was the most important thing to his mother.

Always keep your word.

"Christophe!" Joe gasped. The bobbing of his throat brought the skin close enough to the blade that it nicked ever so slightly, drawing a trace of blood. The prince watched the exchange calmly.

"It might be best if you apologized, Joseph. It's possible you may have offended him." Though the man's face was grave, Ezra could swear he could hear the hint of a smile in the ruler's voice.

"I am sorry for doubting your word, Mr. Toth. Please accept my most sincere apology." Though Ezra rarely believed an apology that had to be coerced, he realized he may have been oversensitive. It also didn't help to further alienate a man he'd be working with closely for the foreseeable future. The knife slipped back into his sleeve and he held a hand up in surrender.

"I overreacted. You were just protecting your friend. I promise not to let you down." Because Ezra understood him. He had said and done some stupid things in the name of defending his friends. Joe was hardly to blame.

"Does that mean you accept the job?" Christophe asked.

"Yes, I accept. There'll be some rules you'll have to follow and privacies to sacrifice, but we can discuss that on Saturday. I assume I'll be allowed to come by the main gate, yes?" He was only half joking.

"We'll send a horse for you Saturday morning and Joseph will be waiting for you."

"Great. Then if that's it I'll just be on my way—"

"Not just yet," Prince Christophe interrupted.

Ezra thumped back in the chair, now thoroughly convinced he was never going to get back home. The gods would throw honey-dos at him until he gave in to whatever they had planned.

"Don't you want to know what you'll be paid?"

So close.

"Yes, normally we agree to the fee before, and then if I believe the job warranted additional compensation, I'll just charge more at the end. What did you have in mind?" At the moment, Ezra cared less about gold and more about sleep.

"And your past employers were fine with such an unconventional invoice?" Joe asked quietly. As if his throat had not yet forgiven the master's last transgression.

"My services leave nothing to be desired. The few failed contracts were due to an omission of vital information, or idiocy on the part of the client. It is difficult to protect an idiot from themselves." Ezra said this with the same straight face but his heart hurt from the half-truth. Despite knowing he had done nothing wrong on those missions, they'd always felt like personal failures.

"Quite," Christophe agreed, pushing a piece of paper towards him. "This would be the sum total of your fee, to be split per your request. You would receive half today." Ezra picked it up and unfolded it.

100,000 GLD

Written in a heavy-handed script, with a calligraphy brush of all things, the number was very clear. One hundred thousand gold. Ezra took pause, seriously reconsidering the idea that this job would not be worth his time.

"That seems…fair." He hoped he wasn't drooling. Ezra saw no quill on the table so he drew a pencil from his pocket, wrote down a number and pushed the paper back across the table. "This is my account with the city Treasury. Please have the funds deposited there discretely. You can give me the deposit slip when I arrive." Joe looked as surprised as if Ezra had asked for a giant wheel barrel full of coins to take back to town.

"One more thing." Prince Christophe nodded to Joseph who grinned rather menacingly at Ezra before walking to the main door and knocking on it. It opened and in strode an elderly, well-dressed man. He wore a measuring tape around his neck like a stylish noblewoman might wear a scarf. Ezra backed toward the tapestry covered door.

"As grateful as I am that you would think of me, I have clothes. And I promise to wash these before Saturday." he added, well aware that he was clad in a fashion similar to that of a homeless lunatic.

"I'm sure you do Ezra. But as you will be at my side through the greater part of this, it would be best if you had a wardrobe better suited to palace living."

Ezra grimaced, thinking about the three pairs of pants and fours shirts that made up his…wardrobe. Every one of them repaired by Marya more than once. The tailor took his silence as consent and a cue to begin groping him with the measuring tape, eventually standing on a chair to get at his shoulders, neck, and chest.

"I won't take anything brightly colored, or patterned, or poofy, or tight. No tights. Think of the simplest styles you can and go with those. Yes? Please tell me you understand." Ezra ticked off instructions as he remembered every horrible thing he'd ever seen noblemen wear. The old man just nodded, but that may have been to humor him. He took some notes and left, leaving Ezra feeling somewhat violated.

"Is that everything?" Ezra asked only out of politeness. He had every intention of leaving either way.

"Yes." The prince stood to see him off. "Joseph will guide you out. Until Saturday, then."

"Your Highness," Ezra bowed, before turning to go. Joe waited at the open passage with a torch and he followed the knight back down the steps.

They descended for a while in silence. Then Joe stopped, having been working up the nerve to speak since they left.

"Spit it out," Ezra burst impatiently.

"How many people have you failed to save? How many have died while under your protection?" Joe's tone was serious, and Ezra was surprised he had been able to wait that long to ask.

"If you mean how many clients have died on my watch? Three. But each of them died via their own stupidity. They took risks I advised against and suffered for it. I can only do so much." And someday Ezra would say that and believe it.

"You will be sure that doesn't happen this time." Joe instructed.

The 'bodyguard/assassin/coddler of lordlings and knights' sighed.

"I will do my best. But, let's just say this happens. Christophe sits next to his brother who, in turn, picks up a knife from the table and plunges it into his throat? I can only do so much." Ezra repeated.

Joe didn't reply, and they continued onwards. And before Ezra turned to continue down the stairs he caught a glimpse of Joe's face. The man was drawn, tired and sickly. However, Joe's eyes, which were tight with concern, showed the true feelings he held back when he thought someone was paying attention. Ezra knew he'd given the knight a lot to think about. So many thought hiring a guard was just about getting some muscle to stand by and look intimidating. But all it took was one wrong move and everything fell apart. He sensed Joe was just beginning to realize the enormity of the task before them.

At the edge of the tunnel, he reached out and clasped arms with the knight.

"I'm sorry for earlier. This only works if we trust each other. Your friend seems like a good person. I'll make sure he gets through this." And for the first time that day, his smile actually reassured someone. Or he hoped it did. The worry lines around the knight's eyes seemed to smooth out as they clasped arms in farewell. It was also possible that Joe was just relieved to see the back of the merc, if only for a short time.

Ezra climbed back into the carriage, slightly more tolerable with only one passenger, and made his way home.

4

HOME

He only stopped by Granny's house long enough to let them know he hadn't been murdered.

"It's a new client," he explained quickly, leaving before they were able to ask any questions.

Ezra knew from experience that, were he to wait much longer, the blood and mud would cake into his hair and it would take help to get out, so he stopped at the bathhouse, paid triple for the fact that they would likely have to change the water, and scrubbed until he once again appeared human. He changed into the cleanish clothes from his bag and, half a day later than he'd planned, Ezra made his way home.

There were four locks on his door. Starting with the top, then the third, then second, then finally unlocking the fourth. This combination disabled a trap on the other side of the door. It used to be a crossbow, but the cats kept tripping it.

The door gave way to a stuffy, dim space. He opened the shutters to let in the day and some fresh air. Or what remained of it. The sun had already begun it's trek towards the horizon, though it still had a ways to go. Tossing his bag to the floor, Ezra collapsed onto the couch, and out of nowhere, they descended.

Black, blue, orange with a bit of white, white with a bit of orange, one named Snow because she was that ghostly pale, and several others with bits missing. Ezra was soon covered in cats. Their communal purring was deafening, and each vied for space to rub their scent on him. Echo forced his head to dip as Luke chewed on one of his braids and after a while, they all settled down, finding space near enough to curl up near him.

"I missed you too." He chuckled.

Most folks figured him for a dog person, and he loved dogs. But cats were self-sustaining, which more than met his lifestyle of constantly being out for days or weeks on end. They were hunters, so he didn't have to worry about them starving, though Marya brought them food every couple of days. And, just like him, they could be assholes. It bonded them.

He almost fell asleep right there, but experience taught Ezra that his back would never forgive him for his laziness. At thirty-one he already had the body of an old man, albeit a very fit old man. Ezra took a deep breath.

"I'm sorry," he begged, standing slowly, apologizing over and over as the cats yowled in protest.

"How about bed? Bed's better. Bed is good, remember?"

Much like the lead in a parade, Ezra half ran for the bedroom, no less than eight cats following in his wake. Sitting at the foot of the bed the Queen rested, his first and only intentional pet, Lucy. She had been a tiny kitten when he found her, but that was many years and many *many* treats ago. Lucy had a prodigious girth and commanded the respect of any feline that decided this was their home. He gave her an affectionate rub, something that would lose anyone else a finger, and climbed under the covers. The bed creaked as he submitted to the deluge of cats that rained down upon him. All but Lucy. She lay on the edge of the bed, leaning against his feet to provide warmth, ever vigilant, the true defender of the homestead.

•　　•　　•　　•　　•

"You're guarding who?" Marya's latest commission lay forgotten on the table. She was too busy being horrified with Ezra's latest poor life choice.

"Keep your voice down," he hushed, "You'll wake Granny." Ezra glanced furtively at the shut door to the bedroom. Granny didn't know yet and, ideally, wouldn't know until he came to say goodbye. And even then, perhaps at a distance. Corrupt royalty was the reason she'd been forced to flee from her home country, Ruskya. She held an understandable grudge against their 'type' as she called it.

Some of that prejudice had clearly trickled down to her granddaughter.

"Why would you risk yourself for that kind of person? At least you know what to expect when the drug lords come calling." She made it sound like courtship and for a moment Ezra pictured himself arm in arm with Brian the Bear, a local slumlord.

Not for two million gold, he thought to himself, his skin crawling.

"Nonsense," he argued, giving himself a mental shake, "With the money I make from this I'll be able to set you up with the shop you wanted and hire some help. Ian can make those repairs to his tavern. I won't ever really have to worry about money again. Yes, I'll take jobs, but they won't be dangerous. I'll be free to do whatever I want." An idea that still baffled him. What did he want?

"But you just got back. Am I really not going to see you for a year?" She sounded like she might cry.

"This isn't where you profess your love for me, is it? Because I've already told you, I'm in a committed relationship with Lucy." He smirked, wiping at her face. Ezra hated to see her cry.

"Shut up," She grinned and punched him.

"And to answer your question, no. If I was attached at the hip with the prince for a full year, I would kill him myself. I'll find the occasional weekend to come and visit. Perhaps in a month or so. And if not, I'll just drag his royalness with me."

"And you'll be careful about…" Unable to find the words, she simply gestured to him. But he understood what she meant. The scars were obvious. There was only that one other thing.

"I can't see it coming up in between the weather and court fashions, but I'll be careful." He tried to keep the joke in his voice but her eyes caused him to falter.

"People are cruel, Ezra. Especially nobles." She looked so worried for him that he pulled her into a hug.

"I'll be fine. Worst case scenario, Christophe dies, I take my gold and flee the country with Kelva on my back for pointers." Marya hit him again.

"Where are you going now?" She asked when he opened the door.

"I need to tell Ian that I'll be busy for a while."

"Great!" Marya ran into her room and returned with a brown paper package. "He asked me to mend some clothes. Drop them off for me and tell him to stop wearing white if he's going to bleed all over it."

"Why don't you come with me and tell him yourself?" he asked, trying to give it back. She only shook her head violently and pushed him out the door.

"Don't be lazy. You're going there anyway. Tell him—tell him I said hello." She slammed the door, but not fast enough that he missed the furious blush on her face.

Ian and Marya, huh? Ezra's brow furrowed.

Saying 'she could do worse' would be like saying 'at least she's dating the local tavern owner instead of the patrons.' They were all a different shade of brown, character-wise, himself included. Which was likely how this had happened. He liked Ian, the man served as the closest thing to a brother Ezra'd ever had. But Ezra was not above flaying the skin from Ian's bones to prove a point, should the need arise.

●   ●   ●   ●   ●

The Sword and Shield was not the nicest, nor the largest, or even the most popular tavern in town. But it did serve as the hub for all the mercenaries that wanted a job in this city. If a new contract became available, you learned about it here. If you wanted to get your start in Ezra's line of work, this is where you'd go.

Ian's father had been the best broker in the country, but his son now easily had him beat.

At twenty-five, Ian had a manic energy and light about him that put people at their ease. In the event of a drunken brawl, all he'd have to do to bring it to a halt is put himself in between the involved parties. Much like fighting with a puppy present, it simply wasn't done.

Though it was only mid-afternoon, the tavern was already half full. Between his business and hers, Marya would certainly want for nothing if they were together. That is unless Ian got himself killed.

"Ezra!"

Speak of the devil...

Ian waved enthusiastically from the bar, his call alerting the entire establishment to Ezra's presence. Because there was nothing he loved more than being the center of attention. Now he had to make his way to the counter, through a bog of back pats, handshakes, and greetings. Not that he didn't like these people. He liked most of them. But he wasn't in the mood to be social, and forced geniality takes an emotional toll. Ian cringed under Ezra's glare as he approached and sat down.

"Sorry," he apologized timidly. "I forgot. Forgiven because I was happy to see you?"

"Forgiven if you make me some coffee. A whole pot." He nudged enough coin over and yawned, his body already anticipating the buzz. Ian rolled his eyes.

"You're the only reason I keep the stuff in stock, you know that right?" Ian asked as he pulled out the beans, filter, pot, and kettle. "Never mind that you can't drink tea like everyone else on this side of the Sands, you ask for this in a pub. Where I serve spirits, and ales and meads. Hard liquor? You've heard of these, right?"

"I'd make it myself, you know I would. It's just so much work to do it at home. And you know just the right bean to water mixture," he argued, slipping into a variant on a conversation they'd had many times before. "I've told you to try marketing it to the morning crowd."

"And I've told you they hate it. Everyone with taste buds hates it," Ian growled, not missing a beat. Each grind of beans inside the pestle release an aroma that had Ezra salivating. "I should make you buy the lot of it so I never have to go through this over complicated process again!" He slammed the pestle on the counter.

"But coffee makes me happy, Ian." Ezra said cheerfully, "and don't you want me happy when you explain what's going on between you and Marya?"

Ian's jaw dropped.

"Right. Listen. I need to talk to you about—" he paused, "What did Marya tell you?" Ezra set the bundle of clothes on the counter.

"She didn't tell me anything. Which is unusual for her. Care to explain?" He'd seen Ian's expression numerous times on the faces of men he'd killed. Perhaps he was coming on too strong. "I'm not angry, Ian. Finish the coffee, then we'll talk."

The tavern owner exhaled, as if he'd been holding on to his last breath, and went to work grinding the beans with renewed fervor.

A breeze ruffled Ezra's hair as a new group entered the tavern. Efrain Crippen and his bodyguards surveyed the room before keying in on him. Great. Ezra slipped one hand into his jacket, fingers closing around the hilt of a short sword. With the other, he drank the water Ian had given him earlier.

"Toth!" Efrain shouted.

"Crippen." Ezra nodded to the stool next to him. He sat down, though the men hung back.

"Do you know how many men you've cost me?" While fully aware of the fact that Efrain's snarl, meant to intimidate and terrify, usually worked, Ezra was of the opinion that it made the man sound a bit garbled, taking away from the whole menacing effect.

"Twenty-three that I'm sure of. But I set some traps farther in the wood so that may be off." Efrain made a fist.

"Twenty-six. Twenty-six men and women are dead because of you. My people! Give me a reason not to kill you right now!" The tavern was silent. Ezra gave his question some thought. As the wrong answer would lead to a fight and he did not particularly want to kill Efrain.

"Because I was just doing my job. And so were your men. I gave them a chance to run every time. I identified myself and they understood what I could do. I didn't really have a choice, did I? They were trying to kill my client. I would expect the same were our roles reversed." Efrain still looked ready to argue, but the assenting murmurs, agreeing with Ezra's words made him stop. Ezra held out his drink hand.

"We're both professionals. I am truly sorry for the loss of your people and the pain it has caused you." All eyes were on Efrain who, hesitantly, clasped arms with him. The tavern relaxed and the sound of chatter rose to a comfortable level. Ian placed a mug of coffee on the bar.

"Would you like to have a drink with me?" Ezra offered up his mug of coveted elixir, which Efrain sniffed then leaned away from.

"Perhaps another time." He stood, then as an afterthought, "I apologize for my behavior. See you around." Ezra waved him off before returning to his beverage only to find Ian watching him.

"What?"

"You truly seemed like you felt sad this time. Were you actually sorry about his men?"

"Was I sorry I killed them? No. When it comes down to them or me, I'm going to choose me. Do I feel bad about it in a way that I will carry for the rest of my life, like some people? No. The loss of life is a pity, though. The trick is thinking about something that honestly makes you unhappy and then it's more believable."

"Terrifying," Ian muttered, shaking his head in disbelief as he poured Ezra a refill.

"Listen, I came in here to let you know I've accepted a job and it's going to keep me away for a while."

Ian froze, eyebrows furrowed in confusion. It was no exaggeration to say that nearly all the Night work in this city came through his tavern. Whether he had a direct hand in it or, at the very least, made the introductions, he had a finger in the pot of every disreputable thing that happened in the capital.

"Who? When?"

"They were waiting outside my apartment after the Shield job. I can't say who for now. I want to be fully settled in before anyone finds out. Suffice to say, you'll know before I find time to visit. This might take as long as a year. So make sure to re-direct any referrals, yeah?" It was a sign of their friendship that Ian didn't pry into the identity of the client or the mission.

"Because of that, I will be buying out your supply." He placed two gold into Ian's more than willing hands. "Have it all ready to go later this week?" Ian nodded, already wiping down the kettle, clearly eager to get the stuff out of his tavern. "And Ian? Ian?" Ezra tapped him on the side of the head to get his attention. "Make sure you take care of Granny and Marya, yes?" Ian nodded again, this time serious.

"You know I will."

"Oh, and one more thing," Ezra stretched as he stood to take his leave. "Marya is family to me and if you hurt her...well...I don't really have to say what would happen, do I? See you in a couple days!" Ezra gave what he hoped resembled a friendly smile, patted Ian on the back, and left.

5

ERRANDS

Ezra's next errand took him back home for his weapons, which would have taken ten minutes if the cats hadn't wanted to play.

An hour later he pulled out a sturdy bag and began filling it with his favorite knives and swords. Ezra placed his long coat and boots on top, both of which had been seriously abused in his recent foray into the outdoors. The bag, strained against the weight and bulk, barely closed.

The market teemed with people. The constant rain during the past month that had kept people indoors had finally passed and everyone was enjoying the sunshine. Children splashed about in puddles that would not dry up for days and every window hung open to let in the warm breeze. He knew the weather would hold, at least through the rest of the day, because the washerwomen had clothes hung on wires across the buildings. They just had this uncanny way of reading the winds. Sadly, as much as they got along, the washerwomen wouldn't touch his clothes anymore.

Too much blood, they said.

Next door to their washhouse was his destination.

Pearline's Armory & Tannery was the only place he trusted with his gear. Oddly enough, he'd met all his friends by saving their lives. He remembered his first encounter with Pearline vividly.

Ezra happened upon Pearline six years ago in an alley by the docks. She had been covered in the blood of one of her would be rapists. She had stabbed him with a bit of pipe, now lying just out of her reach. The other two were busy beating her and shouting all manner of vile profanity. He had intervened, and the two joined their fallen comrade.

Whether she was too much in shock or she understood it wouldn't do any good, Pearline did not run from Ezra. She let him check her for injuries, just in case some of the blood that covered her was her own. It's likely she'd nicked a vein whilst defending herself. Aside from a good deal of bruising, it looked like she had survived relatively unscathed. He managed to get her home without incident, which was fortunate. Ezra had no idea how he would explain their appearances.

It took a while, but she led them back to her home and he knocked on the door. Given her age, sixteen at most, he expected her parents. Instead, they were greeted by two young men on their way to becoming giants. A smaller boy peeked around them, his eyes wide as saucers as the sight of them. They were ushered inside before Ezra had a chance to excuse himself, and from the glances, her brother's exchanged, he realized it was so they could kill him in the privacy of their own home. The larger of the two took his sister by the shoulders and looked her in the eyes.

"Explain," he demanded, shaking her slightly. Not surprising in the least, she burst into tears. Ezra sighed, separating the two.

"You. Small one," He pointed to the youngest of the brood who came over. "Take your sister and get her cleaned up then put her to bed. Don't ask her questions. Go." He gave them both a little shove, and they went into what he hoped was the bathroom and closed the door.

"Please, sit," Ezra did so himself and, after a moment, so did the brothers. "Your sister has been through an ordeal. She fought back and came through, for the most part, unharmed. But she has been through a trauma and any injuries sustained were emotional." He paused, hoping they understood, "I know I am a stranger to you. And you have no reason to trust me, but when she's cleaned up, I'll need to talk to her. She's going to need me to talk to her. There are certain subjects she simply won't feel capable, or comfortable, sharing with you. Things best said to a stranger." The middle brother Kiernan was against it, but the eldest, Rovin consented. Which, in this family, appeared to be the final word.

When the tiny one, Valiant, came back carrying a bucket of red water, Ezra walked past him.

One large mattress rested on the floor in the corner, likely for the boys. Pearline sat up in a small, wood-framed bed on the other side of the room. A sheet hung down the middle to afford her some privacy.

By the light of the candle by her bed, Ezra evaluated her. She was in shock. The tears had been replaced by a glazed stare, directed at her bloody clothes on the floor. Her hands, once bloody from the fight, gripped the edge of her blanket like it was all that kept her from falling into the dark.

Ezra approached slowly, so as not to startle her, but he could tell when she noticed him. Her whole body tensed. Ezra had a lot of practice attempting to appear non-threatening from when he first met Marya, and he tried to employ those tactics now, for all the good they did. She had seen him without the mask and there was no hiding behind it now. He sat on the edge of her bed and waited.

And waited. They sat in silence for minutes. Neither one moving.

Then, "Why did you save me?" Her voice had hollow, raw quality to it.

"Because you needed me. And because you killed your first attacker and showed me you wanted to live. No matter what you're experiencing now, in this moment, just remember that in that moment, you wanted to live. And," he hesitated, not sure whether he was willing to share this with a stranger. But she finally stared up at him, making eye contact, and holding it. And he continued. "And because no one was there to save me." Her stare, which had slid down to her hands, snapped back to attention, and skepticism as she looked him over. He understood.

"I wasn't always the magnificent specimen you see before you." This elicited a half smile. A win in his book. "I was a small, scrawny and sickly child who had been sent to live with my uncle. He was the Doctores of one of the greatest Lude in the capital of Charus."

"A doctores," he said, seeing her confusion, "is the trainer who manages fighters at their training ground. Known as a Ludus." Ezra could almost smell the hot air and imagine the sensation of the ever-invasive sands as he slipped back into his long-repressed childhood memories.

"Most of the fighters were indentured servants. My uncle bought them as slaves with the agreement that, if they won enough for him, they would earn their freedom. Most men in his position would not do as he did. But he came as close to beloved as a doctores had the potential to be. Some of the better fighters even took their freedom and used it to work for him, outside the fighting pits."

"The rest were criminals. The prisons paid him a fee to take them and use them as lion fodder in the fights. Just the ones too dangerous to work in the fields. And Uncle tried to keep me safe, but he wasn't always there. And one night he came for me." Ezra started when she put her hand over his.

"Klar was one of the most repulsive people I've ever met in my life. And I have met and killed some disgusting scum of the earth. I remember his smell, his hands, his hot breath on my neck as he told me not to scream. He had a knife, but he put it on my nightstand so he could...it was over quickly in hindsight. Once he had finished, he lay down, perhaps to sleep. Maybe just to rest before starting again. I didn't know. I wasn't thinking when I grabbed his knife. Or when I plunged his throat. Or when I pulled it out and stabbed him again, and again." He remembered that he, too, had been covered in blood that night. No one ever came at him again.

"My first kill," Ezra said, rubbing at a black dot at the edge of his wrist reminiscently. Then something happened that he didn't expect. Pearline wrapped her arms around him and started crying. Not for herself, but for him.

"I'm sorry," she whispered, "I'm so sorry." He gave her a few seconds and then gently pushed her away.

"I didn't tell you this for sympathy. I just want you to see that I survived. I found a way to carry on. Now, I don't understand how you feel. No one can. Not even if they had experienced this exact night, as unlikely as that is. You are unique in your feelings. I can't tell you that

I know what you're feeling. But I hope you can trust to tell me what those feelings are when you're ready." He stood, tucking her in and wiping the tears from her face. "For now, go to sleep. I will be by tomorrow. And the day after. I will be here whenever you need me. Go to sleep." And, miraculously, she did.

Rovin and Kiernan were waiting at the door. He gave them instructions to stave off questions. Teas and calming herbs to buy. To expect random fits of crying and nightmares. To be there for her and not dismissive of her seemingly abrupt and unpredictable mood swings.

"I need you to be sensitive," he'd emphasized. But the brothers were far more than their rough appearances. And, just based on what he'd seen in the bedroom, they clearly loved and doted on their sister. He left, feeling good about her chances of recovery.

The next afternoon when he arrived, she was jumpy but cheerful. Pearline didn't cry until they were alone. But over time, she healed.

•　　　•　　　•　　　•　　　•

Now her store was always full, and she thrived. Thankfully, there was only one other person inside at the moment. Kiernan rarely spent time in the store proper. Like his older brother, they worked off-site in production. Kiernan in fabrication and leatherworks, and Rovin in the forge. That left Val to split his time apprenticing with them, minding the store with his sister and—

"BOO!" Val jumped out from behind the counter, failing to sneak up on Ezra. The boy had had it in his head since Ezra brought his sister home that Ezra's job was the only one worthwhile. Something Kiernan hated him for. Val was always trying to prove he could get the best of him.

Valiant was every bit as scrawny as Ezra had been at thirteen, but it was already clear that the boy would be every bit as big as his brothers. Val's face fell at the lack of surprise, but he bounced back quickly.

"Pearl's out on delivery, but I can help you, Ez." The boy wouldn't call him anything else. And, as a child, he'd called him Ezzy. Not much better, but it was a start. He hefted the bag onto the counter and began to unpack. The coat and boots he set to the side and carefully placed the knives out. Val stared at them hungrily.

"Everything needs to be cleaned, first off. I need a new coat of sealant rubbed into the grips and all the blades have to be sharpened." He moved over to the coat and smoothed it out. "This has a bit of weather damage and there may be some mud and blood embedded in the stitching. I tried to get most of it out but your brother should check again. Same with the boots. Oh, and there's a small cut on the right shoulder that needs repairing." Val had been taking notes while he spoke and read back the order.

"Good. Now, I know how much your brothers hate rush orders, but I have another job and I need to pick all this up Friday. Is that possible?"

He saw Val falter slightly, but he nodded.

"It'll be fine. Friday afternoon?" Val asked, reloading everything back into Ezra's pack.

"Perfect." Ezra checked to make sure that Pearl hadn't come in, then took a small pouch out of his pocket and handed it to Val. "Don't tell your sister about this. Give the money directly to Rovin, all right? To Rovin."

Val peeked inside and his jaw dropped.

"This is too much!" he argued, reaching in to give some back. Ezra deftly took the pouch, tied it closed, and stuffed it in Val's pocket.

"Think of it as a rush fee plus the rest for the times your sister wouldn't take my money."

No sooner had he finished speaking than the door opened.

"You didn't tell me you were coming!" a familiar voice cried. And, like Val's habit of jumping out at him, he spun around, arms open to be ready to catch Pearl as she jumped at Ezra. He'd instinctively braced himself but still had the wind knocked out of him.

"Hey Pearl, how are you? Anything new?" She hopped down and smoothed her skirts.

"Oh fine. Just fine. I heard Mrs. Harris baked her cheating husband some ipecac pie. Apparently, he's been so busy retching that he can't lift a finger to stop her throwing his things out the window!" She smiled viciously.

"Remind me never to accept any food from Mrs. Harris." He grinned.

"Speaking of food," she grabbed his hand, "let me take you out for a bite. It's been weeks since I've seen you!" Ezra started backing towards the door.

"I'd love to. Really, I would. But I still have so many errands today. I'll take you to lunch before picking up my order Friday." That got her attention.

"Seriously?" She put her hands on her hips and stood in that way that she thought made her look tall and intimidating. "You just got back!"

"And I'm leaving again Saturday. Not the original plan, but what can I do? I'll fill you in Friday."

He made to open the door when she yelled, "WAIT!"

So close. Pearline now squinted at him with a divining stare nearly as accurate as the washer women's. She turned that glare on Val who jumped.

"Did he pay you?" she demanded.

Val shook his head violently.

"I wouldn't dare, Pearl." Ezra interrupted, trying to save the boy, "Where's the trust?" She scrutinized both of them for a moment longer.

"Fine," she finally relented. To Val she said. "Get those things to the workshop right away. If we're to get these back Friday the boys will want them as soon as possible. And you," she said, turning her attention back to Ezra, "I expect to see you noontime Friday. Yes?"

"Yes, ma'am," he saluted, shutting the door before she could throw something. It relieved him to know that the women in his life could take care of themselves. But, if he was going to be absent for a year, perhaps it would be good to have them spend more time in each other's company. Marya and Pearline had never had real cause to be alone together, as he had always been there. He hoped they might make good friends. Ezra would have to suggest that they spend more time together. Just in a way that it wasn't all his idea.

Women were too tricky to be 'managed'.

6

SEVERAL OTHER ERRANDS

Before she died, his mother had been sickly and scarred like him. She was not marked to such a severe degree but, she too was unable to heal as she should. The fact that she survived childbirth was a miracle none of the healers understood. Confined to bed most of the time, she experienced life through the small window by her bed. According to the gossiping neighbors, that was why his father left. He'd been tired of taking care of a frail wife and disgusted with his weak and equally frail son. It wasn't until his uncle took him to an apothecary, or chemist as they were called in the East, that he truly began to grow and live.

It was a disease called Horafur—literally meaning 'time thief' as Ezra later learned. Common enough in the East, though how he and his mother had contracted it, the chemist had no idea. Possibly something his father had unintentionally picked up on one of his many trading trips.

Usually, when caught in infants, the disease could easily be cured. Though that was not to be his fate, she did have a solution for him. The chemist had prescribed a mixture of herbs to be drunk every day, twice a day. He'd been on them ever since. Considering his size and career, one might make the mistake of thinking he no longer needed the tonic. But if he missed even one dose he started to feel it.

That chemist lived an entire desert away from him, but there was a man in the city of equal talent and of discretion. His shop rested between the midwife and the hacksaw.

Someone was always screaming. Mr. Slaght, a mostly deaf-lip reader, didn't seem to mind. Plus, he'd said, the place had come at a great price as no one else had wanted it.

Imagine that.

It was dim inside due to the constantly closed shutters. Dried plants hung from the already low ceiling and Ezra's back hurt in anticipation of the prolonged hunch. The smell of so many herbs, spices, and tinctures filled his nose and made him sneeze.

"Be right with you," he heard from the back. Ezra made his way through the store, careful not to knock anything over or step on something—again. Slaght stood in the back room, scooping powder into a vial and sealing it.

An assortment of unopened crates were visible just past the shopkeep, meaning a shipment had just come in. Maybe he'd only need the one order. Mr. Slaght wiped his hands, saw Ezra, then pulled his datebook out from his apron and walked out to meet him, thumbing through it.

"You aren't due to run out for another week and a half." He frowned. "I wasn't expecting you until at least the week's end."

"An unexpected job. I won't be able to stop in for a while. It's best that I get as much as possible from you now. Before I forget though." Ezra pulled a pouch from an inner pocket and handed it over. The old man pulled a bowl over and upended the bag into it, carefully turning it inside out to make sure he missed nothing.

"I thought I recognized it from one of your books," Ezra said, watching Mr. Slaght examine his find. The bowl was full of bright blue seeds. Each flower he'd found yielded at least fifty of them, and he'd found a cluster of twenty flowers. "I kept one whole," he handed over another bag with a flower he'd pulled from the ground, roots and all, careful to pack it with dirt. It had been beaten up, to say the least.

But still alive. The druggist, as absorbed as he was, did not pay Ezra any mind until Ezra gave him a firm tap on the shoulder.

"I'm guessing I found something decent. How much is it worth?"

Slaght, still not looking up, tipped the contents of the bowl onto a scale and began writing down numbers and calculations. Ezra had never been good with numbers, though his mother had tried. Finally, the shopkeeper made a note and circled it.

"You've never haggled with me and, if I needed help, you were there. You're a good boy, Ezra." Mr. Slaght smiled fondly at him. "How about a half year's supply of tonic now and another half year if any of the seeds take root. Good?" Now it was Ezra's turn to drool. They shook hands on it and Mr. Slaght began carefully pouring the seeds into a jar.

"Now, you said something about another job? Sword or shield if I may ask?" Mr. Slaght had lost his hearing on a Sword job in his youth, but he always liked to stay in the middle of things.

"Shield. Though it sounds more like a shield-wall type job." He rubbed his face, still getting his head around the idea of protecting a prince. "I'll be gone no less than four months, maybe a year." The more times he said it, the more it felt like a trap closing around him.

Mr. Slaght gave him a sympathetic pat.

"I can get you three months, no problem. But I'll have to double my order for next time. It can be here in a month. Good?"

"The best. Do you need help getting it together?" The old man only waved him away.

"It'll be ready tomorrow. Come back then." Ezra had been dismissed. He gave a slight bow and left.

Outside there was quiet. The newly living and the newly dead all took a moment of silence to rest.

•　　　•　　　•　　　•　　　•

Ezra had a unique relationship with the Treasury. They were an ongoing client, with whom he had a rather unconventional agreement. For a fee, he would occasionally break in, knock out guards, identify weak spots, and report to the guild leaders so they could tighten security. They fawned over him, though the day to day staff hated Ezra. Or feared him. Whatever worked. Clerk Elias sin fa Baez was decidedly the latter.

"Mr. Toth. Are you here for business?" Code for 'are you here to destroy things, beat men up, and potentially get me fired?'.

"Just here to drop some things in my box." He considered smiling but decided against it.

The clerk dabbed at his forehead.

"Good. All right. I'll show you down."

They proceeded to the back of the bank, down the steps, and past the vault. Ezra patted it lovingly, thinking of all the times he'd been inside, sans permission. He'd have to write a letter to the guild notifying them he'd be unavailable for the foreseeable future.

At the end of the hall was a locked door with a guard. The guard and Ezra used their keys to open the door. Another man sat guard on the inside of the room—if it could be called a room. The cavernous space within which so many of the city's elite hid their secrets continued on for quite a way. Torches spaced out every ten feet kept things illuminated. On his first visit, Ezra thought it reminiscent of a mausoleum.

Fifty columns down and three rows up. Ezra stopped in front of his little door in the wall. He repeated the process at the door with Elias, their keys both opening the lock. It was his concept, and the guild had found someone to bring it to life. The Olaesta Capital Treasury was one of the most secure in the world. Ezra slid the box out and set it on one of the tables spaced evenly down the room.

"I'll wait outside until you are finished," the clerk said, excusing himself.

Another key, one only in Ezra's possession, opened the box. Inside were letters. Three bundles of varying size. At least a thousand in all. He pulled three more out of his pack and wrapped them in with their allocated groups. Letters for Marya, Ian, and Pearline. He wrote them before every job. Even the smaller ones. Because no one hired him unless there was risk and in his line of work, there were no guarantees.

He did not want to deny them the farewell, the closure that had been denied him all his life. His father who had left in the night without so much as a word or warning. His mother, through no fault of her own, who died in her sleep. To this day, he still could not remember her last words to him. Ezra had thought there would be more of them to come. And his uncle, stabbed to death mere blocks from their home, yet another lost opportunity for closure.

It was not the same. But the letters were better than nothing. A copy of his will rested at the bottom. No changes were necessary there, save that there would be a lot more to go around. He hesitated, then reached back into his bag for a fourth letter addressed: Crown Prince Christophe Rhey. If dying wasn't worth a royal favor, then nothing was. He put it on top of the rest.

Ideally, they wouldn't see these for a long, long time. But it never hurt to prepare for all possible contingencies.

Walking through the Treasury's main hall he noticed a man wearing the King's sigil watching Ezra from behind a sheaf of papers. The man waited until Ezra was almost to the door before falling in step behind him. Whatever this stalker's profession, they had either never tailed someone before or were just incredibly bad at it.

Ezra, now on his way to see his longtime friend and mentor Antony, hardly wanted to involve his friend in the investigation of this would-be stalker. Ezra walked down the steps, momentarily dazzled by the beauty of the setting sun before he assumed a tactical mindset. He pondered—as he walked—upon the best way to catch his irksome shadow, ultimately deciding on the simplest method.

If Ezra's suspicions were, and they usually were, the mystery man was as bad a spy as he was at spying.

He abruptly turned down an alley, backed into a doorway, and waited. Sure enough, moments later, Ezra's shadow peeked around the corner. The man, seeing no sign of his quarry, walked into the alley, an expression of bewilderment plain on his face.

Ezra arm shot out, grabbing the man by the scruff of the neck and throwing him against the wall.

"We haven't been properly introduced," Ezra said pleasantly, holding a dagger precariously close to the man's right eye. "I'm Ezra. Who might you be?"

The man had eyes only for the dagger in Ezra's hand, seemingly lost for words.

"I'll put this away so we can speak as civilized individuals, shall I?"

Ezra put the blade away and the man let out a notable sigh of relief.

"You don't know who you're messing with." The man had seemingly regained some of his swagger in the absence of imminent death. "I answer to powerful people. The smart thing to do is release me and go about your business."

"That's certainly one option," Ezra said, pretending to consider the man's words. "Another, more favorable alternative involves me dragging you out of sight of the public and torturing you for information." The dagger was back in his hand and he used it to point out body parts, as if deciding where to start. He tapped the man's belt with his blade and smiled.

"Have you ever considered the exciting world of opportunities that would be opened to you, should you become a eunuch?"

The man looked down and gulped.

"I'm an agent of the King. My name is Cameron Redding. Please sir, I have a wife and two children to provide for. I beg of you, please do not remove my manhood." the man said all this very quickly, his words streaming together in a nearly incoherent string of sounds.

"If you had any manhood to begin with it's fading fast," Ezra observed drily. Once more he put the dagger away and took a step back to give Cameron some room to breathe.

"Thank you, sir. Your mercy is without equal." Ezra's shadow made to leave but Ezra casually blocked the man's path.

"You can go and tell your master all you've seen up to this point and then you'll tell him that you lost track of me. There will be no mention of this encounter. He is not to know that I know he sent spies to watch me. Understood?"

Cameron nodded vigorously, too petrified to speak.

He made to leave and Ezra put a hand on the man's shoulder.

"I'll know if you tell anyone about this meeting, Cameron. I can find you, no matter where you may hide. Just remember that." On that note, Ezra stepped aside and gestured that Cameron should leave.

The man's first few steps were tentative, then, like a horse who had been spooked, he bolted.

Ezra chuckled to himself before cracking his neck and continuing on his way.

7

FATHER FIGURE

Ezra's father left a scant three days before the boy's birthday, and he was well on his way to a life of thievery by that point. What little savings they'd had, his father had taken with him. One of the many reasons Ezra liked banks. A guaranteed account sum is much more difficult to steal than a box of coins under the floorboards. Though he still kept a lockbox under his bed for emergencies.

He couldn't do anything too hardy, but a crew had let him in to be their errand boy and occasional distraction when they ran a multi-person con. The crew had been made up of children, much like himself. All street rats from the Boroughs, most of them orphans. He was the youngest of them, the most innocent. Ezra had also been one of the few with a parent that didn't beat him senseless. Though he would have happily let his mother beat him if that meant she would have had the energy to stand and swing.

It was inevitable, him being so slow and weak, that he would get caught. The City Guard had asked his name and then, rather than sending him to the orphanage or locking him up with the other street rats, they'd put him in his own cell.

"Wait here until we get your guardian," they'd said. Which had baffled Ezra to no end. There was no way his mother had the ability to get up to collect him.

At the time, he figured they'd only told him that to keep him calm. More than likely they had a deal with some child runner to whom they planned on selling him. It would serve the bastard right if he paid up front, only to end up with damaged goods, or so he'd thought.

Instead, Ezra was released to a man in clean, pressed solicitor's robes. He had the name and the coloring of a man from the Southern Continent. His face was serious, but his eyes were kind, which was the only reason Ezra followed him, rather than running the first chance he got. Not that he would have gotten very far. Despite the hints of gray in his black hair and the beginnings of wrinkles around his eyes, the man looked spry and more than able to give chase. Robes and all.

To Ezra's surprise, the man took him home. His mother introduced him as Antony sin fa Pena. An investigative solicitor for the crown. Apparently, Sir Sin fa Pena was a childhood friend who had been checking in on her more frequently since her husband's departure. His father had not taken kindly to his wife having a male friend according to his mother.

Ezra waited outside while the two of them spoke. Before Antony took his leave he pulled out some cards and played a quick game of God's Luck. Ezra won. One of the many ways he scraped enough money together to feed him and his mother was through gambling. He was a shark at the card table by the age of seven.

Ezra thought he'd seen the last of Antony, but he returned later that week to speak with him. And a few days after that he brought dinner for him and his mother. A week after that he paid Ezra to run some errands for him, and for a while, he worked for Antony in that capacity.

Ezra wasn't fast, but he knew the city and usually managed to hitch a ride on carts where the adult messengers would have had to walk. Soon after that, Antony took him on as an assistant. He learned how to read and write past what his mother had taught him, though they gave up on numbers quickly. Likely due to advise the solicitor had received from Ezra's mother. There were hints at him even being made an apprentice in the future if he'd continued to work hard and prove himself worthy.

But then his mother died. Even then, Antony offered to be his guardian. Despite everything, Ezra felt at peace because he knew that he was where he belonged, and where his mother would have wanted him to be. He felt safe. And that would have happened, had his Uncle not appeared.

To this day, he wasn't sure why Uncle Sam had wanted him so much. He'd never even met the man. And, though Antony had wanted to argue for custody, Sam was his mother's brother. He was blood and had every right to take Ezra away.

The day Ezra had left, his pack loaded by Antony with clothes and books, was one of the worst days of his life. Even worse than the day his mother died. Her suffering had come to an end, and he'd had Antony to take care of him. Instead, at ten, a stranger was taking him away from his home and the only real family he had left. He'd hated his uncle for that.

So when Sam got himself murdered, Antony was the only reason Ezra returned to the capital at the young age of twenty-one. Merely ten years away, but he had changed enough to account for a lifetime.

They'd both changed since that meeting in the cells. Antony had moved up in the world and become a judge, Ezra an executioner.

He walked up the path to his mentor's mansion home. The size of the place had nothing to do with vanity, though. Every room was filled with books, records, and cases he had reviewed. It was likely they would just move the next judge into this house upon Antony's death, rather than face the task of moving it all out.

At this time in the evening, he knew Antony would be home, and knocked on the heavy door. The butler, Andrew, greeted him.

"He's in the study, Master Toth." Ezra's boots echoed in the halls as he approached the door.

"Antony?" Ezra called out, taking a step into the study. The judge had been asleep, though he tried to hide it, drool still ran down his chin. Ezra wasn't surprised though. The man worked harder than any other civil servant in the land. The years, plus his dedication to the job, had taken their toll, turning his hair pure white and carving wrinkles into his skin. Though, truth be told, many of them were laugh lines.

"Ezra," Antony stabilized one of the many piles on his desk before it had a chance to tip, then fully focused his attention on him. "I expected you back days ago. Are you all right?" Naturally, he would have heard about the dignitaries' resolved situation and known Ezra had finished with his latest job.

"I was on my way home from that very job to rest, then visit you, when I was detained. You're not the only one working for the crown anymore."

Antony's eyebrows rose to meet his receding hairline.

"What?"

"The crown prince's personal guard awaited me at my home. I met with Prince Christophe just this past Monday to discuss my protecting him for the foreseeable future."

"The prince has guards. Why would he call for you?" Antony had turned on his 'judge voice'—as if he was sure this was one of Ezra's jokes. He reached for his tea, something that always calmed him.

"Because Prince Daniel and his father want to kill him. So he is understandably suspicious of who he can trust within the castle."

Anthony's teacup hovered near his chin, completely forgotten, as he gaped at his fosterling. Ezra took this silence as encouragement to continue. "You have been saying I need to find more reputable clientele…" but even that wasn't lightening the mood.

Antony slammed his cup down, splashing liquid on what were likely important documents. Something that would normally lead to a prodigiously large vocabulary of curse words. But he hardly seemed to notice.

"No! You must decline this offer. If you've already accepted, say you've changed your mind. You are not prepared for the royal court. You couldn't handle it."

Ezra turned to the bookcases, hiding the hurt that was likely plain on his face. Did his mentor think him incapable of living in his world, even temporarily? After everything, was he still little more than a murdering gutter rat in Antony's eyes?

"Ezra?" Antony's voice sounded tired and sad. "Please forgive me. I meant nothing against you. But the court is a devious place full of self-serving narcissists with no real sense of right or wrong. I don't want you caught up in that. Despite your profession, you're far too naïve and innocent for the likes of that crowd."

Ezra heard the concern in his voice and, when he turned, he saw it in Antony's eyes. He'd had a few father figures in his life, but Antony ranked highest by far.

"You only want what's best for me, I know. But the pay for this is too good to pass up. And from what you've told me about the royal family, it's too important to let someone else handle. I added a letter to the crown prince to my box. If I fail and he dies, see that it is destroyed."

Antony scowled at that. He was not a fan of the letters, or 'death notes' as he referred to them.

"How long?"

"The job is contingent on the king's death, and perhaps a short time after. I was told no less than four months. No more than a year."

Antony chuckled at that.

"I wager you'll go stir crazy in two."

"Your faith in me is touching," Ezra replied dryly. "Though, if the court is as crazy as it sounds, at least I should have plenty to keep entertained."

"Fair enough. I surrender. But be careful. I'm sure I'll see you around the palace. I'm there every other week with the Court of Justice to convene with the King on the state of the capital."

"I'll still stop in to say goodbye, Friday before I leave. We'll have to be all sorts of formal around each other and I won't be able to do things like this," Ezra strode across the room and gave his mentor a hug. Likely the first one Antony had received since Ezra left for his last job.

"Now go to bed, old man. You're starting to look as old as you actually are!" He ducked the paperweight thrown his way.

"Louse!" Antony yelled, his menace severely punctured by the yawn that followed. Andrew couldn't keep the grin off his face as he opened the door for Ezra, who walked merrily into the night.

8

COUPLES COUNSELING

Thursday flew by. Ezra spent the morning brushing every one of the cats, something he never quite trusted Marya enough to do. He discovered that Lucy was pregnant when brushing her stomach. Ezra wondered whether the kittens would be half mountain lion, or if Lucy had been the one to go after some traumatized male. Either way. She was at least half-way through the pregnancy.

"Did you wait until I left to mount the first poor unsuspecting tomcat you could get your claws into?" he asked, scratching her belly. She only glared at him, a response clearly beneath her.

At least now he had a very clear time that he needed to take a day off. With Lucy being due in a month or so, he'd want to make sure, with winter coming, that all the kittens were all right. Clearly tired of his inspection, she nipped at his fingers and ran off to work on her nest. He sighed, wiping at the blood on his fingertips and went in search of some spirits to rinse it with. The last thing he needed to worry about was Cat Scratch Fever whilst guarding the prince.

•　　•　　•　　•　　•

From the screaming Ezra heard a block away he could tell that both the hack saw, and the midwife were already hard at work when he arrived for his herbs. He was on his way in when Mr. Slaght walked out of the door on his right, the sounds of sawing and screaming grew louder until he shut it behind him. His sleeves were rolled up to keep them clean of the blood that covered his hands.

Mr. Slaght vigorously scrubbed at them with a rag when he almost bumped into Ezra.

"Hello, there," he half shouted, likely still used to the volume he'd only just left, "You'd think with all the poppy I provide these two they wouldn't run out, but no. Too kind-hearted. And I can't give them my whole supply. I have other buyers. I'll have to up my order for next time, same as yours. Samson will be thrilled." He pulled a key out of his pocket, unlocking the apothecary.

"They're low on poppy, I get that," Ezra replied, "But it doesn't explain why you're coming out of the butchers covered in blood."

Mr. Slaght scowled at the jab. He knew how Ezra felt about the bone saw's work. Ezra would rather fix himself up than be sent there.

"I was helping out because Julian's assistant has taken ill and couldn't come in today. It's important to stay good with your neighbors, Ezra. Something you should learn to keep in mind." Likely Mr. Slaght was speaking of Efrain rather than Hugh the user. But he did not comment further, so neither did Ezra.

"Gossiping with Ian again, I see," Ezra observed.

Slaght chose not to dignify that with a response.

"Everything's ready," Mr. Slaght continued. "Three months now, and the rest in a month." He pointed to a large package wrapped in burlap. "And I'm sure you've forgotten, but I also threw in a re-stock of your antidotes and poisons. Something tells me you'll need them." He placed a smaller box on top of the package. "The tonic ingredients haven't been ground down into a powder yet. You'll have to do that before you mix them. If you just chip off a bit from the whole you'll get too much, understand? Do you have a mortar and pestle?" When he said that he didn't Mr. Slaght added them to the increasingly heavy pile. "I know you have measuring spoons so you've all you need." Ezra thanked him, forced money into Mr. Slaght's hand for the mortar, pestle, and antidotes, and promised he'd return in a month, before leaving.

Seriously weighted down, he returned to the apartment to drop the medicine and poison off before going to Marya's home. He'd promised he would spend the day with her. But when he arrived at his door, there a linen wrapped package lay waiting on the stoop. This was a surprise unto itself, not because someone knew where to put it, but because it hadn't been stolen. Ezra managed to balance it atop his pile of purchases and bring it inside. The apartment had emptied. All the cats were outside, sunning themselves on the roof. The herbs he set to the side, confident the animals would not try to eat them. Not after the first time.

The package was large but soft and, when he undid the ribbon securing it, he saw why. Inside were clothes. The palace seamstresses were quick workers if they had the ability to turn this around within a few days. He hung it up, not wanting to risk it getting covered in fur. The man taking his measurements had, at least for this one outfit, taken him seriously.

A simple black coat that hung down to the knees, black trousers, and a royal blue shirt. Were they made with a little less skill and cloth of a far cheaper weave, Ezra might even expect to see someone dressed much the same in The Sword and Shield. He tried everything on and it fit perfectly. The message was clear. 'Wear this to the palace.' He felt like a dress-up doll.

Reaching inside for pockets Ezra froze. There were none. No pockets lined the inside of the jacket or the sleeves. At least their timing could not have been better. He bundled everything back up and made for Marya's.

She was waiting for him by the stall, her hair braided up, and she wore one of her nicer dresses. Granny, currently hard at work, had given Marya the day off to spend with Ezra. Marya was going to hate him for this. Her eyes lit up when she saw Ezra but narrowed in suspicion at the package in his arms.

"I need a favor."

Marya didn't say anything. She just got up and marched inside the store, slamming the door behind her. Granny started cackling.

"What?" Ezra suddenly felt he had done something very bad. "What did I do?"

"I told Marya you would have her working today. I said, 'Just you wait, dijetehe will rip big hole in pants and beg you to fix."

Just then Marya walked out, an apron around her waist, and sewing kit in her hands.

"Ezra, what did you do?" Her voice had that tone. If she ever had children, it would be that tone that had them confessing to whatever wrongdoings they had ever committed or ever would commit.

"I need pockets!" he begged, holding the clothes out for her inspection.

Her eyes widened in surprise, but she took them, walking back inside, with him having no choice but to follow. Marya lay the clothing out on the table and spread it out. He stood in silence, watching her work, while she inspected the cloth, the seams, feeling and stretching at things for who knew what reason.

"Ezra," she barked.

"Yes," he started.

"Where did you get this?"

"So, remember when I mentioned the tailor who took my measurements? I'm fairly certain these came from him. But there aren't any pockets. At all. I've nowhere to put my knives. Or sword. Or medicines. Or poisons."

She raised an eyebrow at him, but said nothing, only lifting the coat to drape it over one of her dress forms.

"The fabric is good. It can hold everything you need but still be light enough not to smother you. Whoever made this knew what they were doing," she admitted grudgingly. "If you want the usual, I can have it done in an hour or so." She pulled a pattern out of her *Ezra* drawer, and spread it on the table, making notes as to the number, location and type of pockets and hoops she would need to sew in.

He broke Marya's concentration to give her a quick hug.

"You're the best, you know that, right? As soon as you're done, the rest of the day is yours. Then dinner and dancing at The Shining Star. Sound good?"

Marya waited, arms crossed, until he had finished to resume her work, grabbing leather cord, thick black cowhide, and scissors.

"Just repeat after me, Ezra. 'I have the best friend in the world and I don't deserve her.'"

Ezra decided against hugging her with scissors in her hands.

"I have the best friend in the whole world and I don't deserve her." He chanted, not for the first time.

"Good. Now go away." She waved him off, already absorbed in her project.

Ezra walked outside where Granny's attention was being pulled in several different directions. She saw him and thrust a dress into his arms.

"Make yourself useful, boy. Wrap this up."

And that was how he worked through the rest of the morning. The shop's regulars understood that there was no need to be afraid of him, but because Granny would knock him out and stuff him under the table rather than miss a sale, she had him wear a pink apron to "cut down on his man-ness" as she said. He failed to mention that his own apron, for the rare times he attempted to cook, sported a similar shade of pink from the blood that had mixed into the wash and stained his whites.

Marya finished her work a mere hour and a half later and came out to find him haggling with an old woman over one of her scarves. The prune was far too cheap for her own good but they came to an arrangement and she went on her way, happily scarved for the few days she had left before she died of old age; which he said to Marya before she cuffed him on the head.

Inside, he tried on the coat. It still felt perfect. She had placed the wooden replicas of his knives for sizing inside each of the hidden compartments inside. The coat lay flat, without any outlines to hint at weaponry underneath. He threw a few practice punches without anything pinching or cutting and when he spun around, nothing flew loose. The knives in his sleeves came out with ease and when he sat, the sword was the only thing that puckered the slightest bit. Marya was a genius. Were she willing to step foot in the castle, she could likely make a real name for herself. He took the coat off, and she disarmed it before carefully folding and wrapping it up with the rest of his things.

"I also made sure to sew in lock picks into the seam of your pants and shirts, should you need it." Because she thought of everything. Ezra had little doubt that Ian was similarly outfitted. "Now I'm starving," she said, grabbing her purse. "You promised me a wonderful day and will have to work extra hard to salvage it."

Properly admonished, he held out an arm which she took, smiling.

Salvage it he did. Though she was thirteen years his junior, they were very much in sync. They ate skewers while walking around the lake, talking about all he had missed in the past month.

First and foremost being that Granny had been arrested, again. But this time the guard had been new and didn't understand the catch and release policy Ezra and the patrol had worked out for her. So Marya, escorted by Ian, was forced to go down to the Southside Borough Department to fetch her. It took a pre-signed letter from Antony to secure Granny Kelva's release.

As a thank you, Marya took Ian out to dinner. And that led to another dinner. Then he took her dancing. She confessed to Ezra that they had been friends before, and she had liked him but had never thought of him in such a way until then.

Ezra asked what happened to make her freeze Ian out, and at first, she didn't want to tell him. But after reassuring her that, were she not to tell him, he would assume the worst, she confessed that they'd had a fight.

The two were meant to meet at the Midsummer festival. Marya had waited by the bonfire for hours, watching folk go past until she gave up and went home. Later that night, after Granny had already turned in, there was a knock on the door and she opened it to find Ian, bleeding on her front step. He had a gash in his arm and was pale from blood loss.

Marya had only ever had to stitch Ezra up when he got cut in a place he couldn't reach. But she'd done it enough that she had the skin cleaned and sewn back together quickly. He'd said he was sorry. That there was a last-minute meeting that should have only taken but a moment and he'd make it up to her next time.

Her response was to toss him out on his ass, stating that he would be lucky if there was a next time.

"And that was the last time we spoke," she finished, angrily chewing at her sixth skewer.

"But, Marya, that festival ended over a week ago. You still haven't spoken?" She paused and gave him a look.

"*You're* going to give me relationship advice?"

"Fair enough." And they moved on to other topics. He brought up the idea of her and Pearline getting together every once in a while whilst he was gone, 'so Marya could check up on her', he'd said, and she thought it was a nice idea. Score one for subtlety.

Marya was overjoyed to hear Lucy was having kittens and promised to check in on her and bring extra cream and food for her. From a safe distance, of course. In return, Ezra promised to get his hands on some fabric for her, and maybe a dress so she could tear it apart and examine it. He suggested that she come and meet the tailor that did his measurements, but she froze up at the mere suggestion, as he was afraid she might.

"Not in a million years." She frowned, arms folded. "I only trust you in that den of lies because I know you'll come out." Skewers gone, they went back into town.

At a jeweler's stall, when Marya leaned down to examine something, Ezra pulled a boy aside, slipped him a copper coin, and instructed him to go to Ian at his tavern and tell him to be at The Shining Star that night, no matter what. The boy vanished before Marya leaned back up. He bought her the necklace she'd been looking at just in case his interference went horribly wrong.

However, it seemed that he would not be punished for his meddling this time. They dined and danced and had a wonderful time. Then in the middle of a particularly lively jig, he spun her into Ian's arms and spent the rest of the night at the edge of the dance floor, stomping and clapping as he watched them dance. They would be a good match, he decided. Ian had a sharp mind to match Marya's and would make her laugh. And she, in turn, would keep him in line and give him the sense of family Ezra knew Ian wanted. They balanced each other out.

The three all went out for drinks after that and Ian entertained them with tales about a fight that had broken out the night before in his tavern involving three mercs, a whoremonger, and a very very lost foreign priest. They roared into their tankards and soon had to leave, or risk being kicked out for causing a ruckus.

Walking down the moonlit street, Ezra became very aware that the two were now holding hands, and excused himself on account of 'a thing he'd forgotten to do for a person at the place' and dashed away quickly before they had a chance to ask him to clarify. His work was very clearly done, and he could come for his clothes tomorrow.

At home a note had been slipped under his door. At least, that was what he figured had happened. It had been torn at and played with by the cats so that, by the time he got to it, the paper had been chewed a bit and been moved to the base of his bed. An offering to the High Queen Lucy. The note informed him that a horse would be sent Saturday morning for his convenience. Which was nice because it saved him the trouble of renting one out with the hopes that he'd be able to find an honest person at the palace to return it. Or willing to even venture into his end of the city.

He leaned out the window to breathe in some of the brisk night air and noticed another spy, nearly invisible amidst the shadows of the night. Ezra gave the man a grin and shut the window, sliding the threadbare curtain closed.

He went to bed that night and dreamed of Queen Marya and King Ian, dancing through a blood-soaked Sword and Shield, Lucy accompanying them on the mandolin.

9

THE TOURNAMENT

Ezra woke before the sun in a cold sweat. He rolled out of bed, disrupting several angry beasts, and staggered to the rain barrel by the window. Dunking his head into the cold water, he swore again to never drink alcohol before bed. It did things to his dreams. It made him see things. But worst of all, he remembered, as he flung open the windows and heaved out onto the street, it made him violently ill.

Luckily the street was empty, and he had ruined no one's morning, save his own. Gargling with the rainwater, he sent that out to join his dinner. Elli and Kyra rubbed against him, purring. They may have been troublemakers, but Ezra found that cats were also exceptionally caring creatures when they felt like it.

At this point, there was no possibility of him getting back to sleep, though everyone else had curled into the warm spot he'd left behind and easily nodded off. Ezra slipped into his clothes from the day before, grabbed a towel, and left.

This time of year, the waters were cooler, but not so cold that they were unbearable. Just enough that they were exactly what he needed. He stripped down to his skivvies, leaving those on so as not to give some poor fisherman's wife a heart attack, and dove into the water. Every part of his body jerked awake in the surprising cold and his eyes opened automatically, though he could see no farther than his hand.

He swam from the docks to the deep-water marker, remembering the first time he really swam.

An enemy gang had nabbed him for some slight his leader had committed against theirs, and Ezra had been easy pickings. They'd meant to drown him but, as it turns out, death is an excellent motivator to learn how to swim. And they didn't know how, wanting to be sailors someday, and were unable to catch him as he darted out into deeper waters.

Ezra loved the ocean. It was the thing he'd missed the most when his uncle had dragged him into the desert. He'd befriended a nobleman's son for the sole purpose of using their indoor lake. What they called a 'pool'. The people in the desert country of Charus were almost indecent in their opulence.

By the time his nausea had passed and Ezra felt well again, dawn had finally arrived. He'd planned on stopping by the washhouse on the way home, but nature had other plans. No sooner had he emerged from the water than the skies opened up to remind the people that the rainy season was still very much in swing. It poured so hard that it only took moments for the salt to rinse from his hair and skin.

Ezra's shirt and pants clung to him, drenched as they were, by the time he arrived home. Though it felt good, he quickly changed into dry things and squeezed the excess water from his hair. He may have his tonic, but that didn't mean he wasn't more than susceptible to everyday illnesses, which reminded him he had not yet taken it this morning.

He pulled in one of the many pots he used to collect rainwater and put it over the fire. Ezra checked the cupboard and found he was almost out of pre-made tonic pouches. Mixing the ingredients every day produced better results, but he found that it took too much time. Every month or so he'd lock the door and work his pestle from morning until night.

When the water came to a boil, he dumped some water into his least chipped mug, mixed in the powder, and stirred. Once the smell had driven away all the cats, he downed the whole thing and chased it with wine. A well-practiced routine he only had to experience twice a day for the rest of his life.

Ezra wanted nothing more than to lie on the couch with the book he'd left, half-finished, three weeks ago, but Bluebell began meowing pathetically. Her piteous cries were taken up by the lot until he was being forced out the door, rain shade in hand, to get them some food. It was a wonder they weren't all as substantial as Lucy.

The fish market greeted Ezra with the sounds of haggling, chopping, and general bustling about, heightened by the reek of fish. While most vendors would only sell their catch as is, Miriam saw him coming a mile away and was in the midst of prepping his usual order when he arrived. It took no time at all for her to mince and package one of her fish, a grouper this time, and hand it over. An older woman, aged even older by a life on the sea, her hands were as tough as the leather gloves tucked into her belt.

"How are the babies doing?" She asked, referring to his many mousers.

"They're fine, Mir. Lucy went and got herself knocked up while I was away. She's bigger than ever. Want one of the kittens?" Miriam had five of her own but was always looking to expand now that her human brood had moved out.

"Not me. I'm set for now as Donald went red as a starfish last time I brought one home. But maybe my youngest grandbaby, Martha might like one." He promised to have Marya bring one over once it had weened, paid for the food, and left.

The vultures were all waiting at the door when he returned, rubbing up against his legs and reaching up as if they meant to trip him and bring the food closer once he fell. Years of practice on this obstacle course allowed him to get to the bowl and dump it out. They descended on it like wolves. He'd saved a handful and placed it on a smaller plate in front of Lucy. She gave him a look of disgust before condescending to tuck in.

With the cats taken care of, he left to meet Smudge.

•   •   •   •   •

One might think an inker named Smudge might not be the best of choices to make, but Ezra had gone to him for every death mark since he'd returned to Olacia.

It had started with Klar. His first. After he'd killed his attacker, uncle had taken Ezra to an inker in town. He'd asked only that a small dot be placed on his arm, right above the wrist. Uncle rolled up his sleeve to show off his own arm. It was covered in dots. Ezra had seen them before but he'd never really understood what they were. Until then. Before they left, Ezra asked for a small circle on the back of his hand. The inker obliged. When uncle asked what it was for Ezra only said that it was a promise.

The kill marks that now spanned his arm had long since covered it, and spread in a circular pattern up his shoulder, just skimming his clavicle. Ezra had lost count of the marks years ago. He knew only that it was a very large number, plus twenty-six. Smudge was one of the few people he'd told about the meaning of the tattoos. *Maculata.* That's what his uncle had called it. The art of marking important events on one's self.

Now he rubbed that still unfilled circle, chuckling at the cockiness of his youth and wondering if the circle would ever be filled in. But for the time being, he had twenty-six new marks to add.

•   •   •   •   •

He felt a bit sad, walking down the muddy streets, lined with buildings abused by time and tenant. This was, after all, his home, no matter how much it smelled, and he felt certain that the palace would not feel right. Ezra took a deep breath through the nose, trying to lock it into his mind, and immediately regretted it. He had every confidence that it would take a hot poker to the brain to free him of that scent memory.

Pearl's shop overflowed with patrons. While some might have to weave their way through the crowd, Ezra had always been blessed with the gift of people getting out of his way. He walked forward, and a path opened to the counter where a frantic Val and near manic Pearl were waiting on people.

"What's going on?" He had to shout, hoping his voice would carry over the din. But it was Rovin who grabbed his arm and pulled him behind the counter, having appeared from somewhere in the crowd.

"This morning the King announced a tournament in honor of Crown Prince Christophe. A week of birthday celebrations ending in a grand prize of five hundred gold pieces. Since the announcement, everyone with too much time on their hands has been through here to buy steel. Most of them too green to use it. If they set the rules same as last year I'll bet more n' half die." Rovin left him to dive back in and manage the crowd, forcing them into something resembling a line.

Christophe's birthday was not for another two weeks. That, and his promise to Pearline were the only things that stopped Ezra from grabbing his gear and leaving for the palace right then. The chances of this being a coincidence were paltry, to say the least. Ezra was willing to bet every mark on his arm that this served as the king's latest attempt to kill his son. Birthday celebration indeed.

He saw his bag on the back counter and swung it across his shoulder. Ezra knocked on Rovin's shoulder to get his attention.

"I'm going to take this home and come back in a bit. Let Pearl know I haven't skipped out on lunch, yeah?" Rovin nodded, then winced as an overexcited youth trod on his foot.

Ezra ran out the door and half the way home before slowing down. His mind raced with all the new problems he faced. A royal celebration of that magnitude meant feasts, foreign entertainment, least of all the men with weapons battling right in front of him. That was in addition to the everyday dangers he was already preparing for. If he'd judged the knight correctly, then Joe was likely in the throes of a panic attack, pacing and yelling.

People were gathered by the Announcements Plaque—possibly a plaque in nicer parts of the city but here it was an old door leaning against a tree—with a notice nailed to it.

THE CROWN IS PROUD TO ANNOUNCE
A WEEKLONG FESTIVAL
IN HONOR OF THE CROWN PRINCE'S BIRTHDAY
TO BE HELD TWO WEEKS HENCE
AND END ON PRINCE CHRISTOPHE'S
23RD BIRTHDAY

The announcement continued on, small writing at the bottom about a few contests and the tournament but Ezra wasn't focused on that. His mind was on the monumental task before him.

The crowd buzzed with excitement. It had been a while since the crown had held a tournament and the festivities were always open to the public. They were traditionally events that Ezra greatly enjoyed. Both because he took Marya, and she was so easily entertained that it made the whole event that much better and because it served as the perfect time to kill someone. Not in the tournament itself. He never participated as it not only drew too much attention his way, but he also felt it wasn't fair to the competitors. Events like this brought in crowds from nearby villages and gathered all the city folk in one place. Were he to walk through a crowd and stab someone, he could easily be out of sight before they fell to the ground. Then again, shooting them with an arrow from a rooftop would eliminate any chance of someone placing him at the scene. Or he could poison them with a blow dart. Or break their neck as they stepped into an alley.

All things he'd done. All things he now imagined being done to Christophe.

As he entered his apartment for the third time that day, the cats were expecting attention but he ignored them, completely lost in thought, as he dumped his things on the table and walked right back out the door.

The good news was, he had two weeks to prepare, and then if the tournament was over in another week. Sometimes these things could go on as long as a month. If that were the case Ezra thought he might just kidnap the prince until it was over, hiding him in some undisclosed location known only to him and, perhaps Joe. Ezra's thoughts spun so fast that, by the time he returned to the shop, he was ready to vomit for the second time that day.

When Ezra returned, Kiernan's cart was just coming up the side, full of swords, knives and all sorts of shiny killing things. He may not have liked Ezra, but he had no problem letting him help carry the merchandise inside. Once they'd loaded it into the back, the two entered the store proper, where things had only become busier. Rovin saw them and near tossed Pearline at Ezra.

"Take her with you!" When she tried to protest, he cut her off, "You've been here longer than any of us. Take the cart back then take a break. Bring some food back with you."

Ezra pulled her out before anyone changed their mind, somewhat gleeful in the fact that they were leaving Kiernan to work in the store. A man so impersonable that he was likely happy at the prospect of dying a bachelor.

According to Pearline, once she'd finished exclaiming over the day she'd had "you would not *believe*" she went on to explain their rush. Not only was the tournament freshly announced, Mrs. Harris' husband, Alvin Harris, who ran the other major swordsmith of affordable price to those who were quite desperate for the prize money, was still laid up. Having apparently overdosed on ipecac, he was unable to open his own store. His wife had threatened their sons, so they hadn't dared open without him. Which left her and her brothers as the only real alternative.

Were there other blacksmiths? Of course. In a city this large there were dozens of shops. But none that specialized in weaponry and were willing to barter for work and goods rather than exclusive coin. Ezra could have sworn he saw a man with a chicken under his arm before he closed the back door behind him.

Leo, the donkey hooked up to the cart, waited patiently for their return. An old donkey, at least twelve years old, he had been purchased by Pearl's father before he and her mother died. Nine years ago, just before Ezra returned, a fever swept through the city. The late Frances and Karen Smith were among the many victims.

The wagon seat only fit one so Ezra took the reins and Pearl lay out in the back, using the burlap as an impromptu pillow. It was not a far ride from the store to the stable they shared with the local innkeeper. For the occasional use of his cart, they let him use Leo. That was the way things usually worked in the Boroughs, no matter whether you were north or south side. Coin had far less value than a favor paid or a favor owed, especially when there was so little coin to go around. One of the many reasons Ezra tried to spend as much he could while at home, more than anywhere else. He wasn't rich, but he was certainly better off than his neighbors. Well enough off that he did not have to live where he did. But he belonged here, to the Borough and it's people.

Their arrival at the inn timed out perfectly, because Mrs. Fetner, the innkeeper's wife, had orders to pick up. She took the reins from Ezra and went on her way.

Friendship with Pearline was effortless. She was one of those people that just seemed to gush happiness all the time. Not like those who did it in such an obnoxious way that it made him want to smash their faces into the wall. Pearl radiated a joy, a warmth, which spread to everyone around her. Soon, his panic over the tournament had faded. He would deal with events as they happened. There was nothing he could do now.

Instead, he just listened. Because, along with her amicable nature, she was also a talker.

Pearline never seemed to run out of things to say. She was friends with so many people who told her things and the sanctity of secret keeping meant nothing when it came to gossip between them, so he knew a bit of everything about everyone. Everything she said had substance and held his interest to the point that he felt comfortable just listening. One of the many reasons their friendship worked. While most people would want to speak at some point, he was more than happy to walk in silence all the way to the pub.

Considering the tournament, he knew she would tear into him the next time they met, so Ezra decided to keep the details of his job from her. She might think it would be safe to tell her brothers, including Kiernan, who seemed solid enough, but who Ezra didn't even trust as far as he could throw him. Instead, he promised her details upon his return in a month. Unlike Miriam, she very much did not want a kitten from Lucy's litter. Lucy had never liked her, and the feeling was mutual.

"With my luck, the ambivalence will have passed to her young and I'll be stuck with a devil cat for the next twenty years." It never occurred to her to abandon a cat. Even a hypothetical one. It was one of the many things he loved about her.

"By the way, Pearl. While I'm gone, Marya is going to be on her own with Granny. You know how much time we spend together." He hoped things would go just as well the second time. "Would you be willing to check in on her every now and again? Maybe say you're looking in on Granny then take Marya out to lunch? I'd feel better if you were keeping an eye on her." Ezra took a bite of his sandwich, trying to seem casual.

"I'd be happy to," she agreed. "We girls have to look after one another."

Two for two. Ezra hid the grin on his face behind another large bite, which backfired when he nearly choked on it. He heard his mother's voice like a little scolding spirit, 'Just because you can, doesn't mean you should.' It was a lesson she applied to the oh so many stupid things he'd attempted and sometimes succeeded at, in his youth. But Pearline didn't seem to notice, so he counted it as another win.

They ordered three more sandwiches to go and Ezra carried them to make sure all three made it back. Their return trip was unusually quiet.

"A whole year?" she finally asked, breaking the silence.

"There's no way it will last that long," he reassured her. "And I'll visit. You won't even notice I'm gone." He reached out to ruffle her hair but, unlike Marya, Pearline kept hers pinned up and dodged quickly so he wouldn't muss it up.

"Back off. I'm already enough of a mess today without you disrupting my do." She was certainly a complicated woman. Her appearance mattered to her quite a lot. And if someone did something to ruin it, there were five knives attached to her person that each had a different way of making that person pay. Apart, he was very proud of his girls. But together? Together he doubted Marya or Pearline would ever need his protection again.

He left her at the shop, the chaos within seemingly contained by the sound of it, and went on his way.

●　　　●　　　●　　　●　　　●

Ian was not in the tavern when Ezra got there. Yovany, the new bartender, busily wiped down tables, careful to avoid direct eye contact. He'd have to get over that if he wanted to last. The nice thing about Ian was that he made Ezra, who only had four friends, feel like a socialite in comparison. When he wasn't in the tavern, Ian was at home, in his apartment above the tavern.

That was where Ezra went now, taking the staircase behind the counter up and back. He would have used his key but, turning the knob to Ian's apartment, he found the door unlocked. He was baffled that no one had managed to murder his friend thus far. Inside Ian was working on one of his many books.

He had a ledger for The Sword and Shield, of course. But he also had one that he kept an eye on for the many gambling rings in the city. He had a ledger that monitored the number of jobs that came through his tavern per day, per year, per month. He had ledgers keeping track of foreign and domestic murderers, thieves and lawbreakers in general for hire. Another book contained a list of people he had blacklisted. Whether by a breach of conduct (difficult to accomplish in their world) or a breach of contract, they were no longer allowed to work in the city and he had their names, the incidents, and the dates as to why all written down. A record of every contract ever completed, by year, existed somewhere on these overloaded shelves. Separate books for the ones he knew about and the ones he had helped facilitate. Ezra was sure it frustrated Ian to no end that Ezra's latest contract was in none of these books.

Antony had a massive library, but Ian's system of organization and record keeping would put even the judge to shame. The tavern owner/master of secrets was so engrossed in writing something that he didn't hear Ezra come in, shut the door, or stop right behind him.

"How many of times have I told you to lock that door?"

Ian let loose a high-pitched scream, falling back in his chair.

Ezra couldn't even laugh at him. He'd surprised Ian enough that the experience had lost its charm.

"You'd best stop doing that now that you're stepping out with Marya. I guarantee she'll never let you live it down." Ezra advised, lifting the chair upright.

"Did I know you were coming?" Ian asked, squinting. Ezra had opened the shutters, letting in the first sunlight Ian had likely seen that day.

"You did, but I told you three pints in, so I forgive you." He moved a pile of books from the chair to the floor, making a note to put them back before he left, and sat down. "You're next to last on my farewell tour. I had planned to spend a bit more time at Pearl's, but it turns out every son of a poor man is buying a weapon from her for this tournament. Heard anything about it?"

"About the tournament?" Ian glared at his books, "Plenty. Even more about the people in town for it, as well as complete profiles for the locals competing. The people in for the tournament are only half the problem. There are a couple of players who haven't checked in that don't seem to have a clear motive for being here."

Ezra would have asked how Ian knew about the arrivals that hadn't passed through his tavern, but he had learned long ago that Ian's informational network was expansive to say the least. He likely took the lack of knowledge as a personal insult.

"To be fair," Ezra consoled, "Most people like us aren't known for checking in. This isn't exactly a fancy salon. The fact that most do is a testament to what you and your father built. But if they've come from far enough away, they may not have heard of our rules."

"That may be true of the random vagabond, but I know of at least ten assassins that have entered the city under false names starting last night. And the announcement was only just posted today." Ian left the statement hanging, having long ago come to a conclusion he wanted to see if Ezra could also reach.

When he did, Ezra couldn't help cursing.

"They aren't here for the tournament." The cloud that had been following him since the announcement that morning began to rain.

"The question is, why? The timing can't be a coincidence. But they show all the signs of being independent contractors which makes it all the stranger." Ezra only nodded. Smart men did not hire multiple swords for one hit. Double-booking a contract served as a great insult for the parties hired to facilitate the hit. And he never found it wise to upset people who killed for money.

Unless he was bored.

"Ezra? What do you think? Why are they here?" Ian must be desperate if he was turning to Ezra for information.

Though in this case, Ezra thought, hiding his smile, he actually did know the answer. Somewhere in the castle was a man with at least ten different targets on his back. And as much as Ezra wanted to tell Ian, he couldn't give information like that to the capital's spymaster.

"Who knows? Maybe there's a convention?"

"No, no," Ian muttered, rifling through another pile, "That's not until the spring." And, with his head ducked back down in his papers, Ezra knew he'd lost his friend to near unbreakable concentration.

"I'll be back in a month," Ezra said at him, "Eat something today." Ian didn't acknowledge his words, nor his exit.

Downstairs, Ezra pulled Yovany away from his sub-par customer service to give him a couple of coppers and send him to the market for food. Ian may not eat it, but at least now there was a chance he wouldn't starve. That was the nice thing about the possible Ian/Marya pairing. They would take care of one another. He'd have to worry a lot less about the pair of them.

10

THE CASTLE

Ezra's bags were packed and ready on the porch for the promised horse. His mouth tasted foul from the rushed tonic mixed with tea that morning. At the time, it sounded like a good idea. He had been so very wrong.

Ezra had dressed in the clothes picked out for him—not demeaning at all—with his cloak overtop to protect the dark cloth from dirt. Also, because he well aware of how his state of dress would raise questions in a place where people knew him for his less than put together appearance.

Even worse, he'd felt compelled to spend hours in the bathhouse untangling his dreads and braids. Even Marya had been envious of the result and gave him a bit of ribbon to keep the hair out of his eyes. It was black, bless her, and he'd pulled half his hair back, leaving the rest down to cover his face and neck. He knew there would be staring, best to minimize it.

Ezra said a final goodbye to his family the night before. Granny had cooked some Ruskin stew - the name of which Ezra had never been able to pronounce and had once thought sounded unappetizing—which was so good he would likely kill to protect the recipe. Granny spent the dinner quietly simmering, angry that he had agreed to protect the devil child—the vragijete—and he only ate the stew because she also ate.

Last night had left him in shock when Marya burst into tears at dinner. She didn't like to cry in front of others. But as the dinner wore on a waver crept into her tone until she could no longer hold it back and tears fell down her cheeks. He promised to write. He promised to visit as often as possible. It wasn't until he started bemoaning his fancy new pocketless clothes, that he saw her ears perk up.

"I'm sure everything they make me will be the same as the first set they sent," he despaired theatrically. "If only you were there to help fix everything for me! I'm sure your skills far exceed those of the royal tailor." He saw her preen at that and Marya sat up, wiping away her tears, sniffling a bit.

"Of course, he won't be able to make the necessary alterations and additions to your clothing. He's used to making things pretty. Not practical. I suppose I should probably just go with you to the palace. It wouldn't take more than the day to finish if I don't stop for breaks." Ezra grinned, recognizing the focused look in her eyes. Marya loved nothing more than a project with an irrational timeline. She enjoyed the challenge.

Granny didn't argue about the castle as much as Ezra expected. Likely because her dijete had stopped crying and, next to Ezra, she was completely useless when it came to tears. Another reason Marya was so unhappy that he was leaving. He was the touchy-feely one in this family. Ezra hoped Pearl would help to fill that void.

That happened last night. This morning Ezra and Marya both stood on his porch, waiting in the pre-dawn silence. The only noise, echoing down the empty street, came from the horse Ezra had borrowed for Marya since the palace only planned on sending one. The birds were just beginning to chirp when he heard the heavy clopping of an approaching horse. Heavy because they'd sent a Clydesdale for him.

"Hello, beautiful," he murmured, taking the reins from the stable boy. The boy rode a much smaller horse and Ezra couldn't help but wonder how he'd managed to get his ride to agree to such an uneven pairing, even for such a short walk.

"I am to escort you to the palace, Sir!" The boy's voice cracked at the end, whether from nerves or puberty, Ezra didn't know. Glancing at Marya, the boy hesitated.

"I was only meant to escort you, sir. Sir Burtness's instructions were very clear." Ezra sensed Marya's gaze burning into the back of his head, willing him not to be mean.

"I'm sure he did. And I don't want you to get into trouble Mr.—?"

"Shipson. Thomas Shipson."

"Thomas. Good name, strong name," Ezra wrapped an arm around the boy's shoulder.

"Listen, I know what a blowhard Joe can be, so if he gives you any trouble, just tell him I didn't give you any choice. You have full permission to blame me for everything. Good?" Thomas nodded up at him, eyes as wide. Not with fear, but rather in awe.

It didn't take long for Ezra to secure his things, Marya had long since been ready, and they were soon underway. To his relief, they cleared the busiest part of town and were on the grounds of the palace by the time the sun showed itself.

When they reached the castle gates, the morning mist had cleared and the outer ward, just inside the castle gates, where numerous servants went about their business.

Knights, maids, stable boys; the palace was already a hive of activity. Riding through the gates, Ezra saw Joe waiting for them at the bottom step leading into the palace. The three rode up to Joe and dismounted. The Lord's face was sour, despite the beautiful morning.

"One day your face will get stuck that way," Ezra warned. This only served to deepen Joe's frown, which he then turned on Marya.

"And who is this?" Joe's scowl became more pronounced once he noticed.

Despite his intent, Marya only smiled back at him genially, as she had seen scarier faces on Yovany than Joe was trying to throw her way. It certainly worked on Thomas, who had long since made himself scarce.

"I thought you understood the importance of secrecy," Joe said to Ezra. "This is...not," he finished lamely.

Marya stood back, admiring the palace, and likely checking viable escape routes. Ezra handed one of his bags off to Joe and pulled him close.

"I trust her more than you, or the prince, or anyone. I'm sorry to say, I found the clothing your tailor provided…lacking. She's just here to make some adjustments. That's all. She'll be in my room the whole day."

Joe gave her a once-over that started at her face, ventured down, and then back up to her face. Anyone else Ezra would have threatened, but he just stored the memory away.

"Very well. You! Help with Mr. Toth's bags." A man who responded to 'you' ran up and grabbed one of the bags, then nearly dropped it. Ezra recognized it as the one full of weapons. He tossed it over his shoulder and held the healing/killing bag in his other hand. That left You with a large, lighter bag of clothing and gear. You offered to carry Marya's kit, but she only looked at him with disdain before skipping up to join Ezra who had started up the stairs.

They passed through the gatehouse and the inner courtyard before entering the castle. The entryway was still dim, lit by the occasional torch until the sun could take over, still, Ezra was able to see that it was grand. In all his years, he had never taken a job in the castle. He'd had plenty of offers. But he liked living in Olaesta. And killing a member of the royal court would likely come back to bite him, no matter how good he was.

They climbed up several flights of steps, down hallways filled with more and more people, and ended in a larger, grander wing of the palace. They stopped at a set of large double doors.

"This is your room," Joe handed Ezra a key and took a step back.

Ezra went to open the door, then hesitated.

"Where does the prince sleep?"

Joe gave him a strange look.

"He knew you'd ask," he muttered. "Prince Christophe's suite is next door." Ezra nodded, expecting nothing less.

The doors were solid, and he felt their weight when he opened them. Inside, though not quite as grandiose as Christophe's quarters, Ezra entered the nicest place he'd ever stayed in. It was similar to the prince's in layout, except smaller, and there were fewer decorations. On the bed, he saw the rest of his new clothing.

Just in case some of it gave reason for panic, he didn't look at it, instead, he chose to survey the room. The windows and doors would be easy to secure. Inspecting to the connecting wall he saw that the rooms were not adjoining, but he could fix that.

Ezra always brought his tools just in case he needed another emergency tunnel.

"Do you have everything you need?" Ezra asked, tapping Marya on the shoulder, to draw her gaping gaze from the suite to the task at hand. She combed through the clothing and then looked past him at the large table by the window.

"I'm set, Ezra." She walked over to the table and started clearing it of the candles, a bowl of fruit, and what appeared to be a statue of a lion. Still, she had plenty of room to unpack her things. Ezra set his bags on the floor, removed his cloak and hung it over a nearby chair. Joe looked like he wanted to object but Ezra steered him away.

"Tell someone if you need me, they'll let me know." Ezra directed Marya, over his shoulder, as they departed.

"I'll send someone to stand by in case she needs anything," Joe said, ducking out from under Ezra's arm.

"I appreciate it, thanks," she said, only half paying attention to them. Her gaze fixated on the clothes laid out before her. The knight scanned for any sarcasm in her face but didn't see any so he shrugged and shut the door behind him.

At the intricately carved doors of Christophe's chambers, Ezra went against his usual habit and knocked before entering. The prince was at a similar table by the window—that would have to move—which was covered with papers. Ezra's fingers twitched, resisting the urge to move his client bodily out of potential harm's way.

"Christophe, Mr. Toth has arrived." At first, Ezra wasn't sure if Christophe heard Joe. He had a look much the same as Ian's when he'd said goodbye; intent on the problem at hand. He was focused, and tired, and a little sad. But a king, even a future one, had to be open to distractions. His hair was in disarray from constantly running his fingers through it and there were shadows beneath his eyes. Even now he sighed deeply, setting his quill on the blotter and pushing some papers to the side. The prince put on a professional smile and rose to greet them.

"Ezra! I hardly recognized you! I would have been there to greet you, but state affairs caught up with me," The prince reached out and they clasped hands. Ezra felt compelled to smile back in the face of a human sunbeam, though it was forced and uncomfortable. He broke grip with the prince, looked down the hall, and then closed the doors to his room.

"Listen, your highness. I'm not just here to protect your health. I'll also protect your reputation should the need arise. So, if you could avoid the fake smiles when we're alone, you're creeping me out a bit."

Christophe's eyes widened slightly and then, like a curtain closing, the mask fell away. The change might have been shocking if Ezra wasn't trained to read people. Though the prince now allowed the exhaustion to show, the faint smile on his face seemed genuine.

"I think this will work out," Christophe said, more to himself than to anyone else. "Where would you like to start, Ezra? The day is yours."

Ezra wasn't sure how the prince had managed that considering the tournament preparations but he was grateful. At that point, however, compulsion did win out.

"There are several safety protocols we have to go through, as well as your schedule, your staff and your upcoming birthday murder tournament, but first I have to take care of this," Ezra strode to the table and slid it across the floor until it was positioned away from the window, near a wall. The chair he moved so its back was to the wall. The prince wouldn't be cornered, but he also wouldn't be caught off guard. Ezra scanned the rest of the room, there was nothing so devastatingly wrong he couldn't make minor adjustments whenever they were in the room.

"Two words, your Highness: Situational Awareness. With your back to that window, I could easily rappel down and shoot you with a crossbow. I, or any great archer with a longbow, could set up in that tower," Ezra pointed to the turret to the east, "and shoot you without any witnesses to pin me to the scene."

"Are you trying to make me paranoid, Ezra?" Christophe locked eyes with him, something clients often did when he gave the 'be afraid' speech.

"Absolutely, your highness. If that's what it takes for you to take this seriously then absolutely I am. You can spend the rest of your life admiring the scenery but, for the next year, I don't want you alone, exposed, or anywhere I deem unsafe. If you don't like it, you can fire me, but I am here to keep you alive and if you follow my rules, you'll stay that way. Understand?"

Ezra had expected some sort of outburst from Joe defending his prince's honor, but he was unusually quiet. Based on his expression, it looked like he may have given a similar speech earlier.

"Understood. However, you *will* address me with more respect when we are not alone," There was a new glint in the prince's eyes that had not been there before. Ezra saw fear, yes, but also anger. He did not envy whatever became of young Prince Daniel after Christophe ascended the throne.

"Absolutely, your highness," He adjusted his tone to one of deference, bowing slightly. "I'd like a map of the palace to study later today, but first, where is it you would go if I were not here."

"I already had breakfast so—what?" He stopped, looking at the bodyguard's face.

"We'll deal with that later." Ezra took a deep breath, patting his coat to make sure he had his antidote pack with him. "Next?"

"Training with the knights."

"Lead on, then."

They walked past Ezra's room, the doors were closed but a young girl stood outside. She glanced at him, and then did a double-take, staring.

She was not the first, and hardly the last.

Most citizens of the Borough were used to his distinct appearance and far more discreet in their staring. However, here he was, a brand-new spectacle, and apparently, castle-folk were not known for their subtlety. He thought he had long since become accustomed to it, but, after being stared at by half the palace like a traveling freak, Ezra's face was tight. The effort to keep a neutral expression was always difficult for him; he had a tendency to wear his emotions on his sleeve.

As they walked through the halls of the palace, Ezra made note of their route, and possible escape routes. As a palace by the sea, used to taking the brunt of hurricane season the windows were long and narrow. The subsequent gloom required torches to remain lit around the clock, despite the sunny weather outside. Within the palace, Ezra felt a chill that went even deeper than the briskness of autumn.

The feel of sunlight and the sound of clashing steel were a welcome relief to the whispering as the three stepped out onto the training grounds. Boys as young as eight to men as old as fifty sparred across the expansive grounds available to them in the inner courtyard of the palace.

It reminded Ezra of the Ludus. Except it was clean, and everyone had clothes on. Not to mention that they were here voluntarily.

Ezra couldn't help but notice the difference in the way Christophe was received by those around him in this space. Considerably less deference was afforded to the prince in this place, amongst his fellow warriors.

Ezra liked that. All men bleed red, no matter their caste. He especially liked them for their less than open stares. Perhaps a glance, but at least they tried to be subtle. He didn't blame the children who openly pointed until their teacher began smacking them on the head, finally bringing a smile to Ezra's face.

"Christophe!" Ezra tensed up, but relaxed when he saw an apparent friend run up and clap the prince on the back. He was going to be excessively on edge until he determined who had good or ill intent towards the client. The newcomer looked past Christophe, and they locked eyes. Joe made the introductions

"Ezra, this is Adam, one of the knights in Christophe's cavalry. He's Senschal for the Olaestan Knights of the Realm. That means he is in command, second only to the prince, of the knights you see before you." The man, the boy really, couldn't have been any older than Christophe. He puffed up a bit at the formal introduction and beamed up at Ezra, his smile warm and open.

"Adam, this is Mr. Toth. He has been hired to provide extra security and point out any vulnerability's in the castle's defense." At that, Adam's eyes narrowed slightly. Ezra could see that the knight didn't wholly buy the pretty story Joe had spun. Although, the best lies were half-truths.

"It's nice to meet you, Mr. Toth. We can always use new swords and fresh perspectives." He shook hands with Ezra, a bit enthusiastically for his taste, but he appreciated the welcome.

"That's an impressive title for someone your age. I look forward to working with you. And you can call me Ezra." He grinned, upping his list of likable people on the job from two to three. Adam broke off with him and turned to Christophe, flinging an arm over his shoulder.

"All right, get ready to eat dirt. I still owe you for yesterday!" The two walked away, chatting amicably, to where a squire waited. He dressed the prince in leather gear much like the knights wore, though Christophe's bore the royal crest. Another boy handed the prince his sword, and he nearly skipped onto the field.

The weary man bent over his scrolls and letters had vanished. Ezra could tell that this represented one of the places Christophe felt safe and free to be himself. It just climbed up to the top five of his potential kill zones. With that happy thought in mind, he went to stand by Joe at the edge of the field while Adam and Christophe warmed up.

"Not going to join them?" Ezra asked.

It was the wrong thing to say. Joe stiffened up and turned slightly away from him.

"No."

Ezra waited for him to expand. They stood in silence, for a moment or two.

"Can I ask why?" At this, Joe spared him a tortured glance. Hardly the reaction Ezra expected. "Can you join them?" he prodded further.

"No," he admitted eventually.

"That's why I'm here, isn't it?" Finally, all the resentments and anger during their first meeting made sense. He wasn't just here to help. He was a temporary replacement. The raw pain on Joe's face was answer enough, but answer he did.

"Yes Ezra, that's why you're here," Joe responded, his voice so quiet the assassin almost missed it amidst the clanging of swords and laughter. Ezra no sooner opened his mouth than Joe shut him down.

"Later," Joe said.

Ezra spent the next hour surveilling the area. There were far too many points of entry to cover, with at least ten overlooking windows. He made a note to sew mirrors into the curtains. And Ezra was far from comforted by the constant flow of people that used the courtyard to get from one wing of the castle to the other. A high exposure, high trafficked area like this was a Sword's wet dream. For a Shield, it was a nightmare. His one consolation ended up being Christophe's ability to fight.

Christophe used his sword, different from that of his comrades in that it had no hilt like it existed as an extension of himself. The blade was straight and thin, Ezra recognized it as being from the prince's mother's land. He may not have had the bulk of some of the other knights, but he easily made up for it in speed.

Was he the best fighter? No.

The prince's true talent lay in the wielding of knives and in hand to hand combat than with the sword. But those were not nearly as kingly in appearance. At the very least, Ezra felt confident that, should the need arise, Christophe would be able to hold his own long enough for Ezra to finish the job.

The hour served as a good chance to get a sense of the knight's feelings for their prince. For the most part, they seemed to love him. There were a few outliers. Those who appeared unhappy; whether due to personal matters or dark intentions towards their liege, Ezra himself would have to determine. And then there were a few who showed visible signs of resentment or jealousy. Obviously not to the naked eye as, when he pointed them out to Joe the knight seemed surprised but Ezra was well practiced in facial cues. Sometimes a twitch was the difference between a real and fake smile. He would keep an eye on them.

"What's next?" he asked Joe, as the prince made his way towards them.

"Horseback riding and archery," Joe handed a wet towel out to the prince which he took and the two started moving back into the castle. A shortcut, based on what Ezra could discern so far, to the stables.

"Well," he thought, apparently out loud, "at least he'll be a moving target."

The two stopped and turned to stare at him. Ezra only shrugged. He found that, once his mouth got him into trouble, it only made things worse.

"I noticed you fidgeting on the edge of the field when you weren't doing your sweeps," Christophe said, changing the subject and resuming their journey to the stables. "You wanted to train as well, right?"

Ezra was surprised he noticed. Christophe had seemed entirely focused on his training.

"Your safety is priority. I can't train and watch you." Which he regretted. Unless there were near daily attempts on the prince's life, Ezra would soon begin to lose his edge.

"I'll secure an hour every day for you to train. Will that be sufficient?" It would be half as much as he usually did, not including his morning run and/or swim, but he would make it work.

"You're very generous, Your Highness," Ezra said, bowing slightly.

Christophe nodded like it was the only acceptable response, and the knight and prince discussed one of the new knights the rest of the way to the stables.

The stables were relatively quiet for the moment if the horses weren't taken into account. They were shockingly clean. Several someone's must come through to clean it on the regular.

Three horses were already saddled, one of them being the Clydesdale from earlier. They mounted, after waiting politely for Ezra to check the saddle and straps, and were off. A gate led into the valley behind the palace walls. Soldiers were practicing maneuvers and, in sharp contrast, a group of women appeared to be having tea on the overlooking hill.

In the middle was a valley where a group of horses did sweeps, back and forth. Even from here, Ezra could see the targets in detail. Hardly a challenge. They rode down to the range, and a boy waited with quiver and bow ready for Christophe to take and ride away with. Joe and Ezra rode a bit behind.

"Have you heard of Indlani Syndrome?" Joe asked, suddenly.

In his search for a cure for his mother, courtesy of Antony's access to the city library, Ezra had come across many degenerative diseases while searching for one that fit. Indlani Syndrome had been one of them, though thankfully, it was not the one.

The first recorded case was of a man by the name of Yulian Indlani. Healers today still didn't know how it spread, or why some people didn't suffer the full effects. What they did know was that nine times out of ten, it resulted in an eventual death sentence. First, the muscles started to atrophy and the patient would experience exhaustion after doing things that normally came with ease. As atrophy of the muscles continued, exhaustion usually followed, with the patient needing large amounts of sleep with the more serious cases being accompanied by nausea. Disorientation and sometimes aphasia were the strongest indicators of a fatal strain, as the organs begin to shut down and the patient died in their sleep soon after.

"Are you sure?"

Joe nodded.

"Does he know?"

To this, Joe did not respond, and Ezra cursed under his breath.

"When did it start?"

"I noticed it a little over a month ago and confirmed it with a doctor three weeks ago."

Which, assuming he followed the course of the average patient, left him with less than a year. Maybe even less than that as he would be overexerting himself in an effort to remain of use to his prince.

"You have to tell him," Ezra was loathed to say as he could see that truth was killing the knight. But this situation had the potential to affect Christophe's safety. Which was a problem.

"I know."

11

URSA'S DEMISE

"He's a terrible shot," Ezra commented, watching the prince aim and shoot the last of his arrows.

"Christophe's better off the horse, you'll see." It was the first thing Joe had said since admitting he needed to tell his best friend he would be dead soon. Dying or not, Ezra was not going to let him defend the prince on every little thing.

"Everyone shoots better off a horse. My Granny shoots better off a horse. But I'd like to know that, after I leave, Christophe has the skills to stay alive. It would be a pity if, after all this work, he was to die due to poor marksmanship."

The knight snorted at that, then coughed abruptly to clear out the sense of humor that had built up under his nose.

Christophe had turned his back on the targets when, past the targets, out of the forest, several riders appeared. None of them bore colors of the royal household and all were heavily armed.

Without waiting for Joe, Ezra spurred his horse to action and took off at top speed towards the prince. He heard Joe behind him but right now he only had eyes for the client and the new danger.

Christophe saw Ezra charging down the valley towards him and frowned, glancing back towards the forest. He seemed appropriately alarmed at the cloaked figures approaching from the forest but, by the time he'd brought his horse to a stop, Ezra had reached him.

"Why did you stop?" Ezra nearly shouted, grabbing the hold of the horse's reigns to bring them in line with his own.

"They're probably a returning hunting party."

"Probably," Ezra repeated flatly, eying them carefully. "Do all your hunting parties dress like mercs, your highness?" Just then, the hood on one of them flew back and the man under it yelled out in glee. His horse pulled away from the others and made straight for them. Christophe sighed, clearly recognizing him.

"They do when they hunt with my brother,"

Ezra would have preferred the mercs.

As Prince Daniel approached, Ezra's distaste over the little traitor only grew. The horse was overtired, foaming at the mouth from exhaustion; the princeling didn't seem to notice or care, though.

Daniel was eighteen years old, with blond hair, and blue eyes. The spitting image of his father, though Ezra had only ever seen the King from afar, during parades or while witnessing speeches made from the palace balcony. The brothers shared the king's square jaw and thin lips, but the similarities ended there, thankfully.

"Brother!" Daniel called joyfully, closing the distance quickly and yanking the reins so hard he and his horse skidded the last few feet. "You'll never guess the manner of beast we met in the forest!"

"Then you'll have to tell me, Danny," Christophe replied, smiling for all the world like his baby brother wasn't planning to have him killed. Ezra watched the interaction, frowning. If he didn't know better, he would have thought they actually loved each other. He'd have to be careful around the royals and the court. They might all be as talented at acting like these two.

The prince waved over to two riders pulling a makeshift sled. Once they were close enough for Ezra to get a good look, his eyes widened in shock.

"A Ruskin white bear came this far south?" Ezra asked in shock.

Daniel looked at him like it was the first time he'd really noticed Ezra.

"We sort of met the beast halfway," the princeling preened.

He might well have said he'd trespassed into the Ruskin colony. Ezra was loathed to think what Granny would say if she could see the symbol of her country dragged along like a bag of trash, much as Christophe's grandfather had done to the country itself. He clenched his jaw and said nothing else, not trusting himself at the moment. Joe saw the expression on Ezra's face and cut in.

"It is certainly good to have you back your highness. And with such good timing! Christophe's birthday festivities are less than two weeks away!"

Daniel said something in return, which the group laughed at, but Ezra did not have the stomach to continue listening.

He didn't like the feel of Daniel's hunting companions. They had none of the disciplined air of a knight or a soldier. Save one of them, who sat with the unnatural stillness of a true killer, he would have said they were all ordinary sell-swords.

Diverting his attention from the group, Ezra had also been keeping an eye on a page who had been running at a decent clip towards them and came to a stop a few feet away, breathing heavily but not collapsing as he clearly wanted to.

"Prince Daniel! His Majesty, King Lionel requests your presence in the throne room immediately!"

"Can you use 'request' and 'immediately' in the same sentence?" Ezra asked, not really thinking.

Joe cringed. The brothers, however, like they were of one mind, looked to him simultaneously with identical smirks, eyebrows raised. Christophe sighed and clapped Daniel on the back.

"Our father can," Christophe said. "Go, Daniel. See what he wants. We can catch up later."

On some small cue, the silent rider appeared at the princeling's side. Ezra and this new enemy stared at each other until Daniel finally broke away to greet his father. The rest of his group, some dragging the bear, slowly followed. The three watched their progress, not speaking until they disappeared into the stables.

"So—that's him." Ezra observed, not sure what he had been expecting.

"That is my brother. I know what you're thinking. That I must have made a mistake. I thought so too. But the evidence otherwise is too heavy to ignore." Christophe watched him like he was hoping Ezra may have seen something to prove him wrong. He would be disappointed.

"I'd need to talk to him again, but I think you're right. There's something off about him." For a man who'd only had something he already knew confirmed, the prince looked overly dejected, in Ezra's opinion. No need for sulking. "Where to now?"

"Council Meeting," Joe said and led the way to the stables.

The stables were thankfully empty of Daniel and his attendants. The only signs of his passing were the horses being brushed down and the bear that several men stood around. Ezra dismounted and asked the two to wait for him before approaching the men.

"Sirs, what's happening to the bear?" One of the men, a butcher by the state of his dress, turned on him, clearly frustrated.

"Highness wants the head for mounting and the pelt for his floor."

Ezra saw the corner of his mouth curl in disgust. Clearly, Daniel was not popular amongst the working folk. Good to know.

"And the rest?" He asked, but only received an exasperated glare so he pressed on. "There's six gold in it for you, three now, three later, if you save the meat, bones and the heart to be delivered to me." At the mention of the heart, the man stopped fussing with his tools and really looked at Ezra.

"You Ruskin?" The butcher squinted at him like he might find a label of some sort.

"I have family that is. That a problem?"

Rather than eliciting the xenophobic hatred that Granny's people endured, the man smiled broadly. His features becoming friendly, despite the blood.

"Ne, braat." The man's accent that had been dormant suddenly came bursting through as they clasped arms, "I am ashamed to admit I planned on burying the creature. But her death should not be wasted on sentimentality."

"Her?" Ezra had never been close enough to one of the creatures to ascertain their gender.

"She was pregnant," the Ruskin man said bitterly.

Ezra added another gold coin to the first three to cremate the baby and send its soul to the starry night.

"Better not show the *vragijete* that expression. He will take offense."

Ezra only sighed, turning to return to his client.

"But he is not the master I serve so I don't really care what he takes. Let me know when everything is ready. *Hvala*," Ezra thanked the group, leaving them.

"What was that about?" Joe's tone was impatient enough that Ezra was amazed he hadn't gone over to fetch him.

"Preserving home."

Maybe it was the way he said it, but Joe didn't push further.

"Come on, then. We have to go or we'll be late for the meeting."

"Who makes up the council?" Ezra asked, falling in behind them as they cut through the kitchens. He grabbed an apple and stuffed it in his pocket.

"A controlling member of each of the ruling households. The actual lords stay within the borders of their lands most of the year, though they will likely come in for the tournament. But it is comprised of the Land Lord's brothers, sons or cousins. The topic of today will revolve around crops falling short in the eastern villages. Some sort of blight."

Ezra never would have wanted to attend such an important meeting after the fighting and shooting Christophe had done, but, whilst Ezra had been salvaging the Ruskin White, Christophe had changed his shirt for a clean one and jacket as well as wiped down. Far too much work, in his opinion. But he wasn't the future ruler of Olacia, so he didn't have to worry as much about appearances.

Several men in high-quality dress milled around the entrance of a large set of doors. *Not late*, Ezra mouthed at Joe, behind Christophe's back, to which he rolled his eyes. Christophe, with all the omniscience of a mother, turned to glance back at them, his stare telling them to behave. Then he entered the chamber.

Lords were already in the room, some at their seats around a long table, some still standing and talking, but all of them gave wide berth to the large chair at the head of the table. Christophe stared at it blankly before taking a seat at the table, to the right of the throne. Because that's what Ezra now realized it was.

The seat of the king.

"All rise in the presence of His Majesty!"

12

FAMILY

Ezra had seen King Lionel several times. The ruler had a fondness of speeches from his balcony, regaling the people with the details of his latest victory. Or his parades to and from the battlefield. Were Ezra of a political mind, and in the mood to change his surroundings, he would have taken the opportunity to put the man down ages ago. Gods knew there had been more than enough chances. His only consolation was that nature also agreed and had decided to do the job for him.

Lionel still held the air of someone who had been strong. With a large, tall frame, where a great deal of muscle once rested, he was now almost emaciated. What little remained of his once golden hair gleamed white, and the only parts of him that resisted time were his piercing, sapphire blue eyes that scanned the room before resting on Ezra. Daniel entered right on his heels.

Those who had been sitting now sat back down, and those who had been standing took their seats at the table. Joe sat to Christophe's right and Ezra stood against the wall behind them. Arms crossed, he'd have access to the knives in his sleeves in an instant.

"Who are you?" The king was apparently as good an actor as his sons. Ezra was sure that, as a mass murderer himself, Lionel was at least vaguely aware of the other killers in his city. This was likely just a chance to make his son appear weak in front of the council. But he trusted Joe had planned for this and kept his mouth shut.

"Sire." Right on cue, "I present Mr. Toth. I brought him in as a consultant to provide extra security and point out any vulnerability's in the castle's defense in light of recent threats against the Crown Prince. He works on retainer for the Royal Treasury, and as such, they have failed to have a successful robbery in five years." Joe bragged. Everyone turned to stare at Ezra but he continued to scan the room, trying not to take notice.

"A question, Toth."

Now Ezra had no other choice but to break surveillance and give the king his full attention. The man had the same offness that his son had shown. Instinct was screaming for Ezra to kill now and think consequences later. For once, he ignored instinct.

"If someone attacked us, who would you protect?" Christophe stared at his father, but Joe did a full body turn in his chair, eyes wide as if trying to mentally will a diplomatic answer into Ezra's head.

"Prince Christophe is my primary." He answered honestly. From the paling of Joe's face, Ezra could have chosen a more tactful answer.

"And if I was in danger, what would you do?" The king continued.

Assuming I wasn't the one attacking you? Ezra thought to himself.

"If I was certain that absolutely no threat to the primary existed, I would protect you," Ezra answered.

"And if both of us were in danger?" The king pressed further.

Joe's anxious breathing was notably audible, it was that quiet in the chamber. Daniel had been watching the back and forth between the two, a hungry look on his face.

"Prince Christophe is my primary," Ezra repeated.

All eyes were on the king, waiting for his reaction. But Ezra saw he had impressed the ruler.

"Well said," King Lionel approved.

There was a collective exhale from the room. The princeling looked disappointed. Lionel turned from Ezra and nodded pointedly at the councilor sitting at his left. Taking this as his queue, he shot up, papers in hand and began reading off crop reports.

Two hours later Ezra was both itching to move and to go to the market. If Lord Twitchy information was correct, the price of grain was about to go through the roof. There were going to be a lot of hungry mouths this winter. He would have to find a way to warn Marya.

He also wanted to smack the soldiers stationed at the doors. They had begun the meeting at full attention, more for his benefit than for the sake of the job. By the end, the men were slouching, hands nowhere near their weapons, minds wandering.

The last Lord with business to discuss sat down, silence fell, and then Lionel stood and left. Daniel tried to follow him, but his father held a hand up and his son stayed behind. The overall mood visibly lifted with his absence, as the lords began chatting with one another. Some though were exchanging dark looks. Ezra memorized their faces as possible allies.

Joe leaned over and whispered something to Christophe but he just waved him off and stood, heading for the door himself. Ezra fell in step, Joe next to him.

"His father never comes to these things," Joe explained. "He hasn't actually seen his Highness for a few weeks. I think his presence, as well as his deteriorated health, has given Christophe a shock."

"He's going to see some things with a significantly larger shock value in his life. Best adjust now before he takes the big seat."

Before the knight could scold him on his lack of tact, he heard quick steps approaching from behind.

There was just the briefest whiff of flowers and a woman appeared, hugging Christophe. Ezra's reaction time had been superb. He withdrew and sheathed his knife in record time once he realized he was about to stab the Queen.

"Christophe, I missed you! How are you? You look exhausted. Is he sleeping?" She turned fierce eyes on Joe who nodded quickly. Though almost as old as the king's fifty years, she was still one of the most beautiful women Ezra had ever seen.

Queen Daniella's hair and eyes were black, though the hair, worn loose despite the current fashion, had some gray in it, with tanned skin and wrinkles that framed her mouth and eyes. She cupped the prince's face in her hands, turning it this way and that like he was a child. It surprised Ezra to see that Christophe stood still for her inspection.

"I missed you too mother. How is Grandfather?"

"Bah! He's fine, he'll outlive us all. Who is your friend?"

Did she or her husband know how to say hello to people?

"This is Ezra—Mr. Toth. He's here to help resolve security issues and…" he faded off in the face of her expression. Ezra recognized it from the many times he'd lied to both Marya and Granny. Or, the times he'd tried to lie to them.

"This is Ezra, Mother," Christophe started again. "He's here to protect me against any more attempts on my life." She took a step back and gave Ezra a once-over.

"Are you good at what you do, Mr. Toth?

"Yes, Your Majesty."

"Will you kill for him?"

Christophe looked like he intended to interrupt but she held a hand up to silence him.

"If I must," Ezra answered.

"Because you have qualms about killing?" she questioned, sharply.

"Because it's easier to question a living prisoner than a dead one."

Ezra liked this woman. She was hard, like Granny or Marya. Queen Daniella nodded as if she heard stuff like that every day, and he politely ignored the way the queen wrung her hands.

"I want to hear everything I missed while I was away." Finished with Ezra, she turned back to Christophe. "Your father has me putting this tournament of his together so I have a million things to do. The least of which was getting rid of the clowns." She gave him a knowing glance.

"Thank you, mother," Christophe whispered. She smoothed his hair affectionately.

"We have to catch up. I'm having dinner with your father tonight, but we can have dinner tomorrow." She suggested.

And just as quickly as she'd arrived, the queen dashed away. Mere seconds later a handmaiden rounded the corner, hair escaping her braid, and out of breath.

"Which way?" she gasped.

Joe and Christophe both pointed down the hall after the queen. The woman took a deep breath, gathered her skirts up, and tore down the hall and out of sight.

"She likes to ditch her servants," Joe explained. His face was warm like his own mother had just stopped for a visit, then his expression shifted abruptly to panic. The knight rushed to the window, threw it open and leaned out to vomit.

"Joseph," Christophe cried, running over to him. Ezra watched him comfort his friend until the final coughing ceased. Joe took the water skin Ezra offered and gargled before sending the polluted liquid out after his breakfast. He handed it back with a nod and a silencing look.

Christophe was checking his forehead for fever and asking Ezra if it seemed like poisoning, but the Ezra and Joe both knew what was really at fault. Joe's condition had deteriorated to a point far more grave than Ezra has originally assumed.

He pulled the knight aside.

"You need to get ahead of this now," he whispered so the prince could not hear, "I'm friends with an Apothecary who takes care of me. He works in the Boroughs on Black Bones Lane. Go past the only Inn in the Boroughs and stop when you get to the Butcher and the midwife. He's in the middle."

Ezra pulled a notebook out of his pocket, scribbled a message, and tore it out, pushing it into his hand.

"Give this to Mr. Slaght, tell him I sent you. Go."

"Joseph, what's happening?" Christophe demanded in something Ezra wanted to call a 'prince tone'. He saw the knight shrink a bit.

"He has to see a healer in the city." Ezra cut in, "Joe is going to go out, then come back and explain everything in detail. By your leave," he added.

Prince Christophe frowned, glancing back and forth between the two.

"Go," he sighed, "Be safe. Report back to me as soon as you return." Joe bowed to the prince, gave Ezra a grateful nod, and fled.

Ezra then found himself under the prince's sole scrutiny.

"How is it the two of you already have secrets from me?" Now less stern, more reproachful, Christophe seemed like he was rethinking Ezra's assignment.

"What can I say? People just open up to me. I must have one of those faces." The fact that most people opened up to him under torture was irrelevant.

"I'm hungry," Christophe finally said, "Let us return to your suite to eat so you can unpack.".

He led the way back to the wing that held his and Ezra's suites. It was a new way to the same place and Ezra still needed a guide. He'd have to take some time to do some thorough wandering before he became adequately familiar with the palace.

"Bring food and drink for the both of us," Christophe instructed the girl waiting outside. She curtsied deeply, casting a concerned peek at the door before she did so. Ezra sighed and entered.

Marya had her hair pulled up into a chaotic nest atop her head, her sleeves were rolled up to her elbows. When the door opened, she glanced up, a manic expression in her eyes and pins in her mouth.

"What did you do to the maid?" Ezra asked, pulling them from her mouth before she forgot they were there and started talking. Something she had done more than once with gruesome results. Who knew the tongue bled that much?

"She wouldn't know a joke if it bit her in the—"

"Marya this is Prince Christophe! Christophe, this is my best friend, and personal tailor, Marya Dalcazov." Ezra half shouted, fully aware she got her mouth from him.

"It's nice to meet you," she half nodded at him. Granny would have been so proud. "Now you're here you might as well try this on. Take your clothes off!" She reached up and started tugging the coat off Ezra.

"Gods, woman! Let me do it unless you want to take my arms with it!" He slipped out of the coat as fast as he could and threw it at her, knife side folded in. She caught it deftly and hung it over the chair.

"Try on those." She pointed to the two shirts and three coats. She then turned her eyes on the prince, who froze. Much like a deer, he had the good sense to realize when he should try to hide. Sadly, there was no saving the prince from Marya's ministrations.

Ezra watched with something between amusement and horror as she circled the prince with a measuring tape, poking him and asking how many weapons he carried. When he told her he rarely carried more than his dagger she rolled her eyes and looked to Ezra who merely shrugged, changing as quickly as possible.

In her defense, she was raised in an environment where good sense dictated that you never leave the house unarmed. Granny then smuggled her out of the crime-rich colony and they moved to thief-and-murderer alley where they were more than prepared. Putting his black coat back on, Ezra approached the two.

"So, Ezra," Christophe said, jumping at the chance to get out from under Marya's judgmental stare.

"What exactly does Miss Dalcazov do for you that the Palace Outfitter could not?"

Ezra opened his coat, revealing the fifteen or so weapons, medicine pack, and rope he had secured to the cloth.

"She does this." He let the material fall back where it lay flat against him. An unnoticeable layer of padding evened out the bumps and, as it was made of Pearline's special weave, it would deflect against most knives. "And this," Ezra reached into his sleeves, pulling out the foot-long blades hidden there.

"That is both comforting and disconcerting," Christophe joked.

"I'd like you similarly outfitted," Ezra said. "I saw you with your knives and I'd rather you had those hidden away, rather than a sword, with which you are not as comfortable."

Suddenly Marya appeared at the prince's side, removing Christophe's jacket.

"Where are you thinking? I'd need to see the knives in question before I'd be able to recommend placement. If they're smaller than yours, I should see if they fit in his sleeves. Maybe a boot knife as well?"

"Marya? Perhaps you could stop manhandling the future king." She let go like she'd been struck, then glanced at Christophe to see if she was in trouble.

"Do you have any concept of boundaries?" said future king asked her, less angry, and more like he had reached the end of his patience with the two of them.

"Only when the person is armed," she shot back.

Ezra snorted, then silenced at the expression on Christophe's face.

"Fair enough," he admitted.

Thankfully, that was when lunch arrived. Marya resumed her work, saying she would eat later, and the two took their meal in at the table in the other room.

Once they were alone Ezra pulled the bottle he'd taken from one of his bags out and started pouring drops on their food, then finally in their glasses and the jug.

"What is that?"

"It's a liquid that reacts with poison and turns color when it comes in contact with one. Nothing is black. It's safe. And you'll need to start drinking this." Ezra took a small vial out and poured that into the prince's goblet. The liquid inside promptly turned black.

"And what is that?" he asked, staring at the black liquid.

"The essence of several different poisons. I want you to build up a tolerance." Ezra took another vial out and poured it into his own drink, then downed it.

"See? I wouldn't say perfectly safe, but it's something that was necessary for my survival. And if somehow, someone slips poison past me, an immunity, no matter how small, would buy me the time needed to save you." He refilled his cup with normal water and took a sip, watching his client. After a deep breath. Christophe drank his goblet down, refilling it with water.

"Are there any side effects?"

"You ask that after drinking it? How are you not dead already?"

"Ezra..." His prince-tone began to rise to the surface.

Ezra raised his hands in surrender.

"It's fine. I wouldn't give you anything that would hurt you. It would conflict with my interests. Specifically, keeping you alive." Ezra took a breath, seeing this as a good time to broach the subject.

"I know what is happening, I need you to tell me the why."

"I've told you everything you need to know." Prince Christophe turned away slightly, closing off.

"I'll *tell* you what I need to know. You hired me because you know you need me. Not just because I can protect you, but because I bring a different perspective that will catch things you would have missed. Things I can only catch if I have all the information."

"You should know your place." Christophe's voice was dangerously quiet.

"I know my place, your highness. I am your Shield. I stand between you and all dangers and, should the need arise, I will die in the face of those dangers. But I'd rather not die if I don't have to. You could help with that."

The anger that was building in the prince seemed to deflate. It wasn't the first time Ezra had pissed off a client and, gods willing, this would not be the last. Christophe picked up a roll and began playing with it. A nervous habit Ezra would have to train out of him.

"You know my mother was a princess from Zouszian. She was married to my father as part of a diplomatic contract. But she didn't come here for marriage. That was never part of the original treaty."

13

UNPLEASANT TRUTHS

"As a child, I spent my time divided between the estates of the Zouszian delegation and the Palace. It's hard to keep secrets and feelings from a child, I've found. And tensions between the two parties were easy to see. I'd hear the servants from one side make disparaging comments about the other, the same with the nobles. Though at least the nobles, including my Aunt and Uncle, were careful in how they spoke. They clearly hated—hate—it here, but for fear of being deported, they behaved."

"More than once, as a child, I overheard my Aunt, my mother's younger sister, talk to her husband about smuggling me out of the country. But they were either too afraid, or they decided the risks were too great. Sometimes I wish they had gone through with it, risks be damned."

Christophe stared out the window, lost in thought. Ezra waited for him to continue.

"I'm sure you're aware what kind of man my Grandfather, the late King Eli, was. His name is still spoken with hatred in his conquered countries. Ruskin being one of them. My father was not born in his image, grandfather molded him. As he tried to mold me before his poisonous spirit finally killed him."

"Zouszian is a wealthy country due to its trade routes. For once grandfather understood that conquest would not be the best option – though he would never admit it was due to the size of Zouszian's army. He sent envoys to have a treaty signed, allowing my mother's people to have access to those routes by land, and Olacia to have access to additional routes by sea that were originally blocked by us. My mother represented the royal family as part of the delegation. In her country, women were taught politics as well as business. While not in line for the throne, she was expected to succeed as Minister of Foreign Economic Affairs."

"Grandfather waited until negotiations were almost complete before announcing he wanted an additional item added to the treaty. Princess Jeongseon. The Emperor was notified of course, but he did not want war and knew the future of his people depended on sea trade. He agreed. She was his favorite, most intelligent daughter, and he traded her like a nomad would a camel," Christophe said bitterly, taking a deep breath before continuing.

"The Emperor sent my Aunt, only fifteen at the time, with her betrothed. They were married before making the journey. I never truly knew what happened to my mother's intended. No one liked to talk about it. From the stories they told me as a child, I surmised that he was a good man in love. My aunt often said he died of a broken heart when she thought I wasn't there to hear."

"From the stories Aunt Kyunghye told me, mother tried to love father. She was so much…so much more than a queen consort, but she had prepared herself to live that future to its fullest. The problem was, prior to his engagement, father had been in love with someone else."

Ezra was familiar with the story, it was still the subject of gossip when other sources ran dry.

With a white face and red-rimmed eyes, Christophe had to take several steadying breaths before continuing, his voice betraying none of the emotion plain on his face.

"Mother died in childbirth. She didn't even live long enough to hold me, she was dead before I took my first breath. They had to cut me out of her. And mother's body was barely cold before the Lady

Daniella moved into the castle as father's betrothed. I think his plan, originally, was to send me and the Zouszian envoys away. Possibly back to the homeland. I asked Aunt once why father hated me so much. She said it was because I was a reminder of something he never wanted, and a reminder of his betrayal to his true love.

But something happened that Lionel did not intend. Daniella started caring for me. She all but moved into the nursery and was loathed to be parted from me. Despite her place by the King's side, Aunt loves her for what she did for me.

It took them a while to conceive but obviously, they did. Even when she had Daniel nothing really changed. She doted on him, but I was still her 'firstborn'. When we were young, we had a pretty fair relationship, I was six years older than him and he followed me around like a baby duckling. I taught him how to hold a sword, skip a stone, and climb a tree. Daniel is my brother. I love him. I thought he felt the same."

"When did you discover that they were trying to kill you?"

"Two months ago, my father took Daniel away on a private hunt. One month ago, one of the tasters in the kitchen who sampled my food died. Soon after that, a rabid dog found its way into my room and attacked me upon entry. Two weeks ago, a man tried to strangle me in my sleep. Per Joseph's recommendation, I keep my knives under my pillow, and killed him."

"Did you ever consider that you might just be incredibly unlucky?" Ezra only received a dark look in response. "It's suspicious, I'll grant you, but still only circumstantial. What makes you think these attacks came from your Father and brother?"

"The man I killed. He didn't die right away." Christophe's voice was emotionless, eyes far away, in memory. "He named Daniel as the one who hired him. Threatened him, really. And, even if my father is unaware, though I doubt it, Daniel would have his full blessing."

"Well they're impatient, I'll give them that. They're also terrible at murder, which is fortunate. Though, based on my information, your brother has learned from that mistake."

"What information?" Whatever fog Christophe had been slipping in to quickly dissipated.

"I have a reliable source who told me the other day that at least ten hired hitters have entered the city. Most likely foreign and they don't want anyone to know they're here. Daniel's offered some serious money to bring in that kind of crowd, and he and the king are using the tournament for cover."

"I want to speak to this source of yours. How soon can you bring him to the castle?"

"I can't—Let me explain!" Ezra added hastily, as Christophe half rose out of his seat.

"It's not that I don't want to. And I'm sure he'll be flattered when I tell him you demanded an audience. But he isn't like me. If I work for you, the pinnacle of law and attention, it doesn't affect me negatively. You'll be seen as a big score. Another job that, when over, is over. And then the less than reputable will still feel safe to reach out for my services because they know I'll work with them. But my friend is a broker of sorts. He is in the management business and, if word got out that he had any affiliations with you, it would damage his credibility. It might even endanger him and his friends. All right?"

Christophe rubbed at his temples, eyes closed as though he was tired.

"So what you're saying is, my standing as Crown Prince of the Realm would damage your criminal friend's standing." Ezra only nodded, not trusting himself to speak. Perhaps it was a prince thing, or maybe a by-product of his parentage, but he couldn't help thinking that Christophe might be holding in some serious anger issues.

"Do you have anything scheduled right now?" Ezra asked.

Christophe might have lied if he'd known what Ezra had planned, but he said no.

"Let me change into some less expensive clothes," Ezra continued. "Do you care if those are ripped, dirtied, or otherwise destroyed?" The prince's clothes were fine enough that Ezra answered for him. "Follow me, you can go next."

Ezra re-entered the bedroom, Christophe following more on instinct than anything else. Marya had returned whatever mindset she had to enter that allowed her to work for hours on end. He dumped his clothes out onto the bed, grabbed a ragged, but still presentable shirt and trousers, and began to undress.

"Really, Ezra," Christophe said, shocked. "I must ask that you change elsewhere. A lady is present!"

Ezra had always been a quick stripper and made it to his underpants before Christophe could make his protestations.

"Marya, don't look up, you're a lady."

"Because I haven't seen you naked? Ian has a better butt by the way."

She easily dodged the pillow he threw at her head without glancing up from her work. Ezra finished dressing and dragged Christophe from the room before they had a chance to further offend his delicate sensibilities.

Ten minutes later they were back on the training grounds. The fighters were gone, and the casual audience of nobles had left to have their midday meals. Ezra pulled the knives out of his boots and handed them to Christophe.

"Attack me," Ezra said, stepping back.

"What? No. I don't know what you hope to achieve with this but I don't have time for games."

He tried to move past Ezra, who took a chance and pushed him. To his dismay, the prince had no lightning reflexes to help him dodge. The prince simply stumbled, before tripping on a stone and falling. He waited for the man to pick himself up. Christophe was fuming, rage clear in his eyes. People did not treat him this way. He was to be respected. He would not let this stand! Ezra saw these thoughts pass through the client's head moments before he attacked.

Christophe came in low and fast. Sloppy compared to his earlier play fighting with the knights, but with a ferocity that made up for it. But he was still lacking. Ezra dodged, knocking him to the ground again. Like a bull who had missed his target, Christophe got back to his feet for another run. This time he tried to feint – tried, being the operative word, because he was so full of cues that the attack barely counted as a feint. Ezra knocked him aside again but left him standing.

"This isn't a game, your highness." He paused to knock a stab aside and kick Christophe's feet out from under him. "We're here because you keep emotions trapped inside like they don't need tending to. Over the day, I've seen you repress anger and frustration and that's a problem. It blinds you to real dangers and cripples you against them. It blinds you to the things that have been right in front of you."

Christophe skidded to a halt, mid-charge, eyes wide as he caught his breath staring at Ezra, who could see the wheels spinning rapidly within the prince's mind. Despite the understandable issues the future king had to work through, he was a quick wit.

"This is about Joseph."

"Partially," Ezra admitted. "I was going to respect your friendship and let him tell you himself, but Joe's a tad more delicate now than he'll admit, and I don't want your initial reaction to screw things up. It's also because you need to let loose occasionally, and it's safe to do that with me."

Christophe threw one of the knives at Ezra's face. Ezra caught it with ease, but he was almost as surprised as the prince looked.

"That was a decent throw. Bet it felt good."

Christophe was at a loss for words. Ezra flipped the knife and handed it back, handle first. Christophe took it silently.

"I'm going to tell you something upsetting. Then you're going to fight me until you've excised enough anger that you can take the news calmly when you hear it for the 'first time.' Understand? But first," Ezra was already close, so he closed the distance and disarmed him, sliding the knives back into his boots. He chose a metal staff and gave Christophe the sword.

"Ready?" The prince held his sword up, having come to accept Ezra's admittedly mad methodology. "Joe is dying. He has Indlani disease and will slowly deteriorate until he fades away, likely before your father."

Christophe reacted in about the way Ezra expected him to. His sword arm fell limply to his side as he gaped at him in horror. Then the pacing began.

"This is what you were hiding earlier?" he hissed, pointing his sword at Ezra. Christophe's eyes were red. Exactly the kind of comforting reaction his friend was going to need.

"Yes."

"And he told you before me?!"

"No, I figured it out. I was paying attention. But this?" Ezra waved at Christophe, "This is the last thing Joseph needs. It's likely part of the reason he didn't tell you. That and his fear of disappointing you."

With those words, Christophe deflated.

"Good," Ezra continued. "That's the kind of face you should wear. Sad but serious. I'm going to need Joe in the coming months to keep you alive, which means you need to be there for him." Ezra did his level best to keep his tone of voice empathetic. Marya told him often enough that, when dealing with people he deemed as 'slow', he often infantilized them. He should have had her do this. Her tact far exceeded his own.

"Are we done then," the prince asked. "Are you satisfied that I won't traumatize someone I've known my whole life and you've known for all of a day?"

Surprisingly, Ezra was.

"We could be. But you have a lot of anger built up and I'm offering you a chance to let loose. Don't you want to try a spar free of pulled punches at least once?"

Christophe observed him, considering, then raised his sword and charged.

Calm, Christophe's skills as a fighter significantly improved. Ezra almost had to use effort at times. But still, by the time they were done he'd barely broken a sweat.

"You were good," he reassured Christophe on the way back to their rooms. Ezra was of the opinion no workout was over until you needed a bath, and Christophe was more than in need of one.

"I didn't hit you once," Christophe grumbled, revealing the childish quality that sat in sharp contrast with his overall demeanor.

"Did you expect to?"

"Of course," he said, confused.

"That's good. Ridiculous, but good. You'd have to work considerably to land a blow on me. But it's hard to do so if you don't have the goal in mind. What you do have is stamina, which will come in handy on the battlefield. You may not have noticed it but the sun has taken considerable strides."

In fact, the sun was already blocked from view, within the courtyard, by the high castle walls.

"Is there anyone here who has the skill to beat you?" Christophe challenged.

Ezra thought on the question, remembering Daniel's shadow servant.

"At least one."

Unfortunately, he was certain that the opportunity would arise to see which of them was better.

"If I spend the next year losing muscle tone because no one strong has tried to attack you though, then I'm willing to suffer that."

"Well, I'm thinking on a solution for that. It would hardly do to have you out of fighting form because you spent too much time staring at me from the corner." Ezra felt an evil smile creep up his face.

"How do you feel about pre-dawn exercise, your highness?" Christophe appeared properly alarmed at the concept, likely having a good idea what Ezra's regimen would entail.

"We'll discuss that later," he said, entering his room.

It was late enough in the day that candles had been lit to illuminate the dark corners. And Joe sat on a chair by the fireplace, asleep. The trip must have exhausted him in his current condition. Ezra pushed Christophe towards the sleeping knight, whispering, "Calm, understanding, and tactful".

Keeping an eye on the two of them, the prince having just knelt by the armchair, Ezra went to inspect the paper-wrapped package on the table. The note attached was addressed to him.

Ezra,

Thanks for the referral. Maybe come with him next time so he isn't nearly mugged. He's not gonna be as cocky by the time he runs out of medicine and even I could kick his dying arse. This should last until you come for your re-supply. That's some rare shit he needs.

Happy to see your job's off to a nice, easy start,
Slaght

The man had a delightful bedside manner. Ezra had no doubt it was that, in tandem with Joe's pride that led to such a fantastic first impression. And he'd likely overcharged the knight as well.

He could hear the two men speaking quietly to one another by the fireplace and tried to ignore it, focusing instead on the package. For someone so high strung, it was amusing to see that Joe had been prescribed stimulants.

It was important to find humor in a dark place, Ezra reminded himself. It would entertain him in the underworld.

There were several powders and pouches. Most he didn't recognize but one of them was wrapped separately from the others. When he opened it he recognized the ground powder as the flower he had only just retrieved for Slaght. The label read Ambrea and a little skull was drawn underneath it, which was harsh, even for the apothecary.

Ezra read over the directions underneath everything and saw that the medicine was to be prepared in much the same way as his own. A truly horrible tasting tea with equally horrible consequences if prepared incorrectly; exactly what any man would want to spend his last months drinking.

Ezra waited for what seemed like the end of their heart-to-heart before intruding.

"Joe, do you know someone trustworthy and discreet to help you make this?"

The knight still looked a little numb, but he nodded.

"Their name?"

"Lissa." Joe's voice was devoid of emotion, as was his face when Ezra checked. Admitting this weakness had cost him something. And he lost a bit more of it each time his prince looked at him with pity.

Ezra opened the door and signaled for a guard.

"You know Lissa?" The guard nodded mutely, his eyes focused on Ezra's scars. "Then bring her here. Quickly!" Ezra slammed the door in the man's face, unusually grumpy. After a lifetime surrounded by people who were, more or less, used to him, he was not comfortable with such obvious attention.

He reluctantly joined the two by the fireplace and stood by Christophe's chair to wait. The crackling of the fire was a welcome diversion to the oppressive silence and words left unsaid. Christophe, filthy from the fight, seemed more approachable and less like the royal persona he tried to display. That made it far easier for Joseph to accept the hand his friend used to pat him on the back.

No words passed between them, but those would come in time.

Joe was hunched over on the chair, head hung down either from exhaustion or shame, or a mixture of the two. This was such a personal moment that the silence felt like it was screaming at Ezra to get out. Worse yet, as the prince's bodyguard, he knew that this was only the first of many such moments.

The air was so thick that, when he heard approaching footsteps, Ezra all but launched at the door. Throwing it open in relief, he was greeted by the sight of a startled girl, her hand raised to knock. She gave a small yelp of surprise that she quickly tried to disguise as a cough before curtsying.

"Is my Lord Joseph in?"

Only then did Ezra realize he was blocking the door.

"Yes, absolutely yes. Come in, please." He stepped out of her way and, though she gave him a double take, it was subtle enough for him to appreciate the effort. Lissa swept past him into the room and read the situation immediately.

"You told him, Joseph?" She knelt by his chair, opposite the prince, and put her hand on his. Joe's fingers closed around hers and Ezra watched as his shoulders started to shake. She sighed, whispered something in his ear and then stood. It was a simple motion, but like her walk across the room, everything she did had the sense of a dancer to it—quiet and effortless. Lissa sidestepped the prince, managing to curtsy whilst approaching Ezra.

"What is it you need me to do?" She was all business now, and Ezra found that he liked that about her. He wasn't quite sure what to make of this noblewoman, for she was certainly no less than that. Her hair, hanging in a braid over her shoulder, was secured with a pearl clip, and he recognized the high quality of the cloth from his time spent in Marya's shop. It was the little things that threw him off, such as the worn apron around her waist, the scuff marks on her boots, and the calluses that covered her hands.

Ezra stuffed Slaght's message in his pocket and handed her the instructions that accompanied the ingredients.

"It won't save him, but it will keep him strong and relatively pain-free. The apothecary who put this together is good, I trust him with my life, so it may even extend his time."

At that, Lissa gave him a sharp glare.

"I don't hold with false hope, Mr. Toth," she scolded. There was no other word for it. She reminded him of a governess admonishing a wayward student.

"Nor do I," He straightened, having subconsciously made himself smaller to avoid danger.

"Hope is a cruel joke that keeps you dreaming for the possible when you could be working towards the probable." Ezra took a pause to reflect upon one of the most negative things he'd ever said in his life and then continued.

"He's valuable to the Prince which makes him invaluable to me and my mission. Joe seems like a good man. So far, he's the only one I trust, save my obligatory trust in the client, so I'd like to keep him with me as long as possible." Lissa scanned down at the list but he could see his answer had satisfied her. Honest, straightforward, to the point.

"This seems simple enough." She bundled everything up into the cloth, pausing over the skull drawn on the Ambrea, before hastily stuffing it out sight.

"Make sure no one else gets to the ingredients and that you, and only you, are preparing the tonic." Ezra immediately regretted the advice when she turned to face him.

"Thank you, Mr. Toth,," her voice cutting like ice. "The next time I find myself lacking in all common sense, I will know who to call."

She marched away, despite the full skirts that swept the floor it was a very distinctive march, and knelt by Joe. As her eyes met his, all the ice melted away, and the governess transformed into a beautiful young woman.

"I will return tonight, Joseph," she whispered, wiping the hair from his brow. She curtsied to the prince and, with a sniff at Ezra, swept out of the room.

"Personal servant?" Ezra asked, moving to stand by the prince.

Christophe's eyes darted in panic to Joe. However, he was clearly still in some sort of stupor and had not heard him.

"Lissa is his betrothed," Christophe explained. "They are to be married this coming summer." Ezra heard the hesitation in the prince's voice and understood. There was no way Joe was making it through the winter, much less to the summer.

"Well I think it's a perfect match," Ezra said, raising his voice to try and get Joe's attention. "She's likely the only one who'd be willing to manage a man with such a poor personality as his." Nearly yelling this, Ezra was relieved to see his antics had succeeded, as he could see a reluctant smile on the knight's face.

"Your Highness, I think you should take this opportunity to wash up before dinner. Joe, I want you to sit there and keep an eye on the main door." At this, Joe was suddenly all business. He changed seats for a better vantage point and gave Ezra a curt nod before training his eyes on the door. All it took to bring him back was an order to follow. It was very possible this job was the only thing that kept Joe from sinking into the understandable depression that Ezra perceived just under the surface.

14

NEW ALLIES

Dinner was unorthodox, to say the least, though getting there was half the battle. By the time Christophe was done bathing and changing into suitable evening attire, Joe had fallen asleep by the fire so they left him behind. The whole process took a bit longer than usual as Ezra would not budge on the matter of standing beside the prince while he washed.

He also declined suggestions that included but were not limited to: standing to face the wall, waiting outside the open door, and jumping out the window. Ezra gently reminded the prince that he would be glad of the hovering when he emerged from this ordeal alive. Christophe muttered mutinously from the tub that Ezra's royal favor would end up being wasted on a royal pardon for all the petitions to have him executed.

"That would be a shame indeed," Ezra commented, continuing to watch the sulking prince and all possible entry points. He managed to change shirts and wipe himself with a wet cloth discreetly so that, when the prince had finally finished preparing, so too had he.

The year was quickly coming to the close, shortening the days. By the time they reached the kitchens the sun had set. Torches were already lit all along the corridors and, in the open halls, chandeliers hung. Ezra nudged Christophe around those lest anyone get the idea of cutting it loose while he stood under them.

The kitchen was chaotic, but orderly in the almost dance-like way people wove around each other. It was evident that this was a well-practiced routine. Christophe and Ezra's presence brought that routine to a screeching halt.

"Pay your respects," the head cook yelled, her voice booming over the roar to capture everyone's attention. The kitchen staff turned from their tasks to bow. Ezra noted that some of them had abandoned tasks that needed some quick ministrations. He didn't need a house fire on his first day here.

"Everyone go about your business," Christophe ordered, with a silent 'please' for anyone listening.

"How may I help you today, Highness," the cook asked. She was older, at least as old as the king, with a ruddy face and hair that frizzed where it didn't tuck under her cap. The woman was stout both from the love of food Ezra felt any cook should have, as well as the muscles gained from carrying bags of flour and stirring vats of stew for a lifetime. As he sized her up, he noticed she was doing the same to him.

"Mabel," Christophe said, cutting into their staring contest. "this is Ezra Toth. He's the man I told you about. Ezra, this is Mabel Giska. I've known her since I was a child."

"It's a pleasure to meet you, ma'am," Ezra said, reaching out to shake her hand.

She seemed surprised at the gesture, but wiped her hands against her heavily stained apron and did so. He felt no sword calluses and relaxed slightly. An ally in the kitchens would make his life infinitely easier, especially one with eyes as sharp as hers.

While the two caught up, chatting about whatever may have happened since their last meeting, Ezra surveyed the crowd. Most of the staff went about their business, but there were a few who made a point to work close by. Their careful glances in the prince's direction only confirmed Ezra's suspicions that they were spies of the King.

"Is there a place we can talk, ma'am?" Ezra asked, taking their sudden silence as an end to the conversation. The surprised looks on their faces indicated he was wrong. An ability to read social cues was not his strong suit.

Mabel led the way through the busy kitchen. Christophe was probably confused about the way the staff parted for them with a hasty, life-preserving fervor. If he were only to turn around he would be greeted by a looming, terrifying Ezra. Every time they came within reach of a worker with a knife in hand, Ezra would turn his glare on them and they would scuffle away. If only the job was that easy, he'd abandon smiling for the next year. They left the traumatized kitchen behind for a quieter storeroom.

The pantry was surprisingly quiet, despite its proximity to the meal preparation. It had three points of entry: the arched entrance from the kitchen, a door that led to the dining hall, and a square hatch in the ceiling. No hinges were visible. Entry would be difficult without his tools and conspicuous with them. An unknown entrance into the kitchen was unacceptable though, so he'd have to investigate later. Instead, Ezra turned his attention to page one of his to-do list.

"Mabel," Ezra began, smiling as genuinely as was possible for someone like him. "How long have you worked in the castle?"

"Oh, let's see. Well, Micah's going to be thirty-four this coming spring so I'd say thirty-four years plus change. No clue what the staffer was thinking, hiring me in my state. I was as big as a cow." She held her arms out as far as they would go, puffing out her cheeks as to add effect. Ezra felt his face slip into a real smile which Mabel returned. He made a mental note to investigate the son's affiliations and associates and moved on.

"I'm sure it was a sight to see, ma'am. You've known the prince all his life?"

"Even before that. I'm afraid I'm to blame for Chris's strange obsession with pickled cabbage. It's all his mother wanted when she was carrying him. My kitchen reeked with it for days, I thought I would die." Her nose wrinkled from the memory.

"It's called kimchi," Christophe muttered. Ezra was familiar with the dish and understood why the prince loved it, but all his sympathy rested with Mabel. For someone who had no interest in eating such a dish, kimchi was a punishing thing.

"So clearly I don't have to question your loyalty. You've proven a willingness to risk your life for him," Ezra now found himself in a very different position than when he started this conversation; fighting to stay serious rather than burst out laughing. He liked this woman. Were it not for the fact that he guessed the prince's schedule would not allow it, Ezra would choose to hang out with her as much as possible.

"If you are quite done, perhaps you might return to the original subject matter?" Christophe's ears were red as he made most of his request to his feet. How he'd managed to survive court life, Ezra had no idea.

"Right." Ezra gave a small nod of apology.

"Sorry, love." Mabel went to tidy Christophe's hair, but he dodged her in a well-practiced maneuver.

"Obviously, I'll have my own safeguards, but I am confident in my assessment that you aren't looking to kill the Crown Prince any time soon." Ezra pulled a small book from his inner vest pocket and added her name to the list of trustworthy people. Two people in total. His support was almost overwhelming in quantity. He'd taken her silence for confirmation, but in fact, it seemed Mabel was temporarily stunned.

"You said you told her about me," Ezra said.

"I said I was hiring some extra security, Ezra. Not that people were trying to assassinate me!" Christophe managed to yell whilst whispering. Mabel, in the meantime, had gone to sit down on the nearest barrel and was slowly losing all the color in her cheeks.

"Mabes?" Christophe put a hand on her shoulder. "Mabes, are you all right?"

She grabbed at the hand and held it tightly in her own. The cook's eyes were wide with the panic of a mother whose child was in danger.

"Why didn't you tell me?" She seemed torn between a desire to cry or cuff the crown prince over the ears.

"I didn't want to worry you," Christophe replied, shooting Ezra a dirty look.

Ezra pointedly ignored this and pulled Mabel to her feet.

"That was a stupid idea and protected no one," Ezra chided. "Now, the reason we're here is that the easiest way to kill you without detection is poison. I have a way of detecting poisons once they've been introduced, but Mabel, I'm counting on you to help keep them out of the food at all."

He was fairly certain she'd heard him as she started nodding. Then, like a switch had been thrown in her mind, her face turned from stunned to serious.

"Right, well I'm going to have to get to work straight away. There's some folk in this kitchen who are a bit too sneaky for my tastes. Be gone with you both. You'll have your supper in a moment and then I've got some firing to do." Mabel said with fierce determination, rolling up her sleeves before setting her hands on a rolling pin.

"Just don't kill anyone you catch," Ezra said, unable to repress the smile anymore. "It's so much easier to question the living."

Mabel gave a terse nod, like that was obvious, and shooed them out of her kitchen.

There were several dining halls in the castle. Some were the size of ballrooms while others were like the one they entered now, slightly larger than Ezra's apartment. This was a relief, not just because Ezra wasn't fond of wide open spaces with lots of windows, but also because it would have been awkward for the two of them to dine alone at a one hundred foot long table.

They sat in silence, Christophe because he was still mad at Ezra for blabbing, and Ezra because he was never usually the one in charge of the small talk. They were both relieved when Joe finally arrived.

"My apologies, I may have dozed off a bit." Ezra concealed his snort behind a cough. When he and the prince had finally emerged from the bathroom, it was to find that Joe had abandoned his look-out duties in favor of snoring and drooling.

"Quite all right," Christophe said, glaring at Ezra. He and Joe talked about their friends and matters of state until Ezra got bored and cut in.

"So, what's the plan for the rest of tonight?" Ezra asked.

"This is," Christophe said, patting the large pile of documents that Joe had brought along. "From dinner to bed I review petitions and then I re-review them in the morning to make sure I understood everything. They are usually menial issues but it's better to peruse many trivialities to get to what's important."

"I am stunned that Daniel wants this job so desperately. You haven't even started the real work, and it still sounds so boring."

Joe's face turned red but Christophe, who was surprised at first, started laughing.

"Very true, Ezra. It certainly isn't all it's made out to be. Just a fancy chair, some heavy clothes, and people you hope are supporting your rule and not plotting against you. Remind me again why I want to be king?" Christophe asked Joe.

"Because the alternative is Daniel," Joe responded so fast that Ezra could tell this was not the first time he'd been asked that question.

"Because the alternative is my brother, yes." Christophe agreed. "And while I think we can all agree that he has good deep inside him—" Joe shook his head at Ezra from behind Christophe's back, "—that goodness may be just a tad too deep down to be of much help as a sovereign."

"Right—and tomorrow's agenda?" Ezra prompted.

"Tomorrow I review documents, train, visit my mother's family, and then attend a tea party for which my sister was good enough to send an invitation."

"Your sister? I thought she was away at school." Ezra had never seen the little princess and, truth be told, no one knew much about her other than that she was a supposed savant.

"Yes, well, she wanted to be here for my birthday so she came home early." Christophe seemed worried.

"Don't worry, I'll do my best to make sure your situation doesn't put her in danger." Ezra comforted.

"And your maternal family?" Ezra prodded, trying to fill the silence. "I assume they have been filled in on the situation?" This time it was Joe's turn to choke, though he made no effort to cover it up.

"Yes, that's exactly what we should do. Tell Christophe's aunt and uncle that the man who took away the favorite princess of the Zouszian Empire is now attempting to kill the Emperor's grandson. You go ahead, I'll watch as the entire realm is brought down to flames from the war that follows."

Ezra took a sip of water to stifle any and all smart-ass retorts that might have followed that.

"Bit dramatic, but I see your point." The water didn't work. "Anything else?"

"Training and then dinner with mother. She wants to go over preparations for the tournament."

"Sounds like a plan," Ezra said, and the two friends resumed their chatting while Ezra continued to survey the room.

Another location brimming with weak points. Ezra was slowly coming to the realization that this would be the most difficult job of his entire career.

15

UNLIKELY FRIENDS

The next day did not start well. Unless there is some definition wherein screaming can be construed as an enthusiastic greeting to the day. In this case though, not so much.

"AAAAAUUUGH!" Christophe screamed, jerking Ezra awake.

Ezra rolled out from under the bed, sword ready, looking for the threat. But the only other person in the room was Christophe, standing on his bed, dagger in hand, staring at his bodyguard.

"What is it?" Ezra asked urgently, "What's wrong?" Christophe gaped at him, his mouth opening and closing like a goldfish. When he finally spoke it was with an exhausted, frustrated tone.

"What's wrong? What's wrong is that I woke up to see a foot poking out from under my bed! You have an entire room next door. I meant for you to sleep in it!" Christophe still stood on his bed, brandishing his dagger for emphasis.

It was at that moment the door swung open and the guard charged in. The bells he'd attached to the doors last night jangling like crazy.

Ezra could only imagine the questions generated by such a scene.

"You three," Ezra pointed at the guards, "have an abysmal reaction time. What if I were an attacker? The Crown Prince would be dead.

Best case scenario you would be banished for being so terrible at your jobs, and even worse, my clearance rate would drop. Get out!"

The armored guards positively fled, their cumbersome and unnecessary armor clanked and rattled down the hall.

Christophe sat on the bed just in time to avoid causing an even greater scene in front of the castle. A maid darted around Ezra, giving his sword a frightened glance, set a tray on the table before scurrying out.

Ezra smelled coffee and his mouth watered.

"To answer your question, Christophe, my room is too far away from your room. To be of any real assistance during an attack, I need to be by your side at all times."

"At—at all times?" Christophe asked.

"At all times," Ezra confirmed. "Don't touch the coffee until I've had a chance to test it. I'll go get my kit." He left the still stunned prince and hurried to his room, leaving both his and the prince's doors open. Ezra pulled on a shirt, grabbed his poisons kit, food tray, and a tonic pouch before returning to the prince's quarters.

"Remind me to get you one of these," Ezra said, dropping some solution into the cup and onto his plate. "Your breakfast is safe, go ahead."

Unable to down the whole of his tonic in one go, Ezra rotated between it and his coffee until it was gone. The prince watched him do so.

"What is that?" he asked.

Ezra shoveled some food in his mouth to try and get rid of the tonic's aftertaste before answering.

"It's a bit like what I gave Lissa for Joe. It's a medicine that I've had to take since I was a kid. You don't have to worry though. I'm not sickly or anything. Don't forget to take your poison, by the way."

Christophe went to the table and poured himself nearly a quart of coffee. He took a sip as if to enjoy at least one taste, before tipping one drop of the poison mix into the cup.

"For how long do I have to keep poisoning myself?" Christophe asked while pouring a second cup.

"It took me years to build up a tolerance strong enough that I didn't feel the need to test my food. You'll thank me down the line." Ezra said, pausing just long enough from his own breakfast to speak before digging in again. They ate in silence.

"So," Ezra pushed away his tray, wishing there had been more on it, "Aside from the screaming, how do you usually start the day?"

Christophe took the time to fully chew his food, he wasn't quite done with his meal, but he pushed it aside all the same.

"As you saw yesterday, I have appeals, letters, and legal documents to review first thing in the morning. You're welcome to get in some exercise while you wait."

And that is what they did. For an hour there was no sound save for the rustling of papers, scratching of a quill, and the occasional grunt as Ezra neared the end of a long set of stretches or lifts.

Finally, Christophe collected his papers, shuffling them into what vaguely resembled a neat pile, and placed a paperweight on top.

"Now we go to see my aunt." Christophe announced. "I fear I have been neglecting her since this whole affair began."

"Don't forget your knives," Ezra reminded him, pulling his own armory of a coat on.

"Do you expect me to be armed until this is over?" Christophe asked.

"I expect," Ezra said, "that you will stop carrying weapons everywhere as soon as the king is dead. What I'd like is for you to have at least one knife on hand for the rest of your life." He opened the door for the prince, checked the hall, and then stood aside to let Christophe through. The prince rolled his eyes and muttered something unintelligible before walking out.

●　　●　　●　　●　　●

The embassy that housed Christophe's aunt, Princess Kyunghye, and his uncle, Lord Jungjong, was just off the grounds of the castle. They exited the stables, taking horses at Ezra's insistence, and rode a good two miles until they reached what, in Ezra's eyes, was another palace.

He felt the nostalgia of his past travels wash over him. The Emperor spared no expense in the building of this embassy that, really, looked like a mini version of the Imperial Palace. There was no way King Eli or King Lionel would have offered up the gold to build something like this. Especially when its beauty put the Olacian castle to shame.

Though not nearly as grandiose as the real palace in Zouszian, this was still unmistakably a palace in its own right. With outer, and inner courts, along with a large pavilion for events, and several smaller buildings that housed the royal family and servants, it was nearly a scale model of the original. Ezra had no sooner let his thought's drift to Zouszian palace's inner gardens when they entered the courtyard. It was an exact replica.

From the camphor trees that gave shade, to the mugunghwa flowers that lined the walk, it felt less like an embassy and more like the real thing. It wouldn't have surprised Ezra if they had shipped all building materials from Zouszian. Even the servants were all of Zouszian origins and wore the traditional garb of the Ahn family household.

Just then a woman in a silk hanfu emerged from the main building, walking towards them.

"Aunt, it is good to see you. Are you well?"

She gave Ezra an appraising glance before turning to her nephew with a smile as warm as the Queen's.

"Taejong! What a pleasure to see you. He's always on time. Such a good boy," she added to Ezra. Seeing that his aunt was staring pointedly at Ezra, Christophe rushed to make introductions.

"My apologies, Aunt. This is Ezra Toth. Joseph thought it best to bring him on as a security consultant."

She smirked.

"And when is it, Mr. Toth, that you made the transition from assassin to consultant?"

Christophe paled slightly as he looked back and forth from his aunt to Ezra.

"Just recently," Ezra explained. "Your nephew approached me with the idea that long term protection may bring a welcome respite from the non-stop killing. And where, may I ask, did you hear of me?" He matched her polite smile, which she did not lose in the face of his blunt honesty.

"We tried to hire you several years ago to kill his father," she said, nodding at the prince, "but you declined."

At that, Christophe glanced around wildly, making sure no one overheard the treason his aunt had just uttered.

"But—Aunt why?"

"Because we received information that the king planned to kill you and name your idiot half-brother as heir to the throne." Christophe swayed slightly and Ezra gently guided him to a bench.

"Years?" he asked hoarsely. "Father has been planning this for years?"

"I think I'll have them bring the tea a bit early," The princess said, and left to find a servant.

Ezra sat next to the prince who seemed to be in the middle of a panic attack.

"So, I guess that's a bit of bad news," Ezra said lightly.

Christophe turned to him with an indignant grimace, undercut by his wide, panicky eyes.

"You think?" He asked shrilly. "My father has had years to plan, gather followers, bribe lords and gods knows what else. I might as well off myself now and save everyone the trouble!"

"Now, now. No need to feel sorry for yourself." Ezra said, patting the prince on the back. Christophe didn't respond, putting his head in his hands and staring at the perfectly manicured grass beneath his feet.

The princess returned, followed by a servant carrying a tray. Ezra was already pulling a vial out of his coat when Christophe took his cup. He shook a drop into each and, when nothing happened, handed the prince his cup back.

For the first time, the princess' eyes revealed real emotion. Rage.

"You dare imply that I would bring harm to my family?"

"No offense meant, Your Highness. I would never seek to suggest something so distasteful. But you were not the one who prepared the tea. And your nephew isn't paying me to make exceptions." The energy required to use polite speech required so much more effort. Ezra sometimes wondered if it was worth it. 'No', would have sufficed for anyone else he conversed with. But the princess seemed mollified.

"Your wit seems as sharp as your knives, Mr. Toth. Forgive me, you prefer to be called Ezra."

He didn't ask her by what means she acquired that knowledge. Ezra sensed he was in the presence of someone who would give Ian a run for his money.

"You flatter me, Your Highness." Ezra gave a small bow of the head which she returned.

Christophe watched both of them, his mouth open slightly.

"I can't believe you two, right now. Discussing treason with all the manners of a courtier," Christophe complained.

"It's an important skill for a future ruler to have, nephew. You should pay attention to your bodyguard." Now Ezra could easily see the smile in her eyes, though her face remained serious.

Ezra brought up his last trip to Zouszian, and that conversation carried them for the next hour while Christophe sulked to the side.

• • • • •

"You two seemed awfully chummy," Christophe commented on their way back to the castle. When Ezra and the princess had exhausted the topic of her homeland, they had moved on to stories about Christophe as a child. He seemed particularly resentful about that.

"I wouldn't have expected a friendship to form between the two of you," Christophe went on, "though, knowing what I know now, maybe it makes perfect sense. I can't believe she tried to have Father killed. Why didn't you tell me?"

"Tell you what? That your aunt tried to hire me? She must have gone through an intermediary as I never met her face to face. Or the fact that someone wants your father dead? That can't possibly surprise you. Lots of people want your father dead. If you asked me to, I'd kill him now."

"You don't mean that."

"Of course I do! How many lives do you think would be spared if he died today? Your father is dying, that makes a man desperate. As a clear-headed man, he was a terrible king. Imagine what a desperate King Lionel would be like." Ezra let Christophe think on that, as they rode the rest of the way in silence. It wasn't until they were walking towards the wing where his sister was housed that Christophe spoke.

"We will do this my way. That means no patricide. If he succeeds in killing me, you can do what you want."

"If he succeeds in killing you, I'll be on the next ship out of the country," Ezra admitted. "There's no way I'll be able to continue here if, however unlikely, I fail."

From the expression on his face, Christophe didn't seem to appreciate that Ezra already had his exit planned out.

They entered the west wing of the palace where Joe waited for the two of them in the hall leading to the princess's chambers.

"Have a good visit?" he asked.

Christophe didn't answer, rather, he gave Ezra a resentful look and kept walking.

"Come on," the prince said, "we have another engagement to attend to."

·   ·   ·   ·   ·

Princess Liliana Phrey, Duchess of Iirmadelle, and Deputy Master of Games was about four years old. She had only just recently returned from her first year at boarding school where she would learn the arts of dance, music, horsemanship, and court manners. Reading wasn't necessary as it was rumored she had been reading since she was two. From what Ezra had heard, she might well end up more intelligent than both of her brothers combined. Pity, she had been born third.

Her transport from her school in the mountains must have been of the utmost secrecy, as Ezra had heard nothing about it from Ian, who seemed to privately consider her the best of the royal family. A picture of the king was required in every establishment in the capital, but Ian had added hers, hung in a considerably nicer frame, and placed it a bit higher than the king's.

Her suite was next to that of the King and Queen, separated only by the emergency council chamber. Ezra knew who it belonged to because he doubted they would paint a three-hundred-year-old oak door pink for just anyone.

In front of that door stood a mortified knight. He wore the crest of his house alongside that of the royal family on a jerkin similar to the one Ezra had seen Joe wearing when they first met. However, the knight also wore wings and a dragon head made from cloth that flopped in such a way it made him appear sillier than it might have otherwise. He took on a pained look as they approached and, for a moment, the group just stared at him.

"Ah-hem," a small voice came from the other side of the door. The knight sighed deeply.

"*Roar*," the knight said, hands up and held like claws, "Roar! You must solve my riddle to gain entry, *roar!*"

At this, Christophe drew the training sword he'd insisted upon, and pointed it at the dragon.

"Then tell me your riddle, beast!" His voice was dramatically heroic and even Joe was smiling.

The 'dragon' pulled out a scroll and read:

What has cities, but no houses?

Forests, but no trees,

Water, but no fish?

Christophe seemed stumped. He sheathed his 'sword' and scratched his head.

"Cities without houses, no trees and no fish..." he muttered to himself. Ezra knew this riddle. He also knew the answer. After almost a minute the prince laughed out loud. He stood with one hand on his sword, the other pointing at the underpaid knight.

"You nearly bested me, dragon." The heroic voice was well practiced. Ezra would almost think Christophe was of the city players. "I have solved your riddle. It is a map!"

The dragon bowed, and applause erupted from inside. The door was flung open and there stood what Ezra always imagined a pixie to look like. Her poofy purple dress was covered in sparkles and she wore butterfly wings on her back.

"Congratulations, Christophe! You defeated the dragon!" Turning to said dragon, she handed him a gold coin, "For your hoard," she explained before ushering everyone inside.

Her room was a clash between a little girl's dream world, a scholar's library, and a young knight's imagination. Books were neatly organized in pink and purple bookcases that lined the walls. Each case stenciled with knights and dragons and weapons in sparkly paint. Actual weapons were organized in the corner, all sized specifically for a child. A foal-sized stuffed horse stood sentry at the edge of her four-poster bed and currently, all her stuffed animals were sitting around a small table, ready for tea.

"Welcome, honored guests," she said, curtsying. "Would you please be seated?" She pointed out three child-sized chairs. They appeared disproportionately sturdy so, placing as little weight as possible on the chair, Ezra lowered himself onto the seat that displayed his name tag, written in elegant calligraphy. Christophe and Joe followed suit, sitting fully on the chairs with such practiced maneuvering, that they had clearly sat in them many times before.

She danced around the table, pouring them tea and adding enough sugar cubes to satisfy a herd of horses. Before Christophe had the chance to protest, Ezra dropped some solution in each of their teas, and then he gave the go-ahead to drink. The prince's eyes were wide with anger but, if the princess had noticed, she gave no indication of it.

"To my brother! Another year closer to being really *really* old!" She drank her tea with a flourish and Ezra took a bit longer than usual with his so as to hide his smirk. Ian was right. Princess Liliana was the best of all the royals.

"How are your studies progressing?" Christophe asked Liliana in Zouszianes.

"Quite well, thank you for asking," Liliana replied. Her pronunciation had a rough quality to it but her translations were spot on. Seeing Ezra's confusion, she explained.

"It's a present for Auntie for Yulemas. I want to be fluent so we can speak in Zouszianes together."

"Then don't let me hinder your studies," Ezra replied, being fluent himself in the formal dialect. He was impressed. And she was delighted. Princess Liliana began asking rapid-fire questions about how he spoke the language and where he learned it. Ezra answered best he could, trying to clean up his stories as he went along.

Joe sat drinking his tea quietly. It was clear he didn't understand a word the three of them were saying. The next hour or so passed in that fashion. The three of them discussed their travels—Liliana's being limited to the boarding school—and Joe rested his eyes, or at least, that's what he said he was doing when Ezra woke him up on their way out.

Liliana had managed to extract a promise from Ezra that he would take her around the fair next week. It didn't help that Christophe came to her aid by insisting it was fine with him. Surrounded by strangers, Ezra would get to protect two people, not one. Oh, joy. At least he had a week to find a way out of it.

Joe laughed about it the whole way to the training grounds.

"When those two tag-team someone there's no stopping them." He chuckled.

Per Ezra's recommendation, Christophe trained exclusively with his knives that day. His movements were quicker and more accurate. Deadlier. Ezra could see it in the prince's eyes. Perhaps that was why he usually opted for the sword. Maybe the knives brought something out in Christophe that he'd rather keep hidden.

Joe seemed to notice as well, as he stood a little stiffer and didn't speak the entire time Christophe trained.

"Has he ever been in a real fight?" Ezra asked, unable to take his eyes off the prince.

"Never," Joe conceded. "Sometimes I wonder why the king won't send Christophe out to patrol the border. It wouldn't be unusual for the prince to make his presence known to the generals. And a stray arrow from an enemy combatant would be the easiest way for all of this to end." His pause stretched on, and then, "I think the King doesn't want our soldiers and generals meeting, and humanizing the crown prince. That would make things more difficult if King Lionel ever wanted to take more open actions against this son."

"Ezra, come here!" Christophe called, snapping the two out of the grim mood they were falling into. Ezra gave Joe a nod and then approached Christophe and his knights. The prince held what looked like a crossbow, but the style differed slightly. Ezra had never seen anything like it.

"It fires five shots. See?" Everyone cleared away as Christophe aimed at the target and fired. As he pulled the trigger, loosing the bolt, a cylindrical piece turned, bringing another bolt up, ready to shoot. The time it took between firing and reloading was as fast, if not faster, than Ezra when shooting his bow. And when he looked at the target, he saw that it was relatively accurate too. Only one ring from the target. Though that might also have been due to Christophe's aim than the crossbow.

"May I?" Ezra asked, holding his hand out. Christophe handed it to him. The crossbow was surprisingly light. The trigger had a bit of a longer slide and, when he shot, the bolt changed while he let off the trigger. It was truly an elegant design and, based on his dead center shot, the extra feature did not come at the loss of accuracy.

However, Ezra approached the target to retriev the bolts he and the prince had fired, he saw that they just barely held in wood. These would need to hit flesh to cause any real damage. Against someone wearing armor, they were useless.

"I'll stick with my bow," Ezra decided, handing the crossbow back. "It's a good weapon to keep at your bedside though. Very portable." While Christophe and his men continued to train with the new toy, Ezra pulled a longbow from the shed and started exercising.

For most people, exercising meant going for a run. Or doing push-ups. And Ezra did that too, and more. But if he truly wanted to work the muscles that he needed, he had to fight. Or shoot. He paused after each shot to survey his surroundings. It would take less than a minute for an adept assassin to set up at one of the windows, or from one of the many arched pillars.

By the time he'd loosed a quiver full into the center of the target, accidentally splitting several arrows down the center, training was winding down. Of the people who were still training, most of them had stopped to watch Ezra shoot. Approaching the target, he had to use a knife to dig them out, and then he returned everything to the weapon shed.

Joe, and Christophe, who had his back to the wall, were talking when Ezra approached. Christophe appeared uneasy.

"So mother wasn't sure if she'd be able to get away. But she did. And she wants to have dinner with me, as originally planned." Ezra waited for the ask.

"So," Christophe started again, "Would it be all right if we were alone?" The prince's shoulders were so tense they nearly touched the bottoms of his ears.

"No," Ezra said sharply. "I told you that, under no circumstances, were you to leave my sight for however long this takes. I promise I am the definition of discretion. Nothing you discuss with the Queen would leave the room."

Christophe deflated and Joe gave him a 'told you so' sort of nod.

"Shall we then?" Ezra held out an arm for Christophe to take the lead. They had a dinner to attend.

•   •   •   •   •

Dinner was an awkward affair. They ate in the Queen's chambers. Not a 'they' including the three of them cheerfully discussing the day. This 'they' included two people fully aware that they were being monitored by a very hungry third party. Ezra was starving. And the spread that the kitchen staff brought in, once tested, was enough to make his mouth water.

Queen Danielle, unlike her daughter, did make a fuss when Ezra, just for good measure, sprinkled some solution into her food and drink as well. But Christophe promised it was harmless and ate his own tested food to prove the point. After that, the two settled in for a quiet meal, broken up by the occasional halting small talk that Ezra doubted they had meant to have.

He did feel bad about the situation. Truly, he did. But he was hardly going to let sentiment be the cause of his client's death. After one particularly long bought of silence, Ezra decided to intercede.

"You are organizing the festival and tournament for the prince's birthday, isn't that right Your Majesty? How is that going?" She seemed startled to be addressed as such by someone she likely considered 'the help', but she engaged.

"Yes, I have been very busy since your father's abrupt announcement. Thanks to availability, it won't start until next week, but that's just as well. The whole affair will wrap up on the actual date of your birth," she smiled, toasting her adopted son.

"I am sorry that you have to go through all the effort. All this fuss really isn't necessary," Christophe said, his eyes sad.

"Nonsense!" the queen shot back, "No task is too great if it can bring you a bit of happiness. And I am glad for the project. I fear I have not had much to do as of late."

Like a grating, unpleasant, inner voice, Ezra could hear Granny Kelva sneering.

Oh, the poor queen is bored?

Ezra managed to keep the smirk off his face.

"Well," he said, once more trying to stimulate any conversation, "I'm sure the vendors and performers of Olaesta are grateful to you. And all those excited young swordsmen, eager to compete!"

The queen, perhaps seeing what Ezra was doing, grabbed the topic and ran with it. She spent the rest of the evening detailing all the performers and entertainments being brought in for the festivities.

"Of course, your father is taking care of the tournament, he does seem quite invested in making your birthday something special. Oh, I do love that man," she added, a dreamy look in her eyes. Ezra and Christophe shared a glance before she continued detailing each and every thing she was doing and planning.

When they bid her goodnight and returned to Christophe's room the prince kept to himself, reviewing his appeals, and other documents before heading to bed with only a 'goodnight' to Ezra. Ezra suspected that keeping such a huge secret from the queen was taking quite a toll on the prince. Ezra blew out the candles before sticking two daggers in his belt and rolling under the bed.

16

A DAY OUT

They fell into a pattern that carried them through the next week. Training, council meetings, paperwork, and repeat. The festival kicked off without anyone dying, that Ezra knew of, and several days passed into it before anything happened.

Oftentimes, Ezra would find himself asking how his life had led to a particular moment. Usually, these instances of regret occurred right after he'd fallen from a roof, or into a river, or after he'd been stabbed or shot. Now, as he walked hand in hand with Princess Liliana, he wondered at the events that had led to his altered job parameters.

"*What's one more person?*" Christophe had said.

"*It'll be fun,*" he'd said.

Ezra had never been much for children and they, in turn, had never been very fond of him. And yet, the princess seemed fascinated by Ezra. Her head was on a constant swivel, taking in her surroundings and then smiling at Ezra. Christophe, who walked in front of Ezra and behind Joe, seemed to find this enormously funny.

The knights who were following them at a distance might have made Ezra feel a little better were it not for the fact that they had a great vantage point, should they decide to take him or the prince out. If he really thought about it, the poor life choices that led to his job as a baby sitter probably started when he was seven. More recently, the events that led to this moment occurred yesterday morning over breakfast.

"Ezra, I received an interesting invitation this morning," Christophe had said, holding some pink stationary out to him. Ezra took it, not liking the smile the prince was giving him. Unfolding the paper, Ezra read:

Master Ezra Toth
Has been formally invited to attend the festivities with
PRINCESS LILIANA
&
CROWN PRINCE CHRISTOPHE
Tomorrow morning.
Please RSVP at your earliest convenience.

The formality of the invitation was somewhat undercut by the loopy 'Lily' signed at the bottom next to a happy face.

Ezra set down the invitation and stared at Christophe who was making a show of busily spreading jam on toast.

"You want me to guard you and the princess?" She had broached the subject the other day at her tea party, but when the prince agreed Ezra had thought they must have been joking.

Guarding one person? Fine. Guarding a group with no inevitable danger? Sure. Guarding two people, knowing that one of them is in constant danger? Nope.

"There would be knights assigned to our group to add extra security," Christophe said.

"That's not better," Ezra kneaded his forehead with the heel of his hand, feeling a headache fast approaching.

"All right," Ezra said, "Let's say we go. And then say someone, maybe one of your knights decides to attack you. And what if the range of danger extends to the princess? Who am I supposed to protect? Because I don't just want to get paid, I'd like you to be the next king." In the silence that followed, Ezra watched the prince, hoping to see his mind change.

It didn't.

"Nevertheless," Christophe countered, "this is what my sister wants, and for the limited time that she's home from school I will do everything in my power to give it to her. I've selected knights I trust to work as the 'far guard' and Joseph will be there as well. He knows to protect Lily should something happen, leaving you free to protect me. Does that sound reasonable?"

"No," grumbled Ezra, "but you've clearly made up your mind so to hell with it. We'll go to the festival."

"Excellent," Christophe smiled, "Now the matter of your weapons. Lily doesn't know what's going on, obviously, and I fear that your usual amount of weapons might frighten her…" Christophe faded at the sight of Ezra's face.

"I will be wearing my reinforced coat and carrying as many weapons as I can so long as they don't slow me down. Your sister needs to get used to the idea of armed people following her around. This is nonnegotiable." Ezra snapped curtly. And Christophe did not attempt to broach the subject again.

•　　•　　•　　•　　•

Now, thankful for the cool autumn breeze, Ezra walked through the crowds. Christophe might have been under the impression that people were parting for him, as a sign of respect to their future king. In truth, they took one glance at Ezra and hastily moved out of the way.

The festivities were in full swing, with people not just from the capital, but from the surrounding towns as well, crowding the streets. Old women sipped cool juice in the shade of a nearby stall, while the juice vendor sang out to the crowd to sample his wares. Ezra noted that all the vendors were especially exuberant today. Despite the cost to the crown, an event such as this always brought in more gold than it put out.

A group of children ran past, laughing and yelling, and Ezra felt a tug as Lily unconsciously leaned towards them. It must be lonely, he reflected, to be a princess. Though she looked the part of a peasant— per Ezra's insistence all of them wore the clothes of commoners, they would have figured her out in an instant. Clothes could be changed, but it was impossible to completely change one's own mannerisms. And, when he watched the royal siblings, he could instantly tell that they came from money. Maybe not crown jewel money, but they were obviously nobles. It was something about the way they held themselves. Like the weight of the world did not fall quite so heavily on their shoulders. They had problems, sure, but none of those problems involved surviving the winter.

She seemed down after that so, after an impressive juggling act from a shaved-ice vendor, Ezra bought her a cone. Lily perked up quite a bit, likely having never had commoner's food.

They wound their way through the area within a mile of the castle. That had been Ezra's other condition, still, they had plenty to see.

Animals from all parts of the globe were in attendance in the stadium set up to hold the tournament later today. Lily's scream of delight drew attention from those nearby when an elephant reached out to accept her offering of a handful of peanuts. And Ezra forgot anonymity for a moment, roaring with laughter when a camel spit directly into Joe's open mouth.

The acrobats that followed were just as impressive, their routines reminding Ezra of his gymnastic training when he'd first arrived at his uncle's Lude. Remaining at the stadium for the rest of the morning, they were perfectly positioned to enter the podium set aside for the nobility.

Joe, Christophe, and Lily changed behind a curtain while Ezra surveyed the podium. It was an open space, save for a wall behind the chairs, which meant all seated there were vulnerable to an attack from afar. When Christophe emerged, he appeared a little bulkier than Ezra would have liked, but from a distance, no one would be able to tell the prince wore chainmail.

Christophe shot Ezra a dirty look to show exactly what he thought about that, before sitting down on the right of the large, ornate chair in the middle. Ezra had had to move Daniel's own chair farther to the right to make room for Ezra to stand at Christophe's side.

Soon, the animals and acrobats and all other performers cleared the field and an expectant hush fell over the arena. Ezra actually grabbed for his sword when the king's arrival was announced, via trumpeters. He was tense. Too tense. This was not his first job as a shield and he'd been in far more vulnerable positions than this. It was hard to remember such an instance at the moment, but he was sure it had happened. He hadn't received the bulk of his scars on safe, friendly missions.

The King had taken a turn for the worst since his appearance at the council meeting. His gait was much slower and shakier as he climbed the steps to his makeshift throne, assisted by his Queen. Ezra could actually hear the king's breathing, wheezing and labored as it was. If the rest of the court noticed, they gave no indication of it, cheering for their king with enthusiasm. King Lionel whispered to the announcer who pranced to the front of the podium.

"Ladies and gentleman, let the tournament begin!" He cried out to the screaming crowds.

From next to the podium, the line of fighters that had been forming filed into the stadium. Some, by their dress, were professional fighters, traveling far and wide to compete on the tournament circuit. Some, like those who were clamoring to buy steel at Pearl's store, had naught but the clothes on their back and whatever weapon they were able to afford. All stood proud and tall in the crowd in front of them. Ezra scanned the fighters and saw at least three potential threats. They had the bearing of killers.

Ezra didn't pay much attention to the rules the announcer read out to the fighters and the audience. He was too focused on the newcomer who now stood by Daniel's side. Mere feet from Ezra. Mere feet from Christophe. It was Daniel's silent shadow. An assassin for sure, but then again, so was Ezra. There was no proof that the man served as anything more than a bodyguard. But Christophe wasn't paying Ezra to assume the best. He was being paid to be as paranoid as possible.

With that in mind, he palmed a dagger, shifting slightly so Christophe was blocked from the Shadow's view. He noticed this and gave Ezra the smallest of smiles. One rival recognizing another.

On the field, two amateurs were waving their swords about like clubs, sometimes missing their opponent's sword entirely and hitting only air. It was painful to watch. Luckily, the amateur fights were some of the quickest and they were quickly weeded out in favor of more experienced fighters.

The clang of steel and the roar of the crowd brought Ezra back to his childhood. If it even qualified as such. In this environment, he'd killed his first man at the age of twelve, and his next less than a year later. He'd slept with a knife under his pillow and kept a large rock propped against the inside of his door to block intruders. His uncle had lightly poisoned him on a regular basis until Ezra checked everything that passed his lips. Were it not for the daunting prospect of crossing the desert on his own, Ezra would have run away within the first month.

Nearly two hours passed before the final match began. His assessment had been correct. The three assassins had all made it to the top four, with two of them now standing in the finals. The one Ezra had slotted to win was all muscle, wielding a double-ended spear. His weight should have been a disadvantage when it came to speed, but his movements were every bit as agile as those with whom he fought. When the strong man finally won, Ezra could tell he wanted to finish the blow. The restraint being exerted when he removed the spear from his opponent's throat was palpable.

The crowds were beside themselves. Like Ezra, they had favored the strong man to win and were overjoyed. He bowed to all sides of the stadium before approaching the podium and kneeling before the king.

"What if we make this interesting?" King Lionel asked, turning to Christophe. He turned back to the fighter, "If you can beat my son's guard, I'll double your purse! What say you?"

Ezra tensed, about to slit the King's throat for pulling something like this. And yet, he should have expected it. He'd known that the king would use the tournament as a chance to get at Christophe, he just hadn't known how. Until now.

Christophe looked up at Ezra, nervously, having come to the same conclusion. The crowds had heard the King's suggestion and were going nuts.

Fight, fight, fight, fight! They chanted.

This wasn't about Ezra's reputation anymore, if he didn't fight, the king would use it as a chance to make his son appear weak. Ezra glanced back at Joe who rose from his seat and approached. Ezra pressed the dagger he'd been holding into Joe's hand.

"Don't let anyone near him," Ezra whispered. "And keep an eye on that one," he nodded to the Shadow, now positively leering.

Ezra took off his coat, unsheathing his sword as he did so, and jumped to the ground. The crowds went ballistic. Fight, fight, fight!! It was like he'd never left the fighting pits.

"What's your name?" Ezra asked, swinging a few practice strokes to warm his muscles. The strong man only grinned, revealing many missing teeth.

"I'll tell you when I win," he said, twirling his staff in a bout of unnecessary showmanship.

The two circled each other. One sizing up the other. When the strong man struck, Ezra had a half second warning and used it to dodge as his opponent thrust his spear where Ezra's stomach had been. Ezra sliced down but the strong man used his spear to avoid a quick decapitation, swinging around to elbow Ezra in the gut.

The fight began in earnest. Like a dance, each move from one had an equal and opposite response from the other. The strong man was just as agile as Ezra had feared, but his ultimate flaw was in his overconfidence. They traded minor blows, each cautious of the other.

It only took one false move, overreaching and losing his balance for Ezra to reach down and slice through the assassin's hamstring. The strong man roared in pain and jumped away. He bled profusely from his wound, leaning on his spear for support.

Perhaps this had been the plan from the beginning, or perhaps the man chose, in that moment, to improvise in the face of defeat. Regardless, the assassin didn't even have to look at the podium before he was aiming his spear for the prince.

Ezra didn't think, he just lunged and, somehow, managed to tackle the man mid-throw, sending the spear harmlessly off to the side. Screams sounded from the audience and Ezra heard yelling from nearby but he tuned it all out.

The more immediate problem was the pair of hands around his throat, throttling him. Luckily, he had a few daggers on his person and used one to slice at the delicate tissue of his attacker's armpits. The strong man roared again, sounding almost inhuman in his agony. That gave Ezra enough time to break free, flip the man onto his stomach, and tie his wrists with the cord Ezra always kept on his person.

Guards surrounded them, swords pointed at Christophe's would-be assassin.

"Thanks, guys, I think I've got it," Ezra said, groaning as he stood. Definitely a broken rib, several new future scars, and a full body bruise.

Conscious of the blood spurting from the strong man's leg, Ezra used his belt to make a tourniquet. When Ezra pulled the man to his feet he looked ready to kill. Confident that the guards were capable of handling an injured, bound man, Ezra rushed to the podium.

"Are you all right?" he yelled.

Christophe nodded, his face white as a sheet. Lily sat in his lap, sobbing, and Joe looked very much like he needed to sit down. Sparing a moment to glance at King Lionel and Daniel, he noted their expressions of bitter disappointment. Climbing onto the podium, Ezra took Lily in his arms and pulled Christophe up.

"You, you and you," Ezra said, pointing at the soldiers currently surrounding the would-be assassin. "Take him to the dungeons and place a guard on him. You, you and you," he continued, pointing at three more soldiers, "Follow me to the castle. We are to get the prince back without further incident. Now move!"

The soldiers scurried to do his bidding, one bringing horses. Ezra helped Christophe up and then handed Lily over to him. Despite Joe's sickly appearance, he was already in the saddle and Ezra mounted up as well.

"Yah!" he yelled, and the horses seemed to also sense his urgency, breaking into a trot that carried them all the way up to the castle. The whole time, Joe held a crossbow at the ready and Ezra kept his hand on his sword.

More soldiers joined them halfway through the market and a full armed escort walked them up through town and into the stables before retreating.

Ezra's mind raced the whole journey. He could not believe he'd been so stupid. Even if it had made the prince seem weak, even if it embarrassed him, Ezra should have stayed at his post. He'd been so caught up in foolish nostalgia that he'd lost sight of the mission.

They dismounted, and Ezra sent Joe with Lily and a pair of guards back to her rooms. Christophe was sitting on a bench, staring at nothing, when Ezra finally approached him.

"Are you all right?" Ezra asked, more gently this time. Christophe took several deep breaths before answering, his coloring still as pale as Mabel's porridge.

"I have to be, don't I? We knew this was a risk, but I ordered you to take us anyways. It's just lucky you were able to stop him."

"Speaking of the assassin," Ezra hesitated, "We don't have a lot of time before the king sends someone to silence him. We need to get as much information as possible."

"What do you mean?" Christophe asked, wearily.

"Have you ever been to an interrogation, Your Highness?"

17

A CONVERSATION

Ezra shivered against the cold as they descended the worn, uneven stone steps to the dungeon. Water, likely from the moat above, dripped a slow, insistent beat that was enough to drive a man like himself mad even without the added prison conditions. And from the few prisons he'd broken into, this was far from the worst. The shit smell was barely noticeable and the heckling non-existent as he passed the cells. Christophe, close on his heels, seemed more than a little unnerved to be there. He kept his head on a swivel and gripped the sides of his tunic to stop from wringing his hands.

"Not down here often, Your Highness?"

"No. Only once when I was a child." Ezra wondered briefly how the Crown Prince had managed that but they arrived at the assassin's cell so he stowed that away for later.

"I know you don't want to be here, Christophe. It's more than understandable. But your presence may trigger something in the suspect. Besides, I just can't risk letting you out of my sight this close after an attack."

"Wouldn't my—wouldn't they want to lay low until the guards become less vigilant?" He asked, peering into the empty hallway.

"The problem is, the guards aren't as vigilant as you'd think, because they're thinking the same thing. It would be insane to strike again this soon, which is why it is the perfect time to do so. That's what I would do. Speaking of guards, where is the prisoner's guard?" The last one he'd seen was at the top of the steps.

He felt, more than saw Christophe's shrug.

"Why does it matter? He's not going anywhere." The prince was still so unaware of the complicated nature of the danger he was in that sometimes it baffled Ezra.

"Why does it matter? Why do you think we're here, Christophe? For a stroll? I am here to get information about the people who hired him. And it's well within the power of those people to hire someone to kill him while no one is watching. Which leaves us with nothing but a dead body and a million unanswerable questions."

"Something else you would do?" Christophe asked quietly. Ezra turned on him but the prince had taken on a sickly pallor. Something to deal with later. He chose not to answer and unlocked the door, entering the cell.

The one good thing was that the prisoner had been bound exactly as he would have ordered. Half standing, half sitting, the chair the assassin was bound to was one of his uncle's own creation. He'd used it for torture and reprogramming. As a child, after spending a full day and night in it, Ezra found that his legs lost all manner of sensation within a few hours, making escape impossible. Judging the would-be assassin's face, the cramps preceding the numbness were well underway, and he had already pissed himself going by the smell.

He gave Ezra no reaction but, once Christophe entered behind him, the man let out a near animal cry. Struggling against his bonds until his face was a ruddy red, the strong man had several veins throbbing in his forehead. Christophe was plastered against the far wall in shock. Eventually, the prisoner fell back against the chair, his deep, ragged breaths making the only sound in the cell. Ezra waited for those to cease. Then waited a few moments more before pulling a copy of Ian's registry out of his pocket.

"You already know who I am, and you're clearly familiar with my client, but seeing as you've tried to kill us both I'd appreciate your name in turn. I can't keep calling you 'the strong man', 'the assassin', or 'the man with the anger issues I have tied up in my basement'."

"I am Golok." The prisoner said, with no trace of the accent that Ezra knew he had.

"Golok," Ezra repeated, "you are not a subtle man. You named yourself after the short blade the Primbu of the Island Nation of Mendelai are famous for. It certainly makes a statement. Especially since you aren't from Mendelai. Your complexion, and the accent you hide so well hints at a Charusian ancestry. So you're well-traveled. You're also famous enough to be hired for such a high-profile job as this. I apologize that I have not heard of you, I have not left the capitol in the past years or our paths may have crossed."

Golok scowled deeply, upset that he could be so easily read.

"I also notice you did not sign in at The Sword and Shield upon arrival." Ezra held up the list of names he'd been checking. "Even the newest and lowest of scum know it's custom to make yourself known at our capital's criminal capital." Hopefully, Ian would forgive him for saying such a thing in front of the future King of Olacia.

Golok had proceeded to the traditional 'stare at the wall and say nothing' part of every interrogation.

"Now you're being rude. I'm just trying to have a conversation." Ezra leaned down so he was directly in the man's line of sight. "From one professional to another you know I need answers and it would be a lot easier on you if you just gave them to me." They stared at each other for a moment before Golok's expression switched from apathy to one of determination.

"Don't—" Ezra started, reaching for him. But, with a deep breath, he did what Ezra was honestly surprised he hadn't done before the two had arrived. Golok bit his tongue off.

"Shit! Shit, shit, shit. Come with me!" Ezra grabbed Christophe by the collar and dragged him out into the hall. He tossed the kit he'd left outside into the prince's arms and grabbed a torch from the closest sconce. Pulling the prince back into the cell he took the bag in exchange for his water skin and some rag.

"Stand here," Ezra instructed, directing Christophe to the opposite side of the chair. "Water." He reached out, and Christophe placed it in his hand. He undid the neck straps grabbed Golok by the back of his head and poured the water into his mouth. As soon as his mouth filled, and the gargling started Ezra threw his head forward and a bloody, watery mess spilled down Golok's front. He did this three more times while sensing the horrified, judgmental stare bearing down on him. Once Golok's mouth was mostly clean of blood Ezra took the rag from Christophe's hand and shoved it in the prisoner's mouth. Golok's eyes were full of hatred. It was the only way he had at his disposal to express his feelings as the curses he was undoubtedly trying to scream were muffled by the rag.

"Are you actually trying to yell at me," Ezra asked, pulling his smallest hammer out of the fire. He tried to hand it to Christophe who backed away, shaking his head. "It's either this or the tongs, Highness," he held up a blood-crusted pair of tongs in the other hand. Christophe snatched the hammer, freeing Ezra to put on his gloves.

"I'm going to grab the stump and hold it steady for you, so when I say 'now' you press the hot metal down firmly and hold."

"Until when?" Christophe asked. His pale complexion was quickly shifting from porridge to pea soup. Ezra didn't answer and instead dragged him to the opposite side of the chair. The gloves, a gift from Pearl, were not meant for day-to-day wear. They were stiff and thick, made of a hide that had been treated over and over again with her special soup.

He used them for two things specifically: dogs and torture. In this case, the usefulness was leaning in a more canine direction as Golok bit down on his hand. Judging the pressure, Ezra would have easily lost a finger to this ordeal had he not been protected. As it were, he'd have bruises to remind him of this lovely errand. It only took a few moments to force Golok's mouth open enough to shove the tongs in and grab hold of what little remained of the tongue.

"Now!" Ezra wasn't sure if it was his tone of voice, expression as they locked eyes, or a sudden force of will on the prince's part, but Christophe was there with the hammer and shoved it into the killer's mouth. He took the searing sound, smell, and screaming to mean that it was working. After a few moments, Ezra prepared to tell Christophe that he needn't continue, but he had already removed and thrown the hammer on the floor. The future King of Olacia ran into the hall and began to retch violently; negating any sudden force of will he may or may not have stumbled upon.

Ezra waited until the vomiting had ceased before handing the prince his water skin.

"Rinse and spit, your highness. We're not done by a long shot." Christophe, reluctantly, followed Ezra back into the room.

"Now sit there," Ezra said, pointing towards a stool in the corner, "and don't move. Also, I'd appreciate if you wiped the judgmental look off your face. You knew what I was when you hired me." The prince glanced guiltily at the floor and Ezra turned his back on the prince and back to Golok.

"Well obviously Golok isn't your real name, but I don't suppose I'm going to get it now, am I?"

He was met with a silent, agonized glare.

"If you didn't want me to stick a burning hammer in your mouth you might have just said so," Ezra was never able to resist poking fun at his interrogation victims. Likely the gods would find a way to pay him back one day, but today wasn't that day.

"Here's how things are going to work, Golok." Ezra pulled up a chair and sat in front of the prisoner, "I'm going to ask a question and you are going to nod or shake your head. If I think you're lying, or if you don't answer, I take a body part, starting with fingers. And if we run out of fingers I'll move on to toes, and then your heels, and ears. And if, by the end, if all that's left is a torso and a head, then I'll start flaying the skin from your body. I learned the art from a very sick individual so I can promise the skin will look immaculate. Like a human suit. I'm very creative and there's quite a lot of you left for me to play with. Do you understand?"

Golok stared resolutely ahead, refusing to nod his head. Ezra pulled some clippers out of his bag and relieved the man of his left thumb.

"I said," Ezra yelled over Golok's screams, "Do you understand?"

Golok nodded, tears streaming down his face. He took the hammer which he'd placed back in the fire, and cauterized the stump.

"Let's begin."

•   •   •   •   •

Several hours, several more fingers, a big toe, and a good deal more heaving from the prince later, Ezra and Christophe left the dungeons.

Golok told Ezra everything. The king had hired him and nine others to kill the prince, four, including Golok, had taken part in the competition and were consequently taken out of the running to tend to their injuries. One had killed another to minimize the competition. And four remained, ready and able to kill the Crown Prince at any moment. It took a good deal of questioning to get that information but Ezra knew it would be worthless as evidence. Golok was already going into shock from his wounds when Ezra left him, and someone would certainly be by to finish the job by morning.

The two walked in silence, Christophe swaying slightly as if drunk. When they returned to his rooms Joe was waiting for them. He jumped up at the sight of his prince and guided him to the chair by the fire.

"What's wrong with him?" Joe demanded, handing the prince a glass of water.

Christophe, before Ezra could get his kit, dully pulled a vial out of his coat pocket and tipped a drop into the water, watched for change and then drank it.

"He saw a bit more than he was prepared to see, is all. Golok, the man with the spear, was definitely hired by the king. There's four more out there though, after today, one or two of them may decide it's not worth the money." Ezra desperately hoped that was the case, but he hadn't had much luck so far in this job and didn't see why he would get it now.

"If he doesn't use his real name then why do you use yours?" Christophe spoke up suddenly, staring at the fire. Ezra was surprised. That wasn't the first question he expected to get after the prince witnessed Ezra's most brutal side.

"A man only changes his name to safeguard his family," Ezra explained. "I am the last of the Toths. They no longer need my protection."

And no one spoke for a long time after that. Joe and Ezra sat quietly by the fire.

Ezra stood watch.

18

A FULL DAY

The next morning was subdued. Joe joined them for breakfast and, while not usually the talkative type, spent the meal trying to coax the prince out of whatever shell he'd crawled in to. Not the ideal birthday mood.

Still, Ezra had to give him credit. Most men would not have the stomach to witness another man being tortured. Ezra thought Christophe was handling himself relatively well. At least, certainly better than Ezra had done the first time he'd seen his Uncle take the knife to someone.

"What's on the docket for today, then?" Ezra asked. Finally, the prince spoke.

"Documents to review, training with the knights, and then the ball."

"Ball?" Ezra asked sharply. "What ball?"

"The ball to celebrate my birthday," Christophe answered wearily. "I'm sure I told you about it."

"I'm sure you didn't," Ezra shot back. The prince sighed, kneading his forehead with the heel of his hand.

"My mother decided that, as a good way to finish up my birthday festivities, we should host a ball. It's likely also a ploy to try and find me a bride. We discussed it at dinner, you know."

"I wasn't listening," Ezra responded.

"Well that much is obvious," the prince shot back.

"All right, all right," Joe stood, breaking the angry glaring contest between the prince and his bodyguard. "It's too late to cancel, and it's impossible for Christophe to miss it. We'll just have to make the best of it. Ezra can survey the crowd and I'll make sure Lissa and I are always dancing near the prince. Does that sound fair?"

It sounded fair, though it was nowhere near reasonable considering the prince's circumstances. Seeing that Joe was waiting, hands on his hips, Ezra nodded in agreement.

"At least your terrible dancing will distract from my slightly less terrible dancing," Christophe said, breaking the tension. After they finished reviewing the day's papers, the two of them bickered about who was the worse dancer all the way to the training grounds.

Everyone there was in good spirits as all the knights were eligible to attend the ball. No one was really working as hard as they could have been, opting rather, to discuss who they wanted to dance with and what they'd be wearing.

Christophe was quite the opposite.

The attack on his life had spurred him to fight even harder than before. Joe surrendered and went to stand with Ezra after just one sparring match that landed him on his back. The knights that took his place weren't having much better luck.

A dangerous light flickered in Christophe's eyes that hadn't been there before. His movements were wilder and unpredictable, but also less effective. If he didn't learn to control his emotions on the battlefield, they may one day be the death of him.

Ezra was just on his way to the prince to talk him down when a glint of light caught his eye. Glancing up, he saw that one of the mirrors he'd sewn into the curtains in the tower was moving.

Ezra ran, pulling an arrow from his quiver and docking it. He knocked Christophe to the ground, standing over him, and shot at the window. The two arrows passed each other mid-air, Ezra's going through the window and out of sight, and the assassin's into Ezra's right shoulder.

It took a moment for everyone to realize what happened, and then the yelling started. Knights picked up Christophe and made to move him indoors but Ezra got a grip on the prince's arm with his left hand and pulled him close.

"Sir Adam," Ezra pointed at the only knight he actually trusted. "Take some men and check out the tower, I might have injured the assassin. Go!" Blades drawn, the Knights ran for the nearest staircase. Joe stood on the other side of Christophe, sword in hand, glaring at the remaining people in the yard.

"Let's get you inside, it's not safe," Ezra said. Christophe glared up at him, anger flashing in his eyes, then halted.

"You're hurt."

"Very observant. And I can take care of that if we go back upstairs."

"We have to get you to the healers," Christophe argued.

Sensing, more than seeing the blood he was losing, Ezra took a rag from a shaking stable boy and wrapped it around the entry and exit wounds, fixing the arrow in place.

"I don't know your healers, so I don't trust your healers. If you'd please let me take you back to your rooms, I can get my kit and fix this myself. All right?" Ezra asked in frustration. He was injured for the second time in as many days. Clearly, he was losing his edge.

Christophe looked ready to argue but Joe only pulled the prince along, making for the same staircase the knights had run up.

The path to the prince's chambers took them past the room the assassin had been in. Inside, they saw Sir Adam and his friends standing around a body.

Cloaked all in black, he had the coloring of a man from the southern islands. Where Golok had claimed to be from. But, unlike Golok, this man would not be interrogated. An arrow, Ezra's, protruded from the man's neck. Ezra checked the body, finding an ornate dagger and a letter.

"Take him somewhere cold," Ezra instructed. "I'll want to examine the body later." Adam nodded and his men picked up the body and carried it out of the room.

"If you would accompany us to the prince's quarters, I would appreciate it," Ezra continued, "I need to take care of this and I don't want Christophe unprotected." Adam stood a little taller, perhaps understanding what it meant to have Ezra's trust, and followed them. He stood guard outside the doors and Ezra sat down in the nearest chair, a bit dizzy from the exertion.

"Joe, I have a green bag in the armoire by my bed. Would you get it, please?" Ezra asked. Joe nodded, and ran out of the room, returning moments later with Ezra's medicine bag.

"Good, there's a blue bag inside," Joe was already pulling it out. He followed Ezra's instructions as they were given, putting a metal stick with a flat end in the fire to heat, and then bringing a bottle of liquor.

Ezra snapped off the front end of the arrow and threw up from the pain when Joe pulled the rest out the back of his shoulder. This new injury was not normally enough to elicit such a visceral reaction, but in tandem with the previous day's wounds, he was simply happy to still be conscious.

"Good, now pour this on the wounds," Ezra said, handing the bottle over after taking a good long swig. The manner of curse words that streamed from his mouth as the spirits sanitized his wounds would have curdled milk. Granny certainly would have flogged him had she been there.

Taking a needle and thread from his kit he quickly sewed up the entrance wound, wiping a salve over it after he'd finished.

"Any chance either of you have the wherewithal to sew up the other side?" Ezra asked hopefully. Both shook their heads, but he wasn't surprised, that's what the metal rod was for.

"All right, Christophe. Just like yesterday. Press the red end against the wound and hold for a count of three."

Ezra put a roll of leather in between his teeth and nodded. Christophe was far less gentle this time than with Golok, and the sizzling sound of burning flesh filled the room. Ezra blacked out for a second or two, but he stayed upright.

He gave a different salve to spread on the cauterized skin, and then Joe helped him wrap it with a clean bandage. When Ezra was fully himself again, he became aware that the two were staring at him.

Or, more accurately, at his scars. He'd taken his shirt off when he was cleaning the injuries, and now they had a full view of his torso and arms.

In his life, he'd been stabbed, shot, skewered, burned, sliced, whipped and tortured. Those injuries would have left a mark on any man. But on Ezra? With his slow and poor healing? He was hard-pressed to think of a single space that wasn't marked in some way.

"Ezra—" Christophe started.

"No," Ezra cut him off. "I don't want your pity and I don't want your well-meant words. What I want is a clean shirt and some food." Joe left just as quickly as when Ezra had been bleeding out and returned shortly, with a clean shirt and food on the way.

"Now," Ezra said, turning to the prince. "Are you all right?"

Christophe burst out laughing, the sound bitter and angry.

"You must be joking. All I've done is sit back while you get Gods know how many injuries defending me, and you want to know if I'm all right?"

"Yes," Ezra said simply, knowing the answer.

Christophe collapsed into a chair and put his head in his hands. Ezra waited patiently.

"No," Christophe finally admitted. "No, I'm not all right. Today I watched you take an arrow for me after another man tried to kill me. Yesterday, whilst my baby sister sat in my lap, that thug of a man Golok aimed to throw a spear at us. I have to test all my food and drink and I'm taking a mixture of poisons every day so I can build up a tolerance. I don't know who I can trust and I barely want to be king in the first place. No, I am not all right!"

"That's right," Ezra said, "just let it out."

"If my tyrant of a father wasn't so obsessed with conquering the surrounding kingdoms and more interested in getting to know his son maybe he wouldn't hate me so much." Christophe raged, "or have taken the time to turn my own brother against me! What kind of family even acts this way? Normal people don't have to worry about potential infanticide over breakfast." Breakfast was emphasized by him knocking the tray off his nearby table. Unfortunately, it was the tray bearing Joe's tonic. That was just enough to take the wind out of his rant.

He started cleaning, apologizing to Joe who was insisting the prince let a servant take care of it. Ezra couldn't help but wonder who would be there to keep the prince grounded once Joe was gone. It certainly wasn't going to be Ezra. In the week since he'd arrived he'd already been stared at more than a year in the Borough. Plus the fact that all the courtiers he saw wore a smile that was so fake he could wash them off with a bucket of water.

He'd just have to hope that the prince found a nice girl who would serve as his voice of reason when things got tough. Maybe the prince would meet her tonight.

·   ·   ·   ·   ·

"Are you enjoying yourself?" Joe asked, out of breath from a fast-paced dance with Lissa who hung on his arm. She looked distinctly less intimidating when she was happy. Ezra, who was feeling very much like a dress-up doll after being forced to bathe and dress in clothes laid out for him, was not happy at all.

"I've been in battles that were less stressful than this," Ezra responded. Joe shrugged and pulled Lissa back out onto the dance floor. He was more energetic than Ezra had seen in a long while.

Ezra moved to itch his nose, forgetting about the sling binding his right arm to his chest, and winced. The arm would be fine as long as he kept it immobile till tomorrow. Exactly the kind of thing a bodyguard wants.

Christophe, standing on his left, rolled his eyes.

"Come now, Ezra," he said, watching Joe and Lissa who had returned to the dance floor for a waltz. "There must be some girl here that catches your eye."

And Ezra, who sensed the prince was the kind of person who'd try to fix him up with one of the court ladies, decided that the prince had told enough secrets to earn some back.

"I have no interest in women, Your Highness," Ezra admitted.

Christophe, who had been sipping a glass of wine, choked. Ezra handed the coughing prince his handkerchief.

"So," Christophe said tentatively after getting a hold of himself, "is it—men?"

Based on the predilections of some of the knights under Christophe's command, Ezra knew a fondness for men would not be a problem. If only the matter were as simple as that.

"No, your highness. Not men. I have no interest in romantic attachments of any kind. I feel nothing stronger than admiration or friendship for men or women."

It took several moments for Christophe to wrap his head around such an idea.

"Do you mean you just haven't met the right person?"

"No, Christophe," Ezra said patiently, "Boys and girls fantasize about relations with others. I don't. I have no interest. Nor have I ever had an interest in having intimate relations with anyone. Of a physical, or emotional nature. At all. Ever." Ezra said as emphatically as was possible without drawing attention to them.

It was funny. When Ezra had heard this was even a possibility, it had been difficult for him to get his mind around as well. As a fifteen-year-old boy, the other servants in the Lude were all obsessed with women or men. They acted like it was the most natural thing in the world. But frankly, Ezra was much more interested in reading or fighting than taking a tumble with a girl. He did though. For curiosity's sake. Ezra had thought that doing it with a girl might trigger whatever instincts everyone else seemed to possess. And, while she'd seemed to enjoy herself, he found the whole ordeal a bit disgusting.

It wasn't until he ventured into the local brothel for advice, that a madam sat him down and explained that he wasn't alone. Many others had little to no interest in relations. That he was perfectly fine just the way he was and didn't need to feel like he had to be like everyone else.

And that was exactly what he told Christophe. By the time Ezra was done with his story, Christophe looked more thoughtful than confused.

"It's new to me, that's for certain," the prince admitted, "but I'm sure the lack of distractions gives you the edge in your chosen vocation. I don't suppose you see a woman out there that won't bore me to death, do you?" And that, it seemed, was that.

Ezra was shocked that the prince had been so ready to accept Ezra's less than orthodox approach to love. Or his lack thereof. Every day he found something else about this prince that disproved all of Granny's grumblings about the royal family. At least, this particular family member.

"Well?" Christophe asked, scanning the crowds. Ezra smiled and helped him search, trying to separate the empty-headed courtiers from the sensible ones. He'd just passed over a girl hopelessly giggling in his direction when he spotted something that made his blood run cold.

"Your Highness—who is that?" Ezra pointed to a man talking to one of the noblemen who sat on the council.

"Him?" Christophe asked, following his finger to the figure, "That's our Minister of Trade, Master Erik Irvin. Do you know him?"

Ezra felt numb, his fingers itching for the dagger he kept up his sleeve.

"Ezra," Christophe said, insistently. "What's wrong? You look like you've seen a ghost. Do you know Minister Irvin?"

Flashes of Ezra's childhood flashed before his eyes. A small boy smiling up at a man who held him aloft in his arms. It had felt like flying. They had been happy, he'd thought.

"Yes, I know him," Ezra said, stiffly. "That's my father."

•   •   •   •   •

A clatter made Ezra jump. Christophe had actually dropped his cup in surprise. Several people glanced up to see what the noise was, including Minister Irvin. He merely seemed curious at first, then, slowly, a glimmer of recognition. And immediately following that recognition was a look of horror. He bowed quickly to the counselor with whom he had been conversing and then started pushing his way through the crowd, towards the doors.

Ezra started after him, but he'd only gotten a step before strong hands were on his shoulder, pulling him back. Ezra turned on the person who dared to interfere.

"Who do you—" Ezra snarled but was cut off abruptly by the sight of his old teacher.

"Hello, Ezra," Antony said calmly. Ezra shook his shoulder loose and looked to the prince who still appeared a bit shocked by all the revelations being thrown his way. Ignoring, Ezra's glare, Antony gave a small bow to the prince.

"Your Highness, it is a pleasure to see you outside of the council chambers. I see that you did end up hiring my friend, here." Ezra stared from one to the other.

"Wait—what? You approached Antony about me?"

The surprise had left Christophe's face in lieu of the royal smile.

"Not me specifically, while researching your known connections Joseph learned of your mentor Sir Antony and made inquiries. As I recall, you had recommended against the appointment."

Ezra wasn't surprised to hear that. Following such a recommendation, Antony would not have expected that Ezra be offered the position. Which was likely why he'd been so surprised at the news, in the first place.

"I'm more than confident that Ezra can keep Your Highness safe, I just wasn't sure it would be a good fit."

"No," Ezra interrupted, "you didn't want me here because you knew my father was part of the royal court. How long have you known?" he demanded, fighting to keep his voice level.

Antony looked guilty and, to Ezra's surprise, sad.

"I've known for a few years now. Since he was made Minister of Trade. I didn't realize who he was until I saw him since he's changed his name. I told him that you were in the city. He's known where to seek you out. He just chose not to. I'm sorry, Ezra." Antony said quietly.

Ezra's good hand curled into a fist, nails digging into skin.

All this time.

After all this time.

Ezra had assumed his father had died in a ditch somewhere or had been killed by the many men to whom he'd owed money. His father, who had gambled away all their savings and when those had been depleted, he disappeared.

He still remembered that day. Ezra had woken up in the middle of the night from one of the coughing fits that had plagued him as a child. He had gone to the kitchen for some water when he saw him. Father, standing in the doorway, a sack swung over his shoulder. He'd looked stricken, clearly not expecting to be caught. And with one last glance at his only son, he walked out, closing the door behind him.

Ezra had thought he was going on a trip somewhere for work. Off trading in far away, exciting places. Places about which his father had told him the most wonderful stories. But the weeks turned to months which turned to years, and he did not return. Leaving him, and his mother alone. Until now.

"I'm going to kill him," Ezra growled, making for the doorway. This time it was two pairs of hands that held him back, both the prince and Antony, who seemed more than shocked by Ezra's expression when he turned on them.

"Aren't you forgetting something?" Christophe asked.

There was a ringing in his ears that made the prince's words sound distant. But yes, he had been forgetting something. He was an overpaid babysitter. Ezra's mind raced for a possible solution.

"I don't suppose you'd be willing to come with me on a murder trip?" Ezra ventured.

"No, no I don't think I do. I appreciate the offer, though."

"Just a thought," Ezra sighed, rubbing the back of his neck.

"I'm sorry, your highness, I lost my head for a moment. I will not leave your side."

Christophe still looked worried, but he nodded in forgiveness.

"It's quite all right. I'm the last person you would have to explain father issues too," Christophe added dryly. Ezra smiled at that. They were quite a pair. One with a murderous father, one a murderous son.

"Ahem, pardon me, Your Highness."

The bravest of the court ladies had finally shown herself. A beautiful girl wearing a deep blue gown She gave a deep, full curtsy before beaming at Christophe; a smile that was warm and genuine. "If you might grace me with the honor of a dance?" she asked, holding out her hand.

Christophe gave a quick glance to Ezra who scanned the crowd. Joe, seeing the situation, was already steering Lissa closer to them. He gave the prince a nod and Christophe took the lady's arm and off they went.

Antony and Ezra watched them in silence. Joe hovering nearby, Christophe careful not to dance too far away from his bodyguard's watchful gaze.

The prince and his partner seemed like they were having a grand time, not keeping entirely in time with the music as they were too busy talking.

"That's Lady Sara of Thiuda," Antony said. "Her father has never been a full supporter of the King and has not made a secret of his eagerness for Christophe to assume the throne. I've been to his estate a few times on business and had occasion to meet her. She's a bright, engaging girl."

Ezra relaxed slightly, no longer fearful that Christophe's dance partner would try to stab him mid-twirl. Antony's information was nearly as good as Ian's and Ezra always trusted it.

Ezra glanced once more to the doors, but his father had long since vanished. An interesting reaction, to be sure, after seeing his son for the first time in twenty years. He wasn't sure what he'd expected, if he ever, in fact, saw his father again, but it hadn't been this. He felt almost consumed with rage and despair. Flashes of his mother's last moments appeared to him. Would she have died if they hadn't been abandoned like that? Would she have succumbed to the disease?

It didn't matter now.

Ezra rubbed the empty circle on the back of his hand. A promise he'd made to himself when he was still a child, too young to understand what he was doing. In the heat of the moment, Ezra had lost his head entirely. He was fairly certain, given the chance, that he would have killed his father then and there, witnesses be damned.

Antony remained silent, perhaps, allowing Ezra to have a moment to collect himself. The music changed but Christophe and Sara showed no signs of slowing down. The prince's face was transformed in such a way that it made Ezra realize something. He'd never seen the prince honestly, truly happy before. It stripped away the shadows under his eyes and the tight worry in his mouth. He seemed almost as happy as Joe, who looked disgustingly so, in the arms of his intended.

"I know you must be angry at me, for not telling you," Antony said, "But I never thought your paths would cross, and killing him won't change the past and it will do nothing to diminish your pain. Potentially it might leave you feeling worse."

Ezra didn't answer but nodded to let Antony know he understood. The two watched the dancers for a while in silence before Antony was called away by an associate, leaving Ezra alone.

It was a magical night for all who attended. Just not for him.

19

JANUS DAY

"Your Highness? Your Highness, wake up," Ezra said, shaking Christophe.

The crown prince muttered something unintelligible and burrowed deeper down into the nest of quilts and sheets he'd made for himself.

Using both hands, Ezra took hold of the blankets and gave a sharp tug, unearthing the now shivering prince.

"What? What, Ezra? What in the name of all that is holy could you possibly want at this ungodly hour?"

"We're going out," Ezra said with a grin, holding up a mask.

"Janus day," Christophe asked blearily, "That's a festival of the people. The royal family does not participate."

"Neither does Prince Christophe. Today you'll be a friend I made, whilst working across the desert. Your name is Hyul."

"Does Joseph know?"

"This was Joe's idea. He thought we could use some time away from this place. We've been planting the idea that you're coming down with a cold for days now. No one will be suspicious when Joseph announces you'll be sleeping in your room the whole day."

"And you don't think anyone will be suspicious of the fact that you happen to have a companion with the same physical description as the prince you've taken on as a client?"

"Not after I'm through with you they won't," Ezra assured him.

An hour later the two made their way through the old tunnels towards the back of the palace. Ezra was dressed in his armored long coat and, after some persuading, Christophe dressed in the patched and worn clothing Joe had procured for him.

"Try not to scratch your head too much," Ezra cautioned. "Those extensions should hold until we soak them out but no sense in straining them."

Christophe stopped itching his head and gave a martyred sigh. Ezra had to admit, Christophe was sporting some of his best transformative work to date.

The crown prince was nearly unrecognizable to any, but those who knew the truth. Gone was the sleek, shiny black hair and unblemished face. Ezra used wax to twist the prince's hair into a length of dreadlocks that hung past his shoulders. He also applied an unsightly burn scar to the prince's right cheek, stretching down to his neck. Christophe's teeth were no longer white but instead a dark tan. Ezra assured the prince the dye would wash out.

Eventually.

They reached the mouth of the tunnel just as the sun began to peak over the horizon. A light fog clung to the grass in the empty field, lending an additional layer of cover as they snuck out of the palace. Joe waited for them with a pair of horses, mouth agape as he took in the prince's new appearance.

"That's remarkable, Ezra," Joe said, handing over the reins, "I will admit, I doubted your powers of metamorphosis but even I can hardly tell it is Christophe. Well done!"

"Well thank you kindly, Joe. It's some of my best work if I do say so myself."

"Yes, yes, fine work you two," Christophe grumbled. "Let's go already."

Joe rolled his eyes when the prince's back was turned to mount his horse.

"Best get his highness a pick-me-up the first chance you get," Joe advised. "He's never been much for mornings."

"I've noticed," Ezra said dryly, mounting his own horse.

Joe gave them one final wave before entering the tunnel and disappearing into the dark. His sole duty that day would be to turn away anyone who wanted to see the prince, claiming he was too ill to be disturbed.

Ezra had a sneaking suspicion Joe was looking forward to a quiet day to himself.

They rode in silence until they reached the city center, and Ezra had, at first, been worried the prince's sour mood would last all day. He only spoke up when they turned down a side road that would lead them to the Borough.

"Are we not going to the festival," Christophe asked, pointing down the main road towards the many multi-colored tents that had already been erected.

"We'll get to that," Ezra assured him, "But things won't be ready until noontime at the earliest. I have some stops to make first."

Deeper into the slums of the city they ventured, with Ezra acting the part of a guide, pointing out all his old haunts and favorite places. The city was just barely waking up, with the only evidence of activity present as they passed the washerwomen, already hard at work. Most businesses were closed on Janus Day, but not the washerwomen. They'd work through Yule itself were such an act not an affront to the Gods.

Ezra had a strong suspicion that Marya was still sleeping, otherwise, he would have greeted her first. But a woken Marya was far more fearsome than Christophe had any hope of being, so they passed her apartment without knocking.

"What a dump," Christophe exclaimed when they finally stopped.

"I'll admit, it could use a coat of paint and some new shutters," Ezra said, rubbing the back of his neck, "but that's for the landlord to worry over, not me."

Ezra pulled out a ring of keys and began the process of unlocking the front door.

"I—ah—I'm sorry Ezra, I didn't realize this was—"

"My home? Don't trouble yourself, over it, Hyul. Even I know it's not much to look at. Tie your horse up next to mine," He instructed, having just fastened his horse to one of the wood pillars that held up the porch.

Skeptically, Christophe asked, "And they'll be here when we return?"

"The last person to steal from me was relieved of his right hand," Ezra said simply. "People know better than to take what's mine."

Christophe made no further comment, opting instead to hastily dismount and tie up his horse next to Ezra's.

Having finally disabled the booby trap Ezra opened the door, hand out to catch the copper piece he left. No one had disturbed his home since he'd left it to go to the palace.

"It's safe," Ezra said, stepping aside, "Won't you come in?"

Christophe climbed the steps, pausing at the entrance to look down, perhaps for a mat with which to wipe his muddy boots.

"Here," Ezra said, taking a hold of the doorframe for support. "Just do this." He thumped his boots on the frame of the door, causing dried bits of mud and hay to fall onto the porch. Christophe repeated the motions, though with considerably less gusto, and followed Ezra up the stairs to the assassin's apartment.

In the early hours of the morning only a few cats were up and about, the rest still piled together on his bed. Lucy looked up from her perch on the corner of the bed and gave him a slow blink, the closest she could come to an enthusiastic greeting.

Squinting in the gloom, Ezra was just able to make out the fuzzy shapes protruding from Lucy's stomach. Newborn kittens, five of them if he counted right, all suckling at their mother's teat. They were ginger, like their mother, but bigger than any kitten he'd ever seen. He reckoned they were part mountain lion or some such blend.

"Ezra...are all of these yours?" Christophe's voice was heavy with concern and subconscious judgment.

"Sort of," Ezra hedged, pulling a bottle of cream from his coat. He took a bowl from the cupboard, filled it to the brim then, carefully scooping them up, he arranged the kittens around the bowl. "Most of them come and go as they please. These littlins and their mum are mine, I suppose. Lucy is the only pet I ever had on purpose."

"I see. I've always been more a dog person myself," he said, his stance rigid as one of the tabbies rubbed against his leg.

Ezra shrugged and poured more cream into the bowl.

"That's fine. Nobody's perfect. Shall we go?"

"Wasn't there something you needed to do here," Christophe asked in confusion.

"Yes. This was it," he said, waving a hand at the kittens that paid him no mind, focused intently as they were on the cream.

"You woke me up before the sun just so you could feed cats," Christophe growled.

"I woke you up at the ass crack of dawn because it was the only way to guarantee we slipped out of the castle unseen. How about some breakfast? And coffee?"

Christophe nodded curtly and led the way out of Ezra's apartment. He stopped the prince before he could open the door.

"Time to put this on," Ezra said, holding up a black and gold mask designed to cover the top half of the prince's face.

Ezra helped secure it to the prince's face, double knotting it to ensure it would not fall off. He was fairly confident no one would recognize Christophe, but an added layer of security wouldn't hurt anyone.

Outside the air was still brisk, but it held a tinge of warmth from a sun trying so desperately to break through the clouds that covered the city like a thick blanket.

They stopped at Mother Dharma's bakery and bought a basket of sweet rolls and a loaf of bread. She gave Christophe a once over and added two muffins.

"Your friend is too skinny," she complained to Ezra. "Make sure he eats these," Ezra assured her he would, and they exited the already packed bakery, goods in hand, making their way to The Sword and Shield.

"Now this tavern is a little bit rougher than what you may be used to. No one knows you're a prince, but you'll get a fair amount of respect for being associated with me. Don't talk to anyone unless they talk to you first and remember, your name is Hyul."

"Understood."

They turned the corner and Ezra lay his eyes upon the pub. His home away from home.

Some might say that calling an establishment such as this a "home away from home" might not be the best indicator of that person's character. Those people were also the kind who judge a book by their cover, so Ezra rarely paid any mind to what they said.

The assassin took in a deep breath, inhaling the putrid stench of the Borough with a sigh of nostalgia. From inside Ezra could hear the sounds of a fiddle, its cheery tune carrying outside and into the street.

"Gods, I missed it here," Ezra exclaimed and, holding open the tavern door, he ushered the crown prince inside.

20

A MAN OF MANY FACES

Though it was still early, the tavern had filled to capacity. Few people worked on Janus day, lest they offend the Great Father's favorite brother.

The general chatter ceased the moment they walked in the door. The music halted and everyone paused from their drinks and talk to take a gander at the prince's bodyguard.

"Are ye here on official business then, Toth," a man amidst the throng yelled out.

"Aye," Ezra confirmed, "His Highness the Crown Prince Christophe respectfully requests that you take a bath. He can smell you all the way up in the palace!"

The crowd burst into laughter and the fiddler resumed his song. Ian waved them over to a pair of open stools at the bar and Ezra led Christophe to them.

Ian, who loved Janus day as much as most people loved Yule, sported a festive half-mask with feathers glued to it for added flamboyancy. Ezra also noted the tavern keeper was wearing a vest with Marya's handiwork embroidered into it. Things must be going well between the two of them.

"Ezra, I have missed you, my friend," Ian yelled above the din. "Who's your companion," he asked, looking curiously at the prince.

"This is Hyul," Ezra replied, "A friend from out east. He's in town making a study of the varying festivals put on by different cultures. After this, he goes to the Isle of Maan to observe their celebration to the island God Stepoawtu."

"The indigenous people worship Stepoawtu by throwing flowers into the active volcano that lies on the easternmost edge of the island," Christophe added, to Ezra's surprise.

"Fascinating," Ian said politely. "What can I get for you two?"

"Coffee for both of us," Ezra said, laying down some coin. Ian scowled but retreated into the back to get the equipment needed to make the 'foul brew' as he so often referred to it.

"No one is looking at me," Christophe whispered to Ezra in awe.

"Why would they," Ezra asked, "You're just a random foreigner in town for the festival."

"I suppose you're right," Christophe/Hyul said, looking around the tavern, "Still, it's an odd sensation to no longer be an object of scrutiny."

"Sounds like an exhausting way to live," Ezra empathized. "I understand what you mean, though. My scars get their fair number of stares on the regular."

"I can only imagine how hard that must be for you," Christophe said softly.

"It doesn't bother me as much as you'd think. At least, not anymore."

"Here you go. Two mugs of putrid sludge," Ian said, handing the coffee over.

Christophe took his mug in hand and sipped at it thankfully. Ezra had long since gotten the prince hooked on the rich elixir.

"So I'm curious," Ian said, "Did you quit your position as bodyguard to His Highness or did he fire you?"

Christophe stiffened but Ezra only laughed.

"Nothing of the sort," Ezra said. "His Highness has taken ill and is currently resting in his rooms."

"Nothing serious, I hope," the tavern-keeper said.

"Ill humors or something of the like," Ezra lied. "The prince has been feeling poorly these past few days, so he's resting at the moment."

Ian poured himself a tankard and raised it, "To his health," he toasted.

"To his health," Ezra and Christophe repeated, raising their mugs.

"Have you been to see Marya yet?"

"No, I thought I'd let her have a bit of a lie-in. She's my next stop. How are things going with the two of you, anyway?"

Ian flushed and took a gulp of mead that was just a little too large, causing him to cough.

"Things are good. She gave me this vest as an early Yule present," he said, running a finger down the embroidery.

"Very nice," Christophe complimented.

"Thank you. If you'd believe it, she's even more bonnie than her handiwork."

"I'll drink to that," Ezra agreed, draining his mug. "Almost done?" he asked Christophe, who tipped his own mug back and emptied it.

"All done," the undercover prince confirmed.

"I trust I'll see you for the festival later today?" Ezra asked Ian.

"Oh yes," he confirmed, "I promised Marya I would take her. But the more the merrier!"

"Until then," Ezra waved goodbye and held the door to the tavern open for Christophe to exit.

Signs of life were now visible as even those who'd chosen to sleep in were now up and about. Children were running about, wearing whatever manner of mask their parents managed to cobble together from spare bits of cloth. In the alleys Olacia's homeless were just beginning to stir.

The winters were hard on that population, culling half of it without fail by springtime.

Listening to the church bells, Ezra counted out nine rings. At nine in the morning he would certainly hope that Marya was awake, holiday or no.

He led Christophe down the muddy streets of the Borough to the home of Kelva and Marya.

Ezra knocked on the door and waited.

To Christophe he said, "You've met Marya so it's possible that she will recognize you, but if you introduce yourself as Hyul that is how she will address you. Understood?"

"If you trust her so do I," Christophe said as the door opened.

Kelva stood in the doorway with a scowl so deep rivers could run through the creases in her brow. In her weathered and arthritic hand she gripped a dagger.

"Expecting someone else," Ezra asked, amused by the reception.

"That *vradijete* Ian says he takes Marya today for festival."

"And that is how you choose to greet your future Grandson-In-Law?"

"No, I greet him like this," she growled, pointing the end of her dagger at Christophe's throat. "Why you bring stranger to my home?"

Ezra put a hand on Christophe's shoulder and pulled him a few steps back out of range of Kelva's dagger.

"Granny, that's no way to treat an honored guest, especially on Janus day. This is a dear friend of mine from across the sands. His name is Hyul."

Granny Kelva glared up at the hidden prince, scrutinizing his appearance.

"Good job laying the hair for beard, Ezra. But you forgot to dirty face. He too clean to be anything but royal."

Ezra looked around quickly but there was no one in the street that might have overheard Kelva outing the prince.

"Oh, Granny," Ezra laughed nervously, pushing Christophe inside. "You're such a hoot!"

He glanced up and down the street one more time before closing the door behind them. Kelva sheathed the knife in her flowery apron and returned to the fireplace where a pot was boiling.

"Granny, was there someone at the door," Marya called from the other room.

"Just the royal *vradijete*," Granny called back.

There was a thump from the other room followed by some quick footsteps. Marya appeared in the doorway, her hair half braided and took in the scene before her.

"Ezra," she cried in delight, running into his open arms. She then smacked him on the arm. "You should have let me know you were coming. I would have cooked all your favorites."

Ezra rubbed his arm in mock pain.

"Exactly why I didn't tell you," he said. "I didn't want you to fuss. Besides, the fewer people who know we're in town, the better."

Marya turned from Ezra to Christophe and asked, "Who are you supposed to be?"

"Hyul," Christophe replied, "I'm a friend of Ezra's, visiting Olaesta to make a study of the local festivals and celebrations."

She gave a nod of approval to Ezra before joining Kelva by the fireplace. The girl dipped her fingers in the ash and proceeded to smudge up the prince's face.

"He was too clean. It's suspicious to be a commoner without a dirty face," Marya said by way of explanation.

"That's what your Granny said," Ezra smiled, admitting to himself that the prince's disguise was much better for the dirt. "What do you think? Will anyone else recognize him?"

Marya circled the prince, rubbing her chin with ashy fingers that smudged her face.

"It would help if you slouched a bit," she advised Christophe. He did so, and just like that, any residual regality diminished, leaving only Hyul, the humble scholar.

"Come here girl," Granny Kelva said, waving a wet rag that she used to wipe Marya's hand and chin, much to the girl's embarrassment.

"Ian should be here any minute and then we can go," Marya said, drying her face with her sleeve. She returned to the bathroom and the mirror within to finish doing her hair. No sooner had she returned, did the door open, revealing Ian. He wore a nervous smile and carried a bouquet of wildflowers.

"Good morning, Dalcov family! I come bearing good tidings on this lovely Janus Day!"

Kelva marched up to the tavern keeper and snatched the flowers out of his hands.

"Next time, knock first," she growled.

"My deepest and most sincere apologies, Granny. I was simply so excited at the prospect of seeing you that I took leave of my manners," Ian said with a small bow.

"*Jste take prazdni jako vase krasna slova,*" Granny muttered to herself as she went into the kitchen to retrieve a vase, putting the arrangement on the small wooden table by the window.

"Happy Janus Day, Ian," Marya called cheerfully from the doorway, having finished pinning her braids up in a crown that encircled her head.

Ian gave her a chaste kiss on the cheek, well aware of the death glare he was currently receiving from Kelva.

"Shall we go, then," he suggested, one foot already out the door.

"Lets shall," Ezra agreed, and the four of them walked out to join in the festivities.

21

AMONG THE PEOPLE

Janus Day was a favorite of Ezra's as a child. He wore clothes that covered his skin and a mask to hide his face and appeared to the world just like any other boy. Perhaps a bit underfed if one were to take a close look at the bagginess of his garb, but healthy nonetheless. No one stared at the half-healed scars and lingering bruises on Janus Day. It was the one day out of the year that he was just like everyone else.

Since then Ezra had shed most of the insecurities that made today so special for him as a child, but the fond association still remained.

The group followed the crowd of people making their way to the city's Holy Sanctum, a series of altars, each with its own monk to manage the offerings and upkeep.

Janus' altar, along with that of his son, the Trickster god Fili, were overflowing with all manner of offerings. Masks made out of rice paper and flowers were secured to the pillars surrounding Janus' statue and someone had even so bold as to affix masks onto the faces of the two-faced God.

Looking close, Ezra thought he saw the slightest curve up in the god's mouth. Janus was happy which meant that his children, Fili the Trickster God, and Meri the Goddess of Justice were happy.

Happy Gods were far less likely to meddle in the affairs of mortals, leaving everyone better off for their lack of intervention.

Ezra lay down a mask made up of blue jay feathers he'd been collecting along with one of raven feathers that he'd brought for Christophe to offer up to Janus. He whispered a quick thank you to Ezra as he handed over his offering to the monk.

Behind the Holy Sanctum stood the marketplace where foreign merchants would set up their wares. Today, they shared the space with local sellers who wanted to make an extra profit on this Janus Day.

Given the cool weather, the stench that emanated from the nearby Ruskin refugee camp did not carry its usual potency. Still, Ezra noted the instinctive crinkling of Christophe's nose.

"I'll admit," Christophe whispered to Ezra, "This is my first occasion to walk amongst my people as one of them, rather than above them. It is a rare feeling, indeed."

"I imagine the view is different than you're used to down here rather than astride your horse and surrounded by guards."

"Indeed," Christophe agreed. "It is a nice change of pace. Though I do admit, I miss the way crowds usually part for me. This is a tad claustrophobic."

"One of the many joys of being tall," Ezra said with a smile, "My head sticks above the throng like a meerkat from its hole."

"Beg pardon, but I am not familiar with such a creature."

"It's a rodent that lives underground. They have them south of the Great Desert," Ezra explained. "Ah, here we go, Hyul, a meerkat. Though it looks a good deal different without its fur."

Christophe looked like he was about to be sick as they passed a food cart bearing a spit upon which several of the critters were roasting.

That was far from the most disquieting thing they witnessed in the market. Eyeballs, entrails, and all manner of body part not meant for traditional consumption were available to them. By the time they cleared the edible section of the festival, Christophe had turned positively green.

In fact, Ezra pointed out with a laugh, he was almost the exact same shade as the shakes one of the vendors was selling. Supposedly it promoted wellness and long life. After taking a whiff Ezra took a hard pass. Sometimes the cost of long life was too high, even for him.

"That smelled worse than the tonic I drink," he added with a wrinkling of his nose. They meandered around the city for an hour until the group ended up at Pearline's door.

A 'Closed' sign hung in the shop's window but Ezra could see her inside. Janus day was usually the day Pearline used to scrub the shop from top to bottom. Last year, the wood floors had actually shone from a polish layered on top of a sealant.

At the time, Ezra had been certain she was going to slit his throat after he walked on those newly polished floors with his muddy boots. Thankfully, she forgave him, but he decided to ere on the side of caution this year and knock rather than barging in.

"We're closed," she shouted from inside.

"Even for an old friend," Ezra asked, raising his voice so his voice penetrated whatever manner of cleaning induced frenzy she was in. The door flew open seconds later and Ezra, who had already braced himself, was ready to catch Pearline's flying form.

"You bad man, Ezra. Why didn't you tell me you were coming?" Ezra set the girl down and she shook out her skirts, dusty from kneeling on the floor.

"It was a last-minute thing," he apologized, following her inside. Once the group had gathered in the store's front room Ezra closed the curtain and locked the door.

"Pearline, may I present his Royal Highness, the Crown Prince Christophe." It was hard to tell who was more surprised: Ian, Pearline, or Christophe.

"What happened to keeping my identity a secret," Christophe asked.

"It's fine," Ezra assured the prince, "I trust everyone here with my life. No one in this room would betray your confidence."

Pearline, meanwhile, had flushed a red as rich as the rosy embroidery on Ian's vest. She smacked Ezra on the shoulder. He could practically feel the bruise forming. While Marya usually held back,

Pearline was not quite so considerate when it came to Ezra's fragile constitution.

"Here I am dressed like a house maid and you bring in the next king of Olacia. Fantastic," she said wearily before spreading her skirts and dipping into a beautiful curtsy.

"It is an honor to meet you, Your Highness. Please forgive me for my current state of dress. Had I known you were coming I would have worn something a little less filthy."

"You need not worry about it," Christophe said hastily, "Please stand." She rose out of her curtsy and shot Ezra a look that, were it made of steel, would have killed him where he stood.

"I've brought the prince here for a fitting, Pearl," Ezra explained. "I want a vest made for him out of the same shingled armor that makes up my coat."

That caused Pearline to perk up right away.

"Just a moment while I get my things," she said, rushing into the back room.

"You couldn't have warned me," Ian whispered to Ezra when Pearline returned and began measuring Christophe.

"You have a terrible poker face," Ezra whispered back. "I didn't want the whole tavern to know I had the prince with me."

"Fair enough," Ian acquiesced.

"Marya, dear, come here," Pearline said, writing down the prince's measurements. "Would you make some linen linings to lay under the vest?"

"Not a problem," she said, folding up the paper and tucking it in her dress pocket. "I'll start on it first thing tomorrow."

"Excellent," Pearline said with a satisfied smile. "Now I don't mean to be rude, but I've scant hours left to clean and a good deal still has to be done. Out, all of you, out!" She shooed the group out the door and down the steps before locking the door behind them.

"She's—she's certainly something," Christophe said, staring at the closed door.

"She is at that," Ezra agreed. "Shall we take in a show or two before returning to the palace?"

They spent the rest of the day taking in the various plays being put on by local and traveling theatrical troupes. Janus Day served as an unofficial holiday for actors, after all, who had more faces than one who lived on the stage?

By the time Ezra and Christophe returned to the palace they were too exhausted to do much more than removing the prince's beard and extensions before turning in for the evening.

"Thank you for today, Ezra," Christophe yawned. "It was an illuminating experience, to say the least."

"I'm glad, your highness. I hope your time among the people gave you some valuable perspective."

"It did," Christophe confirmed. To Ezra, the prince sounded a million miles away. Despite the number of wonderful things they'd witnessed, the group had also taken in their fair view of refugee encampments and homeless beggars.

A result of his father's negligence. Ezra had a feeling that those scenes were weighing heavily on Christophe's mind. The prince had his work cut out for him when he finally ascended to the throne, and Ezra didn't envy him one bit.

22

BROTHERS

The next morning, a noticeable shift in the atmosphere alerted Ezra to danger. He glanced around the training grounds where Christophe and the knights were fighting until he found the source of the threat.

Daniel, Shadow in tow, had come to train.

He appeared younger, out of his usual regalia, opting instead for simple cotton tunic and trousers. Though Ezra would bet that even those cost more than Marya usually charged for a dress. His Shadow wore his usual cloak and was likely the most comfortable of them all, in the face of the biting wind that made Ezra shiver.

Ezra had never seen the training ground so still. Even the younglings, too small to really understand, remained quiet, watching the faces of their elders with confusion and a little fear.

"Brother!" Christophe's voice served as a signal to everyone, to act as though nothing was wrong.

Which was interesting.

Because, to Ezra's knowledge, none of them should know that anything *was* wrong.

"Christophe!" Daniel replied, embracing his brother. They patted each other on the back with some unnecessarily excessive gusto.

"How are you, brother?" The younger prince asked.

"Oh fine. Just fine. Keeping fighting fit. Want to be ready for father's next war!" They laughed jovially, though Ezra had never heard a faker laugh in his life.

"Would you like to spar a bit," Daniel ventured, cutting Christophe's laughter off abruptly. He glanced quickly at Ezra who had been watching the prince's Shadow, unmoving and unresponsive after the proposal of this potentially deadly 'sparring' match.

"Of course," Christophe said, his voice the essence of cheer. "It's been too long since we had a proper fight."

The knights had cleared a space for the brothers to fight.

Ezra walked over to where Joe stood and leaned over.

"Why is everyone so tense? It's not like they know what we know."

Joe gave him an exasperated look.

"Because Daniel has been burning anthills and pulling the wings off flies since he could crawl. No one wants their Crown Prince within a mile of that deviant. It's the one thing the royal court can agree on."

"You know," Ezra said, "I've heard just about every rumor about the royal court but none of them said anything about the youngest prince being psychotic." Frankly, Ezra was amazed that something so huge hadn't gotten out.

"It's the best-kept secret in the kingdom," Joe said bitterly.

Meanwhile, the two princes circled each other, practice swords held at the ready. The two had styles and stances vastly different from one another.

Christophe was cautious but direct, each step placed methodically. Held his sword in the way Ezra had shown him earlier that week and he stood sideways, presenting the smallest target possible.

Daniel was more like a jungle cat. He moved with a slow, sinewy gait, slinking around the ring. His sword rested at his side, but Ezra recognized the position. By keeping it low it gave that much more room to gain speed for the killing blow.

Whoever had trained Daniel was dangerous, indeed. That was a move reserved for people like Ezra, rather than knights. Despite the use of training swords, Ezra kept a dagger in each hand. A well-placed jab from a wooden sword had the power to impale just as well as a steel one.

Daniel's arm twitched moments before he lashed out. Christophe had seen it and was ready, his sword raised to parry Daniel's blow. Swords locked, he pushed back until Daniel forced back to the edge of the circle. Daniel leaned precariously over the edge before kicking the crown prince in the shin, causing him to disengage and retreat.

They were almost evenly matched, blow for blow, and it was easy to see they'd had this same fight many times before. But Daniel was starting to lose steam, his vicious blows, meant to stun, took their toll, and Christophe had saved his energy by deflecting those blows, rather than blocking and taking the full brunt of it.

So when Christophe struck out, Daniel was too exhausted to get his sword up in time, and he was hit with a sideswipe to the ribs. Christophe dropped his sword immediately and knelt by his brother who had collapsed on the ground. Daniel's shadow approached quickly, prompting Ezra to move to Christophe's side, not so subtly flashing his daggers.

The spectators held their breath, waiting for someone to make the first move.

In the end, Joe was the one who broke the tension when he fell to his knees and began vomiting blood.

Ezra and Christophe were with him in a flash, supporting him until the attack stopped. Joe wouldn't look Ezra in the eye as he accepted a water skin to wash out his mouth. He spat pink water into the dirt. Joe's shirt was soaked with blood, but it still wasn't redder than Joe's face. The shame was plain for everyone to see, though it wasn't as obvious as the shock of his fellow knights. Clearly, they'd had no clue about his condition.

Ezra pointed to Adam.

"Get a healer and send him to Joe's quarters," Ezra ordered, and together he and Christophe helped Joe up to the castle.

Ezra had never seen Joe's room before. He'd always imagined it as a militarily neat and obsessively organized place. What he didn't expect was a cluttered, small, one room suite. It was larger than Ezra's bedroom, but that was because it housed a bedroom, washroom, desk, and wardrobe. It was not the kind of place Ezra expected for the Crown Prince's right-hand man.

Seeing the expression on Ezra's face, Joe smiled.

"It's not much, but I don't need a lot of space. Anything more would just be excessive." He started coughing again, thankfully without blood, and they hurried him to the bed and helped him onto it. Christophe helped Joe remove his shirt while Ezra retrieved a clean one from the wardrobe.

Inside, he found the anal-retentive Joe that he had expected. Everything was folded uniformly, by color and level of formality. Even the socks were stacked in a perfect pyramid. It made Ezra smile.

A rustling sound came from under the bed and Ezra drew his sword, only to find himself pointing it at the oldest dog in the world.

Seriously.

Ezra would not have been surprised if someone told him the dog was older than Joe.

The dog, a bloodhound, trotted out from underneath the bed and gave a yawn that revealed a profound lack of teeth. He then sneezed, sending his many, many wrinkles flapping and shards of spittle across the room. He squinted up at Ezra before turning to paw at the edge of the bed.

Christophe handed the washcloth off to Joe so he could, with a grunt, lift the dog onto the bed. It inspected Joe, gave the smallest of whimpers, and curled up by his master's feet.

"I didn't know you had a dog," Ezra commented, scratching the hound behind the ears.

"He was a gift when I was a child. His name is Ferdinand."

"Of course it is," Ezra rolled his eyes at the overly formal name. Though he had to admit, the dog seemed like a Ferdinand, but he doubted it suited him one hundred years ago when he was born.

Joe was wiping at his red-stained chest with a wet rag when Lissa arrived, a healer in tow.

"Joseph!" she cried out, rushing to his side.

"I'm fine, Lissa," Joe comforted, but she only had eyes for the blood-stained shirt on the floor.

"Were you training, again?" she asked, her voice shrill.

"No, no, dear. I wouldn't dare. Just a little overexcitement. I feel fine now, right as rain," he said, thumping his chest and provoking another dry coughing fit. The healer swooped in, a medical horn already in his ear, and he held it to Joe's chest.

"Fluid in the lungs," the healer muttered to himself. Then he moved the horn up to his sternum, "and an erratic heartbeat." Lissa's face as white as Joe's by this point, her hands clenched at her side as if to stop herself from reaching for Joe. The healer finished his examination and offered up a bag.

"For the pain," he explained, before bidding farewell and leaving.

Ezra picked it up, peered inside, and sniffed. They were Buja Leaves, famous for their numbing powers. They were also highly addictive and had some serious side effects, so he was surprised that a palace healer would traffic in such an herb.

"It's meant to be brewed in a tea," Ezra said, moving to put the kettle over the fire. "I would only take it before bed though, as it makes a person drowsy."

Lissa took it from Ezra.

"Can I mix it with milk?"

"I wouldn't," Ezra cautioned. "Milk undercuts the potency."

She nodded and then turned away, busying herself with the kettle.

Ezra approached Joe and the prince who had been having what appeared to be a whispered argument.

"You have a council meeting to prepare for," Ezra reminded Christophe. The crown prince nodded and stood, shaking his head severely when Joe seemed like he wanted to say something.

"Get some rest," Ezra told Joe, following Christophe out the door.

They walked in silence for a while before Christophe finally broke the silence.

"Joe wants me to cut him loose. Those were his words. To *cut him loose*. He thinks he's become a burden, more trouble than he's worth. I don't know how to convince him otherwise."

Ezra didn't know what to say. For the most part, he agreed with Joe. The day-to-day stress of this life was shortening whatever time he had left, and likely causing undue suffering. The prince had enough to worry about without the added strain of watching his closest friend waste away before his eyes.

But that was not something Christophe was ready to hear, so Ezra didn't speak on it. Neither of them did. And they walked the rest of the way to the council chamber in silence.

· · · · ·

The next morning, Ezra came to Christophe with an idea.

"You go through a lot of unimportant paperwork just to get to the relevant stuff," Ezra commented to Christophe, who sat behind several stacks of paper.

"Your point?" The crown prince asked tersely, his hand on top of a pile that threatened collapse.

"You might want to consider giving Joe something to do that will make him feel useful. He wants to know that he isn't a burden. Why don't you have Joe review and sort all the documents you spend hours on every morning into a more manageable pile?"

Christophe scanned the mountain of paperwork thoughtfully before pulling out a clean piece of paper and writing.

"That's a good idea, Ezra." Christophe approved, folding up the letter and walking to the door. The prince returned with a guard.

"Take this letter and these papers to Joseph's chambers," Christophe instructed. The guard bowed and collected the papers, leaving Christophe's desk cleaner than Ezra had ever seen it.

"That brings me to my next suggestion," Ezra said. Something in his voice seemed to alert Christophe because the prince sat down.

"Yes, Ezra?"

"Now that you have a chunk of time every morning freed up, this might be your chance to follow up on your promise to allow me training time."

"And where would I be in the meantime?"

Ezra tried not to smile.

"With me of course. We could even start now."

Understanding was quickly replaced with a look of dread.

"I hardly think I'd be able to keep up with your regime."

"Don't worry," Ezra said, handing Christophe his boots, "I'll match your pace. Today is the perfect morning for a run!"

Christophe appeared torn between keeping his promise and using his influence to save himself from a run. Resigned, he took the boots from Ezra and yanked them on.

Mist clung to the grounds as they trundled along. Though he was running much slower than he usually would, Ezra made up for it by having them lap the entirety of the castle walls three times. By the time they were done the sun was well established in the sky, and Christophe appeared ready to collapse.

"Usually after a run, I go for a swim, but you don't have a lake nearby so we'll just have to call it a day," Ezra said.

Christophe gave him an exasperated look, too out of breath to say anything.

"Yes—such a pity."

Ezra ignored the sarcasm, opting instead to do some stretches.

"Well," Ezra said, "time for your horse riding practice." Christophe sat on the ground in response to that.

"Give me a second. Not all of us are one hundred percent muscle."

Ezra scanned the area before sitting down next to the prince. From their place on the hilltop, they had a great view of the castle.

"It's ugly," Christophe commented, surprising Ezra who had been thinking the same thing.

"It was built for defense," Christophe continued, "not as a pinnacle of Olacian building prowess, or a symbol of a great nation. It was built with a military mind. Just like this country." The bitterness practically dripped off the prince's tongue. Those words were a little bit too heavy for Ezra to tackle this early in the morning.

"Time to ride some horses and shoot some stuff," Ezra said, dragging the prince to his feet.

The prince shook his head, as if to clear away the bad thoughts, and smiled wearily at Ezra.

"That sounds like a good idea," he said.

It's a good thing I'm not claustrophobic, Ezra thought from underneath the prince's bed. About a half a foot of clearance separated the tip of Ezra's nose and the bed frame. Still plenty of room for him to shimmy out and stand in under three seconds. He'd timed it.

He slept in a rolling nap cycle. Half an hour awake,, five minutes asleep, and so on. It was how he did all his long jobs. These days though, it was more like an hour awake, five minutes asleep. Christophe snored with such volume that Ezra spent his nights casually contemplating the murder of his client. In the morning, putting the prince through his paces during his hour of training was his own personal way of getting revenge. It was on one of these torturous runs, that they ran into the King.

He wore a simpler outfit, still trussed up with the regalia of the crown, but less pompously so. Wrapped around his shoulders was a fur cloak to protect against the cold, kept around his shoulders by a heavy, gold, jewel-encrusted chain. The queen walked by his side, their arms entwined, the picture of love.

Though, after looking into the King's eyes that morning in the council chamber, Ezra wondered if King Lionel was even capable of love. Ezra found his stare to be almost dead, like that of a shark. Now, however, those eyes were full of light as they gazed adoringly into those of the queen.

Behind them, a procession of members of the court followed at an appropriate distance. Far enough to indicate respect, but close enough to eavesdrop on the royal couple's conversation. The women, fans out despite the cold, hung on to their male counterparts who appeared equally ridiculous in the latest fashion. This year, it was popular to wear poofy shorts over tights. Gods only knew why.

Christophe quickly wiped his face with a rag before putting on his genial mask and striding towards his parents.

"Father! Mother! What a pleasant surprise!"

"Christophe," King Lionel grunted in acknowledgment.

"Christophe! Mr. Toth! How nice to see the both of you," The queen exclaimed. Wrapping her arms around her son.

Ezra and Lionel stared at each other stiffly as Christophe and his step-mother chatted happily. After a few minutes, the King started coughing violently, and the Queen rushed to his support. Courtiers crowded around him, offering their compliments and concerns. Like vultures descending on a carcass.

Ezra and Christophe used the chaos to excuse themselves and ran back towards the castle.

23

A DAY OFF

Over the next month, life fell into a steady rhythm of caution countered by Christophe's responsibilities. Though every time the prince wanted to go out, there were no incidents, Ezra did not let up on his protective measures. Christophe may not have appreciated the constant hovering, but when his food was actually found poisoned by an outside foe, he was quick to thank Ezra for his hard work. Ezra tracked down the poisoner—not one of the assassins, rather, a terrified lackey who killed himself upon seeing Ezra coming after him.

The body of the assassin who had shot Ezra surrendered none of the secrets Ezra had hoped to find. No letters, money, or sigils associated with the numerous assassin's guild's that spanned the world. The lack of markings was more disquieting than the rest of the man's anonymity put together. Even Ezra had a small tattoo of a sword crossed over a shield. It was a way of ensuring safe passage from one guild to another and proving your qualifications once you got there. It was also a badge of honor.

Ezra was grateful that this one had gone down so easily, otherwise, he might have caused more trouble than the rest put together. With the archer and Golok gone, if Ian's count had been correct, there were still three people out there anxious for the prince's blood money. Ezra was willing to bet all the gold in his vault that one of them was the Shadow that followed Daniel around, leaving two unknown entities.

Being a shield involves the willingness to throw yourself in front of your client to protect them, fighting off the people who want to harm your client, or risking the client's wrath when they just want a moment to themselves. But the biggest part of the job is waiting. Ezra hated waiting. The tournament was long over, no one had attacked the prince, and Ezra was bored to death.

After training in the morning Ezra endured meeting after meeting after meeting. When he wasn't in meetings, Christophe spent his time with Joe. They would talk about things Ezra had no point of reference for, leaving him feeling distinctly left out. And if Christophe wasn't with Joe, he was reading.

The man ploughed through several books a week. Ezra liked reading almost as much as Christophe did. But the least interesting thing in the world was watching someone else enjoy a good book.

At times like these, Ezra liked to allow his mind to wander. More often than not, those thoughts wandered to his future. Did he really want to go back to working as a sword or shield after this? Yes, he enjoyed it. And yes, he was good at it. But there was always the risk that every job might be his last. He wouldn't need the money after this.

It was almost a certainty that Christophe would need a head of security when he became King. And Ezra, thanks to a very patient Christophe, had already mapped out every square inch of the castle. He was familiar with all the threats, all the players, and most importantly, he had become friends with the future king.

The feeling had snuck up on him, for sure, and before he knew it, he found himself genuinely liking and caring for the wellbeing of the crown prince.

Ezra didn't allow many people into his circle of trust, and even fewer of those people were considered friends. But he found that Christophe and Joe had joined both groups while Ezra wasn't paying attention.

Could he really see himself working in the castle for the rest of his life? At moments like these, the answer would be an aggressive no. But he wouldn't be standing watch over Christophe every day if he took the job. He'd be responsible for the security of the Royal Family and the entirety of the castle.

He'd have to work with people.

Ezra had shuddered at the thought. One of the best parts of his job was that, usually, he worked alone. He loved his friends but, much like his cats, he needed his alone time. And years of living with an excess of alone time had left his social skills a bit rusty.

This was, of course, all predicated on the assumption that Christophe would even want him for the job. He might be worried that Ezra's reputation was too tainted. A more reputable option, Sir Adam for example, might be more to the crown prince's taste.

With Sir Adam's help, Ezra increased the prince's security when he was training on the fighting grounds, or if on horseback in the fields outside the castle. He even, with the princess's permission, assigned a detail of elite Zouszian warriors to monitor from a distance when the prince went on one of his unscheduled trips to the local orphanages. Christophe may not have seen them, but they saw him. From rooftops, alleys and strategically placed points in the crowd. Knowing that Ezra was able to actually relax a bit and enjoy the sight of a toddler vomiting on Joe's shoes.

Christophe also started spending a good deal of time with Lady Sara. Walking through the garden, discussing their favorite books over meals, or playing chess, the prince was constantly seeking her out, that is, when she wasn't busy studying in the castle infirmary. Training to be a healer, someday, despite her father's protestations that a lady shouldn't do that sort of work.

Ezra was happy for Christophe. Not only were the two of them compatible, but they would also be a good political match, as her father was warden over one of the largest farming provinces in the country.

He also found something unexpected in the palace. Friendship.

Friendships are a funny thing. Most of his friends were either people he'd saved, or tried to kill. Certainly, his relationship with Joe hadn't started off in the best place, but over the months it had evolved into one of the stronger bonds in his life. Joe spent most of his time with Christophe, and by extension, with Ezra. Between Christophe's time training and his time reviewing documents, the knight and assassin spent a lot of time talking. It turned out they had a great deal in common.

Many evenings found the two of them sitting by the fire, sipping their respective tonics while discussing all sorts of things. Their excessive love and devotion towards their pets, a mutual dislike for hot temperatures, their political stances, and their hopes for the future of Olacia.

Christophe said they were like a pair of old women, clutching their tea whilst gossiping by the fire.

•　　•　　•　　•　　•

On the morning of his second month, Ezra got up early. It was his one, and possibly only, day off for the duration of the job. Christophe had impressed upon Ezra the importance of them having some time apart before Ezra went on a stir-crazy killing spree.

The only way Ezra would even consider agreeing was if Adam's forces, and those of Princess Kyunghye worked together to guard him.

Before leaving, Ezra had also reminded Christophe that he was not to leave the safety of his quarters for the day. He placed Joe as near guard and watchdog, a guarantee that the prince wouldn't try to escape during Ezra's one day of 'freedom'. He'd considered having Sir Adam in the suite as well, but he didn't want to undermine his faith in Joe, who, despite his rapidly deteriorating state, was still quite capable with a sword.

Barely dawn, Ezra walked down the empty halls to the stables. He was just about to take the stairs down when he glanced out the window and saw Prince Daniel. Ezra paused, then decided to investigate, taking the stairs up instead, to the tower.

The autumn air was brisk, the wind stinging Ezra's face. Daniel was bundled up, but also pale enough to suggest he'd been out for a while. Seeing Ezra, the prince beckoned for Ezra to join Daniel outside.

"I love the sunrise," Daniel said, as Ezra approached him. "It's my favorite part of waking up early. I'm out here almost every morning. I find it to be a wonderful way to start my day. Don't you think?"

"It is a beautiful sight, Your Highness," Ezra agreed. The sky was a striking shade of orange, with pinks and purples clinging to the horizon.

"You're going back into the city today, are you not?" Daniel asked, causing Ezra to stiffen slightly. He'd tried to keep his trip a secret but secrets were a rare thing to behold in the castle.

"I am. Just for the day, though. I need to check on my home." Ezra explained, choosing his words carefully.

"I should think it would be fine, in your absence."

"You'd think so," Ezra said, allowing himself a smile, "But my cats are likely angry with me for my prolonged absence, and may have taken it upon themselves to destroy everything I own. In addition, the kittens are likely almost ready to be weaned and will need new homes.."

At that, Daniel tore his eyes from the sunrise to face Ezra.

"Kittens? You must bring one back, for me. I've been trying to figure out a birthday gift for Lily but she doesn't really need anything. She has never had a pet, she was too young before. Would you, please?"

Ezra was momentarily stunned by the prince's earnestness and his use of the word 'please'.

"I'd be happy to, your highness. But the kittens are only a month or so old. It will still be several weeks, possibly four, before they can be separated from their mother. And their mother wouldn't likely be parted from them before then anyway. But I promise the cutest in the bunch as soon as they're old enough."

Daniel's face lit up, and he actually took Ezra's hand in his, shaking it emphatically.

"That would be wondrous, Ezra. I'm sure she'll be thrilled."

"Yes, well, I should be going. Thank you for sharing the view." Ezra said, waving goodbye. A tinge of sadness crept onto Daniel's face, but he hid it with a jaunty smile and wave.

All in all, it proved to be one of Ezra's stranger encounters with the royal family.

•   •   •   •   •

The city hadn't changed in the slightest since Ezra had left his home for the palace. The bakers were still up before anyone else, washerwomen following close behind, and streets still smelled faintly of shit. Ezra took a deep breath, letting the homesickness wash away.

He purchased several breakfast buns and pastries on his way to Granny's house. The sun had established its place in the sky when he knocked on their door, so he had no fears about waking them, earning their wrath.

"Who is it?" Granny called from inside.

"Your long-lost grandson," Ezra said through the door. There was a shriek from inside before the door was thrown open. He had a brief view of Marya before she jumped into his arms. He managed to keep the baked good safe from being crushed as he scooped her up with his good arm. His right still twinged slightly from the arrow wound.

"I can't believe you managed to come back so soon!" Marya exclaimed, smacking him on said shoulder. Ezra tried to hide the wince but Marya saw it, scrambling down out of his arms so as not to hurt him further.

"You're hurt!" She exclaimed, taking his bags and pulling him inside.

"You needn't concern yourself with that, it's nearly healed," Ezra comforted. "And I'm sorry I'm late. Things at the palace are a little more complicated than I'd previously thought." She still seemed worried until Ezra pulled an envelope from his jacket.

"Do you want to worry or do you want to open your present?"

Marya snatched it out of his hands, beaming.

"Presents are good." She said, opening the letter.

Marya read it once, then again.

"We're going to a wedding?"

"I don't know if you remember Joe, the stiff man who greeted us on my first day? Well, he found someone willing to marry him and he's not waiting about for her to change her mind. They're having a Yule wedding one month from now and I've been given the option of a guest."

"And you're inviting me?" She asked slowly.

"Yes, but if you don't want to attend I understand. Perhaps Pearl might—"

"No, I want to go! I want to go!" She said, abandoning her aloof pretense for real excitement.

"Excellent, I'll leave the invitation with you so you have the date. I have a few other things to attend to while I'm here, but would you like to have dinner with me later?"

"Actually, I'm meeting up with Pearl for dinner. But you're welcome to join us." Ezra agreed to meet the two of them at Marya's house later that day and, with a quick hug he was off. Seeing Marya and Pearl both, that night meant one less visit and gave him the time and excuse to make a special trip.

•   •   •   •   •

It didn't take long to find the house of the Minister of Trade. Those with that kind of information were always happy to exchange favor for favor. He had more than a few information brokers eternally in his debt. It turned out, despite his illustrious title, his father was not living up to the means of the other ministers, opting instead, for a house by the docks.

It made sense, Ezra supposed. His father would want to have a quick getaway should the crown ever figure out what a slimy weasel he truly was. In fact, Ezra wondered how he'd managed to maintain a single job for so long. The highlight of his father's life as a merchant was that he traveled too much for any one person to get wise to his schemes.

Keeping in character, his father's apartments resided above the local pub. Though, unlike Ian, Ezra was certain his father sampled the merchandise quite often. As it was midday, the pub was mostly empty. Only the most degenerate of the degenerates occupied a few stools. They paid him no mind as he passed them by, making for the stairs.

"You can't go up there." Ezra turned to the barkeep who was wiping a glass clean with a rag. "That part of the building belongs to another tenant. You can't go up there." The barkeep repeated.

Reaching into his pocket, Ezra pulled out a gold coin and placed it on the counter.

"I'm a relative come to pay my respects. If you might just pretend you didn't see me?"

The coin disappeared off the counter and the barkeep nodded, resuming his futile work on the glass.

Climbing the steps to his father's home, Ezra felt something he hadn't truly felt in a while. Dread. Theirs had not been a positive relationship. Especially in the last few years before he'd left, when Ezra's symptoms presented themselves. Ezra felt fear.

His father had hated him, no matter what his mother would say Ezra knew it to be true. There was no hiding the sneer of disgust on his face whenever he looked at his son. His one and only son. And Ezra had tried to toughen himself up and eat as much fruit and meat as they could afford, but back then he hadn't had the tonic upon which he now relied. He'd had no way to make himself healthy. Or his mother.

Ezra sometimes wondered if, had he been healthy, would his father have stayed? Would his mother have lived? Those were the kind of dark thoughts that led Ezra down a path eventually ending in a long period during which time he abstained from all liquor and spirits.

He was so lost in thought he almost ran into the door at the top of the stairs. He paused, frozen, unable to turn back but too afraid to knock. Both choices were eliminated when the door opened, revealing his father.

The two stared at each other in silence, both afraid, although his father's fear was far more obvious on his stricken face.

"Hello, father," Ezra said. His words broke the spell that his father had been under and he moved if only to scramble back away from the door.

"I don't know what you mean by coming here, but you aren't welcome. Get out!" his father shouted. Scrambling, he grabbed a knife from the table and swung it wildly in Ezra's direction.

"Is that any way to greet your son?" Ezra asked, stepping over the threshold. He noted a bag on the bed, partially packed. "Going somewhere, father?"

Erik Irvin's eyes darted from the bed to Ezra, to the open window.

"Yes, not that it's any of your business." He was regaining some of his composure now that he was certain Ezra would not kill him immediately.

"Well, you'll need a bigger bag than that. It's far too small for me to fit your mangled corpse in," Ezra said nonchalantly, twirling a dagger in his hands. His father squealed in a way, not unlike a pig for slaughter.

"What do you want? An apology? I'm sorry I left you and your mother. I was devastated to hear of her death—"

"Don't you talk about her!" Ezra yelled, not expecting the rage that filled him but doing nothing to diminish it.

With a clatter, Erik dropped his knife and backed up until he was against the wall.

"I'm not going to kill you, father. At least, not today." Even as the words came out of Ezra's mouth, he had a hard time believing them. But he continued, nonetheless, "You will get on a ship, any ship, the one leaving soonest. And you will leave this city and never return." His father started to cut him off but Ezra held up a hand for silence.

"If you do return, and I'm able to get my hands on you, your death will be long and agonizing until not even I could identify your mangled, fractured corpse. Do you understand?"

Lost for words, his father nodded quickly, sweat drenching his clothes with a fear Ezra could almost smell.

"Good. Then I suppose this will be the last time we see each other. Goodbye, father." Ezra said and, with one last glance, he turned and fled the apartment, slamming the door shut behind him.

He ran down the steps, out of the pub, and all the way to the docks before he stopped to catch his breath.

For years. Years! He'd imagined how good he'd feel when he finally killed his father. When he got that circle on his hand filled in and finally had closure. Even now, part of him wanted to go back and finish what he'd been too chicken to start. But something else held him back.

Marya, who had looked at him with such trust only an hour before. Antony, who had faith that Ezra was a better man than the many rumors suggested. Christophe, who was counting on him to return. All of those people believed in a him that he truly wanted to be. An Ezra that was a good man.

And, while he was far from an authority on the subject, he had an inkling that good men did not kill their fathers. Christophe certainly wasn't going to, though he had more cause even than Ezra to do so.

Ezra sat on the docks for a while, listening to the waves and the gulls, before going to find comfort in a friend.

•　　•　　•　　•　　•

The Sword and Shield was packed. In the month before Yule, not many people felt in a murderous mood, too busy with final preparations for winter, or end of year festivities to consider all the people they wanted dead. It served as a yearly vacation from work for the mercenaries of the city. And what better place to vacation than at a tavern?

Failing to see Ian by the bar, he waded through the crowds and climbed the stairs, getting a nasty sense of deja vu. Ian's door was, of course, unlocked, and Ezra entered without knocking.

Inside Ian sat at the kitchen table, actually eating for once, and not at all surprised to see the assassin.

"Ezra! I heard this was your day off, come in!" He pulled out a chair which Ezra sank into grumpily.

"How in the hell does everyone in the godsforsaken country seem to know my secret schedule?"

"You are many things, Ezra, but a spy is not one of them. I could certainly offer you some classes in the art of deceit and subterfuge, but

I fear they would be wasted on a man such as yourself. Not a subtle bone in your body. Tea?"

"That may be true," Ezra said, accepting the cup, "but at least you always know I'm telling you the truth."

"Speaking of truth!" Ian set his plate down, turning on Ezra.

"Bodyguard to the Crown Prince? When did that happen? Who facilitated the job? I could hardly ask you in plain sight of his highness." There was a burning curiosity in Ian's eyes that must have been eating at him these past months.

"It's not as exciting as you'd think. Through some recommendations and research, a friend of Prince Christophe's sought me out and brought me to the prince who then offered me a deal."

"He brought you to the prince before a deal was even made?" Ian exclaimed.

"I know, right? A rookie mistake, but neither of them were built to think as we do. How would they have known the number of times I'd been asked to kill members of the royal family? Anyways, we agreed on a sum and here I am, on my Nationally Celebrated Day of Rest before I return to the castle."

Ian ignored the sarcasm, fervently writing down everything Ezra said.

"When did the prince's man approach you? Considering your normal prep time and rest between jobs it couldn't have been any later than—"

"He was waiting for me with an armed escort whilst I was returning from that job you got me for the Duke."

"Ah, yes. That one had quite the body count attached to it. Twenty-two, wasn't it?"

"Twenty-six."

"That's a record for you, I think. Drop any more bodies on this job?" Ian asked, glancing at the arm that bore all of Ezra's tattoos.

"Two. If you watched the tournament, you would have seen one of them."

"That was a great fight, you know. Maybe hard for you to appreciate since you were in it, but the crowd absolutely loved you. If you went in for the fighting pits you'd be set for life."

"No," Ezra barked, causing Ian to raise an eyebrow in surprise. "I've done my time fighting for another's enjoyment. I'm done with that. In fact, after this job, I might be done with the life altogether."

"He's paying you that much, is he?"

"And more."

They drank their tea in silence before Ezra realized he was in the presence of the one person who wouldn't ask too many questions.

"I saw my father today," Ezra confessed.

"Do you need help with body disposal?" Ian asked simply. The mark of a true friend.

"No. I—let him live."

Ian leaned over the table and put a hand on Ezra's forehead.

"You let the man who abandoned you live? Ezra, are you quite well?" Ezra waved Ian off, scowling.

"I don't fully understand it myself. I just found myself there, facing such a pathetic specimen of human existence, and I realized it wouldn't make me feel better to kill him. After all these years, I've outgrown my hatred of him. I can honestly say I don't care whether he's dead or alive. He's out of my life. And out of this city. I told him if he ever set foot in the capital I'd do most unspeakable things to him." Ezra smiled at the memory.

"I suppose you'd like me to make sure he actually does what you've told him?" Ian asked.

"I would appreciate it, yes. I'm sure if you put his name on the wind your spies would be happy to keep an ear out for it. You don't need to do more than that."

"Easy enough." Ian agreed.

"Now," Ezra said, "I must be off. I've supplies to gather and a dinner with Marya and Pearl to attend."

"You're seeing Marya, tonight?" Ian tried to sound nonchalant and failed miserably.

"I am. How are things between you two?"

"Things are wonderful," Ian said, sounding like they were anything but, "The only problem is Granny Kelva. She absolutely despises me and I'm afraid her opinions may sway Marya away from me." He sounded thoroughly downtrodden.

Granny Kelva was a formidable opponent, to be sure, and Ezra didn't envy Ian one bit. Ezra patted him on the shoulder in what he hoped was a comforting manner.

"That doesn't sound like the Ian Rehner I know. He's a much more persistent sort of man."

"Ezra, she threatened to have her friends in the Ruskin underworld spirit me away in the dead of night."

Ezra actually laughed at that.

"Everyone in the underworld owes you one favor or another. They'll not risk your wrath just from fear of an admittedly terrifying old woman. I think you'll be fine. Just keep showing up with gifts for Marya, sweets for Kelva, and she'll warm up to you in no time."

"You think so?" Ian said hopefully.

"Absolutely." Ezra said on his way out, "Besides if she was going to set the Ruskin Mob on you, she'd have done it already."

Leaving him with that comforting piece of information, Ezra let himself out of Ian's apartment and waded back through the tavern to the dwindling sunlight.

·　　·　　·　　·　　·

It was unseasonably cold for the time of year, accentuated by the early snows that started to fall as Ezra made his way down the streets of the borough. Aware of the time, Ezra knew he had scant moments before Slaght closed for the day so he cut through the market, winding his way through back alleys, until he arrived at the Apothecary's shop.

The sign said 'Closed' but when Ezra tested the knob, the door was unlocked. The inside was dark, illuminated only by the light from the windows. On the counter sat a paper-wrapped package with a note.

Ezra,
Sorry to have missed you but I was called away on business.
Lock up behind you,
Slaght

Ezra wondered vaguely whether someone had taken up an advert on the Town Bulletin, listing the day he was to be home and where he'd be going. He gathered up the medicine and made for home.

•　　•　　•　　•　　•

It was a good five minutes of petting, scratching, and dodging his cats before he was able to take off his coat and go to the bedroom. On his bed, of all places, sat Lucy, surrounded by orange fur balls. He hoped fervently that was not where they had also been born as he had no time to buy a new mattress. One of the kittens, pure white with yellow socks approached him and gave a tentative nudge of his hand with her head. He picked her up, she fit in the palm of his hand, and she curled up and fell asleep.

"Lily will definitely like you," Ezra said, more to himself than the sleeping cat.

Scanning the apartment, he felt the slightest twinge of homesickness. His mattress wasn't perfect, but it was better than the floor, and his kitchen only churned out poison-free food. Ezra thought of himself as a relatively simple person, with simple needs. Antony had been right the night Ezra had told him about this job, he was not a fan of the palace intrigue and the complexities accompanied it.

He left his things in the apartment, planning to pick them up on his way back to the castle, and left for dinner.

•　　•　　•　　•　　•

Dinner that night only accentuated his feelings of missing home. Pearl, after smacking him for not revealing the true nature of his latest job, gave him a hug that made his ribs twinge.

Far from being upset that she wasn't invited to the wedding, Pearl seemed overjoyed for Marya, and they spent most of the evening talking about what she would wear and the networking she could do. He wasn't quite sure how they managed to talk about dresses for an hour, but they did, and then some. Ezra was not in a talkative mood, so that suited him just fine.

His mind was elsewhere. Up at the castle, hoping he wouldn't return to find a dead prince. Once the pair realized their friend was a million miles away, they tried to re-engage him, pressing for details about the prince and the castle.

He told them about the secret rooms and tunnels he'd found, though he didn't tell them where, as well as the excessive extravagance that could be found throughout the castle. He told them about a woman who fainted in the hall after nearly bumping into him and a knight who clutched at his sword every time they were near one another. He told them about Mabel and Joe and Christophe and Adam, as well as Liliana, Lionel, and Danielle. He told them about preparations for the wedding and how, some of them, he would have rather avoided.

"It's purple, I hate purple," Ezra had said flatly, handing the jacket back to Joe.

Christophe, as Joe's best friend, would stand at the front as his Best Man. That meant that Ezra had to be a groomsman. And that meant that he had to suffer for things as random as Lissa's favorite color. Purple.

"It's more of a pale aubergine," Joe said.

"I don't care how many fancy words you use. I am not wearing purple." Ezra folded his arms.

"Ezra," Christophe hedged, "You agreed to obey all orders not related to my personal safety, did you not?"

"Yes..." Ezra said slowly, not liking where this was going.

"Then I hereby order you to wear this jacket to Joseph's wedding."

Ezra scowled, but his brow softened at the relief on Joe's face. This was the last party Joe was ever going to have, the least Ezra could do was look stupid in front of hundreds of people.

The two girls laughed at that, promising that he would look great in anything. Ezra knew they were just humoring him though. He looked terrible in purple. Like a scarred eggplant.

After dinner he walked them back to their respective houses and then made his way home, hoping to finally get a comfortable night's sleep.

Taking a shortcut, he passed through the market, where what appeared to be a rally was taking place. A man stood on a crate, yelling to the crowd who had gathered around him. Ezra paused, curious.

"People of Olaesta, I bid you think on what I have said. If we do not rise up against King Lionel, he will continue to oppress and deprive us of our rights! He adds countries to his collection with a ruthless, cruel force that drives its people to impoverished despair. And that's if they're lucky! So many Ruskins and Veldirs are dead and buried in mass graves with no one left to mourn them."

The man continued, oblivious to the three soldiers shoving their way through the crowd. They pulled him down from his makeshift podium and dragged him away. The man's screams cut off abruptly as one of the soldiers hit him on the head with the pommel of their sword.

Ezra glanced around to see if anyone else was surprised, horrified, or at least frightened by what had just transpired. But most of them wore an apathetic, glazed expression. The Ruskin man already forgotten in their minds.

Shuddering slightly, Ezra went home.

24

FUN AND GAMES

The biggest danger on a Shield job is the waiting. Usually, once the threat has been encountered, the job is done. But the waiting was Ezra's least favorite part. That and being stabbed. It was an honest tie, which one he found worse. It seemed, to the inexperienced onlooker, like Christophe was in the clear. No one came after him again and, for weeks, Ezra kept watch. No more archers, or javelins, or poisons. Just seemingly endless days of nothing.

Despite the considerable danger to all of them, Ezra actually welcomed the news that Christophe wanted to throw Joe a Stag Party in the city. According to Christophe, there was a high-end club at which the nobles gathered at. Joe didn't, because he was Joe, and Christophe didn't because he was the prince. But apparently now was as good a time as any to start living the bachelor lifestyle. Just in time for Joe to get hitched, with Christophe, if Ezra wasn't mistaken, not far behind. Sir Adam, and a few other knights agreed to accompany them.

So, on a cold, blizzardy night, the group set off in their carriages for The Hound's Club. Ezra had only agreed to this event if the entirety of the establishment was vacated, and he found that his instructions had been followed to the letter. Their party was the only one present in the whole of the gentleman's club. Even the staff had been given the night off.

Christophe patiently followed Ezra through the building as he made sure all doors and windows were securely locked. When they returned to the main sitting room, it was to jovial music. Sir Adam, it seemed, was something of a savant when it came to instruments. He spent the whole night flitting from the fiddle to the piano, playing music throughout the night.

The men played card games, drunken checkers - wherein shot glasses take the place of pieces—charades, and drinking songs with inappropriate titles and even worse lyrics. Ezra's favorite part was the stories the knights told. All about how Joe used to be wild, rebellious, and foolhardy.

"I'd pay good money to see that!" Ezra said to Joe, who made a gesture that sent everyone in attendance into fits of laughter.

The party carried on well into the night and, true to their natures, both the prince and the groom-to-be fell asleep in the carriage on the way back to the castle. The excitement of the evening had far exceeded any of their usual exploits. Ezra got them to bed as quickly as possible before settling in, himself. Ezra was almost too excited to sleep because tomorrow was his favorite holiday of the year.

Yule.

·   ·   ·   ·   ·

Though Yule came, and went, without any serious mishaps, Ezra was unable to relax for the duration of the festivities. Work had, once again, managed to ruin his favorite holiday. Though at least this year he wasn't freezing his manhood off in an igloo. That had been unpleasant.

The worst part about the day was the sheer number of people packed into the Great Hall. Nobles, ministers, lords, and senators. All were welcome for the royal Yule Day feast.

Ezra had already had to save the prince's life once that morning. A servant came by with some toast and eggs which turned black when introduced to Ezra's solution. The prince had been about to take a bite without clearing it with Ezra when the bodyguard shouted at him from across the room to "put the fork *down*". They didn't mention this to Joe who had been looking severely under the weather as of late.

At the feast, Ezra was gifted a Zouszian Imperial sword with a dragon etched into the blade, courtesy of Crown Prince Christophe. It was the most beautiful thing Ezra had ever seen, and he immediately buckled it to his belt, liking the new weight at his side. For Joe and the prince, courtesy of Marya, Ezra gave two embroidered handkerchiefs to be given to the women in their lives. Joe's relief was palpable, as he had clearly forgotten all about a present for Lissa.

On the day of Yule, a grand feast was held in the great hall. Presided over by the royal family, lords, ladies, merchants, and soldiers crammed into the hall to partake. Ezra, who normally would not merit an invitation to such an event, found himself sitting at the head table, between Christophe and Lily. The princess who had apparently found out exactly what it is Ezra did for a living, peppered him with all sorts of questions, some of which were not appropriate for someone her age. For instance: How many people have you killed? Where have you traveled? How many tattoos have you gotten? Is that how many people you've killed? Wow, that's a lot! Where'd you get that scar? How about that one?

On and on and on until she eventually fell asleep at her seat and was carried away by her lady's maid.

Christophe and Joe descended to the lower level of the hall and joined the soldiers in a set of drinking songs. Ezra would have preferred to go his whole life without hearing Joe sing. There was no doubt that he had passion, but the enthusiasm that he put into the song only seemed to make the screeching sound coming out of his mouth that much worse.

He looked to the main table and met eyes with Daniel, who raised a glass to him. Ezra had handed over one of Lucy's kittens that morning, hoping he was making the right decision by giving the prince a defenseless animal. But the prince had seemed so excited at the prospect of giving her to his sister that Ezra had relaxed.

Obviously, he hadn't presented the kitten to her yet, or that's all Lily would have talked about. At least then Ezra might have been able to contribute to the conversation. He knew a thing or two about cats.

What they discussed most was how upset Lily was that she had not been invited to the wedding. Despite the fact that the day was only a week away, she was returning to school the morning after next.

"I think it's ridiculous to send me there," She ranted in between spoon-fulls of plum pudding.

"I am hardly a child anymore and am perfectly capable of learning from the palace tutors that instructed my brothers." Ezra privately agreed with her, but for the sake of family peace, he insisted that it was better at the school as she would have girls her own age with whom to play.

This mollified her slightly, and she spent the rest of her waking moments talking about her friends.

Ezra missed his Yule dinner with his friends, but, as he watched Lily sleep, he admitted that this wasn't so bad.

25

A WEDDING

The home of Lord Joseph Burtness the First sat in the middle of a dense forest. Snow-covered pine trees were visible from the windows of the great hall where Ezra stood.

The ceremony was beautiful. There wasn't a dry eye in the temple as Joseph and Lissa exchanged their vows. Partly, because of the reason that they were having such a rushed ceremony, but also because, as it turned out, Joe was actually quite the poet. He described, in verse, the first day they met. How she'd been covered in dust and dirt from a long hard ride and the world seemed to stop for Joe, his heart, his mind, all of it. He described the most perfect moment in his life as he laid eyes on her for the first time. And when she smiled at him it was as if the sun had come out just for him. Even Ezra was a bit misty by the end. Next to him, Marya had let loose a honk while blowing her nose, such was the depth of her emotion.

Now he stood, side by side with the prince, in the great hall. He had not seen it with all the furniture that had been moved to the foyer for the feast, but with all the men and women dancing to the string quartet, he had a hard time imagining it as being used for anything but this. Scanning the crowd, he spotted the happy couple.

Ezra had never seen Lissa as carefree and buoyant as she seemed at this moment. She radiated joy as her new husband whisked her across the ballroom floor. Not just radiant, she was glowing.

"Joe didn't waste any time," Ezra chuckled to himself.

"What was that?" Christophe asked, glancing over towards the couple, lost amidst the dancers but for Lissa's crown of flowers that stood out in the crowd. Ezra was convinced it wasn't the crown that added the height, but that Lissa was actually floating from the happiness of it all.

They were going to be a repulsive couple.

"Nothing, Highness. I just need to hold on to Marya's knitting needles a little bit longer."

The last time he'd made footies and onesies, Ezra had had babies to borrow for the measurements. Now he'd just have to do it from memory and hope for the best.

"You mean Lissa is—?" He pointed to his stomach. Christophe had either developed observational skills of his own, or he was just that much better at interpreting Ezra's.

"Very subtle, Your Highness. And I'm no doctor but I'd put money on it, yes."

Christophe appeared overjoyed, but then he remembered why they were here and the smile fell.

"I expect that will be of some comfort to her after he's gone."

"He won't truly be gone, highness."

"If you want to use the business of souls watching over us as a method of comfort then let me tell you…"

"I wasn't going to," Ezra said, hands held up in surrender. "I merely meant that you should think of the impact his life has made. You have your life thanks to him. He told me he was the one who suggested my hiring in the first place. His friendship is the reason, these last few months, that you didn't give over to the kind of paranoia that I see so often in potential assassination victims. His child, or children, will be friends with your children and every time you see one of them, you will see him. It might be the shade of their eyes, or the way they pout when they don't get their way, or the occasional nostril flare. But you will see him."

Ezra turned to face the prince and was thoroughly discomfited to find that Christophe was crying. Not in the way that any normal person would cry when discussing the imminent death of a best friend. Even his tears carried decorum and would only deign to fall in two perfect lines down his face. He didn't even have a runny nose.

"Thank you, Ezra. That means more than you know."

He said nothing and only steered the prince towards the pastry table in the hopes that it would cheer him up.

Ezra was just demolishing his third piece of cake when he noticed something was off. One of the windows, previously closed and latched, now hung open an inch or two. Several men who he hadn't recognized, and had assumed were friends of Joe's, were now making their way off the dance floor and into the hall. Ezra scanned the crowd, panic gripping him, but he was able to find Marya easily.

Thank the gods for traditional Ruskin designs. Brighter than peacocks.

"We need to move," he urged Christophe, taking him firmly by the bicep and steering him towards Marya. She was explaining the way she dyed fabrics to a group of women when he came upon her.

"Marya I need to talk to you outside." She barely had time to register surprise before he took her hand and proceeded to drag both of his charges towards the hall.

They only just made it to the door when it happened. Ezra heard the ting of metal on stone and then an explosion knocked the three of them off their feet. Having wrapped his hands around their heads to protect them, Ezra was almost certain he'd broken the knuckles in at least one of his hands when they hit the stone. A sharp pain in the back of his leg signaled shrapnel. By the time he'd decided on a plan of action, the ringing in his ears had dissipated and he could hear the screams. Many of the ladies Marya had been speaking with lay unconscious next to Sir Adam who, it appeared, had been running towards them when he was knocked out.

Men and women cried out while the few children in attendance just cried. Rock still crumbled from the arched windows and rubble and glass were strewn everywhere. A snowy wind blew in from the broken windows, bringing the temperature down quickly.

He released his charges to flex his hands. The left had almost certainly broken, but the right was only bruised. Christophe had a hard head, go figure.

He examined the prince for obvious signs of injury first before moving on to Marya. Once he determined that both of them were fine, shaken, but fine, he turned to the leg which had a large piece of glass sticking out of it. He pointed it out to Marya, who immediately began tearing off pieces from her dress which she helped him to wrap. Without knowing how deep the shard of glass had embedded itself in his leg, he was unwilling to remove it without a healer present. She wrapped the bandaging as tight around the shard as possible and then made a sling that kept his left hand up against his chest. That, in and of itself, caused considerable pain. It seemed that he had broken his healing ribs, along with a few more.

He stood carefully and despite the pain, kept a firm grip on his sword.

"You two stay close to me," Ezra ordered. They only nodded, too stunned to say anything.

The men who had evacuated beforehand had fought their way through the panicked crowd of wedding guests and were filing back into the room, fixating on the prince and heading in their direction.

"You might have to defend yourselves." Ezra told them. "Are you armed, Christophe?"

To Ezra's relief, Christophe drew twin daggers from the sleeves of his jacket. Ezra turned to face the enemy but Marya grabbed him.

"You can't!" Marya cried, gripping his arm. "You're barely standing as it is!" Ezra shrugged her off and attempted to give a reassuring smile.

"That's the job," he said, kissing her forehead. "Let's get to it."

Four men charged him from the front while he sensed two behind him.

"Duck!" Christophe and Marya crouched as he swung his sword in an arc over their heads, easily batting aside the men's swords and slicing their throats. He continued the arc around to catch his first opponent in the ear, rooting his sword in the man's skull. He kicked the man away with his injured leg, the sound of his sword pulling free and his roar of pain called everyone's attention to them. He disemboweled the second, decapitated the third, and then turned to face the fourth man. His heart dropped. It was Daniel's shadow holding two scimitars in hand with no obvious injuries to speak of.

Ezra didn't stand a chance.

The funny thing is, Ezra had been looking forward to this fight. They both had. He could see it in the assassin's eyes, mixed with disappointment at the knowledge that Ezra had been seriously injured. This would not be the true battle they had been hoping for.

Of course, Ezra had a bit more to be upset about because he was the one about to die.

Ezra only hoped he could take Daniel's assassin down with him.

"Be ready," Ezra said over his shoulder before turning to face his doom.

And for the first time, Ezra heard the Shadow speak.

"I'm sorry it had to end this way."

That was all he said, but Ezra understood.

Ezra nodded. He was ready.

Surveying the room in a last-ditch attempt to rally some form of aid, Ezra was disheartened to see that Adam, the only knight remaining, remained unconscious.

The Shadow shrugged off his cape and drew his swords, twin scimitars of a simple, but deadly design. They shimmered in the candlelight, having been lovingly polished to a mirror-like finish.

Ezra's vision blurred around the edges as the blood loss began to take his toll. The broken windows, and the blistering cold wind that blew through them into the hall, were of great service. The cold kept him alert and the adrenaline coursing through his veins did the rest.

When the Shadow attacked, it was without warning, his movements lending themselves to the name Ezra had given him. Shadow became a dark blur, speeding towards Ezra with silent steps. Ezra just barely brought his swords up in time to block the assassin's attack, which nearly knocked him over.

Ezra kneed his opponent in the groin and used the time in which the Shadow was temporarily incapacitated to jump back, giving himself some room to breathe and settle into a defensive stance. His lungs burned, with each breath more difficult than the last.

Then the dance of blades began in earnest. In a fair fight, Ezra was certain he would win, for here, in his weakened state, they were evenly matched. Almost. As the fight continued Ezra began to lose ground, sustaining blows and cuts to his already battered body.

In a move so dirty that Ezra was not prepared for it, the Shadow kicked him in the thigh, driving the shard of glass deeper into his leg.

Ezra fell to the floor, swords too far away to reach.

The Shadow raised his sword to deliver the killing blow.

Ezra was ready, knowing he had done all he could.

It was time to see his mother.

What he hadn't been ready for was Adam picking himself up and stabbing the assassin in the back. It was hard to tell which face registered a greater level of surprise, Ezra's or the Shadow's. He looked down at the sword protruding from his chest, coughing up blood and spittle that ran down his chin, onto the floor. After that, the life left his eyes, and he collapsed, Adam's sword still impaling him.

There was a moment of silence and then—

"*What. Were. You. Thinking?*" Each word was accentuated by a slap from Marya on one of his less obvious injuries. "You could have died! And you just knelt there like a moron? Idiot!" she yelled, hitting him again.

"Joseph!" Lissa's scream grabbed their attention. It was raw and harsh.

Ezra knew what that scream meant.

In the center of the ballroom, Lissa knelt on the floor with Joe's head in her lap. He was smiling, talking to her. But for the table leg protruding from his stomach, he might have simply been resting. Sadly, that was not to be. He would never rest in the arms of his beloved again.

Christophe broke from Ezra's grasp and ran to his friend's side.

"No! We have to do something. Ezra, you must have something in that bag of yours. Save him," the prince ordered. Sara, who had escaped the brunt of the blast, limped towards them and laid a hand on her prince's shoulder. He reached up, taking her hand in his, seeking comfort in a comfortless place. She and Ezra exchanged a glance. They both knew what such an injury meant. Nothing in Ezra's medicine bag was capable of the miracle Christophe was asking for.

Ezra gave a small shake of his head, then turned to Joe, smiling.

"You really do know how to throw a party, eh Joe?"

Joseph laughed, blood spurting out of his mouth as he devolved into a coughing fit. Lissa leaned over him, shoulders shaking with silent tears.

"How else was I to keep your interest?" Joe shot back.

Ezra chuckled, kneeling next to the newlyweds.

"You have to tell him, Lissa." She glanced up, surprised. "Tell him now."

And it seemed as though that would be what would take her down, the edges of her mouth twitching violently. Instead, she took a deep breath and nodded, wiping her face.

"I'm pregnant, Joseph. You're going to be a father." She choked on the last word, her hands clutching his so tightly that it probably hurt.

Joe smiled wider than Ezra had ever seen before. It was the happiest Joe had probably ever been.

"A father?" he repeated. "Oh Lissa, thank you." Joe shuddered, a bubble of blood bursting at the corner of his mouth. "I don't think I ever really showed you how much I really loved you. I do though, Lissa. I love you more than anything in this world. Ever since I first saw you. I thought, 'that is the most beautiful woman in the world and I'm going to marry her someday'."

Tears now cascaded down Lissa's face and she made no further attempts to quell them. They fell from her cheeks to land on his.

"Don't cry, darling." Joe tried to wipe her tears away. Ezra could tell by the way his arm twitched and raised an inch from the ground before going still.

"You'll have the baby, and Christophe and Ezra to keep him safe."

"I don't know if it's a boy or girl," Lissa cried.

"Then they'll keep her safe. It doesn't matter—" Joe's voice began to fade. "The child will be of us, and they will be perfect." Then, with renewed energy, Joe's eyes widened.

"Christophe!"

"I'm here," the prince said, leaning over his best friend. This time Joe managed to reach up, pulling his friend down to whisper something in his ear. Then his grip on Christophe's collar loosened, and his arm fell to the floor.

"Joseph? Joseph!" Lissa clutched at Christophe, sobbing into his shoulder. Leaving Christophe to his grief, Sara knelt down and took Lissa in her arms.

Ezra reached out and felt for a pulse. He took a deep breath and then stood.

"I'm terribly sorry," Ezra said to the two of them. That was as far as Lissa was able to make it though, and she fainted into Christophe's arms.

The time for mourning had ended. They were in the middle of a war zone with no clear sign that the attack was over. Ezra pulled the leg from Joe's stomach before covering him with a tablecloth.

"Have someone find a healer and bring him here," Ezra addressed Sir Adam. "We don't know what injuries she may have sustained or if the baby can cope with the stress. Be careful, there may be more attackers," Ezra added before the knight vanished through the crumbling archway.

"Marya, find whatever clean cloth you can and start making bandages. Christophe, you come with me."

The two of them went to the kitchen where they gathered a pot of boiling water and some strong spirits. They dragged everything back into the ballroom where many of the guests had reappeared, clamoring to find out what had happened.

Ezra was irritated to see several knights amongst them, a handful of injuries between the lot of them. Where they had been when Ezra was fighting for the life of their future king, he did not know. One thing was certain, they were going to get a talking to from him, and they weren't going to like it one bit.

"You're going to need to address them," Ezra told Christophe. "It's important that everyone remain calm." Christophe nodded and turned to face the expectant crowd.

While Christophe did that, Ezra handed the water, alcohol, and his medkit over to Marya.

"Set up triage," He instructed her. "Find people you think are trustworthy and have them help. Keep an eye on Lissa." And, while still keeping an eye on Christophe, Ezra surveyed the damage.

It did not appear as though the room was at risk from any further collapse. From the bodies that scattered the floor and their distance from the blast radius, Ezra estimated around five dead with countless more injured. The movement that caught his immediate attention was from one of the attackers. He was still alive. Ezra worked quickly, tying off the man's wounds before securing him to the one pillar left standing. And, just so he didn't get any ideas about his tongue, Ezra stuffed a gag in his mouth.

With Sara by his side, Christophe was giving what appeared to be a rousingly inspirational speech. The people well enough to stand around him looked fiercely determined. Ezra walked up in time to catch the end.

"– swear to you all that I will find the people responsible for this and they will be brought to justice! Now, we need our fastest rider to get a message to the palace for aide. Adam, are you well enough to ride?"

He was favoring his wrist, which looked like it had been wrapped in a bit of Marya's skirt, but he bowed and gave a "Yes, sire."

"Then go. And only bring back people you trust." Adam put on the cloak someone handed him and was gone.

"Lady Marya is working to aid the injured, but anyone else with medical knowledge needs to help her. We don't know how soon a healer can arrive and, unfortunately, the healer that resided here has fallen." Christophe gestured to a man lying on the ground, the blue shroud of the healers wrapped around his waist.

Ezra had to give Christophe credit for not only being so observant but also not going into shock. He supposed it was unfair to judge Christophe's courage based on the past brushes with danger. The prince just needed a true disaster to bring out the leader within. And he was grateful that Christophe was, at the moment, surrounded by the knights Ezra trusted.

He approached just as the people were dispersing.

"That was well done," Ezra said. "We have a lot of work left to do, though. Is there a large space where we can transport everyone? The temperature is dropping quickly." The area around the shattered windows was already coated in snow.

"The foyer is large enough, if only just. We can move them there." Christophe started to give new instructions, asking that the people who could move, do so. Soon, only six injured were left. Three of them, women Marya had been standing next to, were dead from the explosion. Another two were in shock, a mother and her child clinging to one another. Ezra got them up and pushed them gently toward the foyer with everyone else. The last man was one of the assassins. While Ezra had tied the one up, and the others were dead, this one's gut wound had not been as deep as he'd thought. Well, two witnesses were better than one.

He dragged the unconscious man to the opposite side of the pillar and tied him up as well. Then he was alone with Lissa and Joe. Christophe had reluctantly left her with her husband so that he could attend to the rest of the wedding party. Ezra would not have let him out of arms reach, but the prince was surrounded by knights that Ezra had vetted. Christophe was safe for now.

Lissa sat still, her head bowed, Joe's head still resting in her lap. Were it not for the blood, he might have been sleeping. And in a way, Ezra supposed, he was. Joe had suffered the effects of his disease in relative silence, but Ezra had seen the signs. Much like the king, he had been getting slower, gaunter, in obvious pain. The only difference was, Joe didn't deserve any of it.

Ezra was suddenly overcome by rage. Rage at the unfairness of it all. Bad enough that Joe was already going to leave this world so soon, but to be taken in such a way? Unable to contain himself, he punched the remaining window, shredding the skin of his fractured hand in the process. He stood there, panting, almost overwhelmed by the pain. But he welcomed the pain because it gave him something else to focus on.

"Ezra," Lissa tugged on his sleeve and he turned to see her peering up at him with what were usually such cold eyes. Then they'd been warm with happiness. And now overflowing with tears.

"I'm so sorry, Lissa." Ezra pulled her into a hug and she sobbed quietly in his arms, at times, gasping for breath as she hyperventilated. He knew he should be in the foyer with Christophe, if not guarding him, then at least seeing to the wounded. But he just held her tight, and they both mourned.

Snow swirled around them in the empty, silent hall.

26

THE CALM

When help arrived, it came in full force. Thirty knights, escorting five healers rode in that morning, a miracle considering the distance. They lost another one of Marya's prospective clients during the night, but everyone else had survived. Most of the scars incurred that night had been emotional, not physical.

Ezra wished fervently he could say the same for himself. Lack of sleep, combined with the medical aid he'd provided while in his injured state, had left him unable even to ride a horse back to the castle. He was forced to sit in the carriage with Christophe, wincing every time they hit a bump.

Marya had wanted him to take some milk of the poppy to dull his pain, but it made him drowsy so he suffered through, fully cognizant of just how exposed their caravan back to the palace really was. Miraculously, the assault on the wedding seemed to be all of it. It had been a desperate, callous plan without regard for casualties. Ezra reflected that, even if he hadn't sensed something wrong in time, there still wasn't a guarantee that the prince would have been killed in the initial blast. He supposed that was what the assassins, now walking behind the carriage, were for; to take care of the prince, were he to survive, along with any witnesses.

The world seemed dimmer somehow, foggy around the edges and dull to the senses. He was exhausted, not just physically, but also emotionally. Logically, he knew the events that transpired were not his fault. He had done everything he could possibly have done and had counted on the knights assisting him to do the same. But one lone bomber was difficult to spot. Still, the depression washed over him, rising above his head, drowning him over the several hours it took to get back to the castle.

At one point, Christophe tried to say something, but whatever it was, he changed his mind. Marya spent the whole of the ride curled up, sleeping, her head resting on Ezra's lap.

They rode in silence.

•   •   •   •   •

News of what happened spread through the castle long before they arrived. When they did, it was to an intensified military presence and terrified staff. Christophe, Marya and Ezra were ushered up to the prince's quarters where Adam handpicked a pair of knights to guard the door.

Marya was escorted next door to Ezra's quarters for a bath and change of clothes and Mabel brought in hot bowls of soup. Christophe ate while Ezra changed the bandage on the prince's arm. A superficial graze, especially compared to Ezra's own injuries, but it was an injury nonetheless.

All of his sanitizing efforts, however, were for naught. Just as Ezra finished wrapping the bandage, he coughed up some blood onto it.

"Ezra!" Christophe cried although it sounded faint. Far away.

A faint ringing sound echoed in Ezra's ears and he was having trouble staying awake. Objectively, this didn't come as a big surprise. Considering his injuries and the fact that he hadn't taken his tonic in over a day, it was no wonder he was passing out.

Was he passing out? Perhaps he was just feeling poorly—

•   •   •   •   •

The first thing Ezra saw when he woke up was the canopy of his four-poster bed. Despite the months, he'd stayed in the palace, this was the first time he'd actually lain in the bed Christophe had intended for him, rather than the floor. It was quite comfortable.

He became aware of a hand, holding his, and turned to his right. Marya was asleep in a chair at his bedside, her hand clutching his with the same strength as when she was a child, reaching for an anchor in a tumultuous sea.

"How are you?" came a voice from his left.

He turned to see Christophe sitting with a book on the other side of his bed. Ezra struggled to sit up but all it took was a firm hand from the prince to keep him down.

"Embarrassed, mostly," Ezra admitted, causing Christophe to roll his eyes.

"Ezra, you had a shard of glass embedded in your leg, five broken ribs, one broken hand and the other cut up to all hell. The healer's also suspected a concussion and if you looked in a mirror, you're more purple than anything else. They say it's a miracle that you're even alive."

"Ezra?" Marya had woken up. He smiled at her and, after one second of smiling back, she burst into tears. He reached out to pat her on the shoulder and saw that his hand was wrapped in bandages. That's what he got for letting his frustration get the best of him. Of course, he'd had to go and break the one remaining window in that family's hall. He patted her on the head, wincing at the contact until she calmed down.

"We thought you were going to die," she sniffed, wiping her face with the handkerchief Christophe handed her. "They said you got most of your injuries protecting us from the blast." And that was enough to send her over the edge again. Ezra gave her some privacy and turned back to Christophe.

"How long was I out?"

"Only a few hours. And before you ask, I've made sure the prisoners are secured in individual cells, guarded by Adam's most trusted men. We will have their testimony." There was a steely look in his eyes and Ezra had a feeling Christophe wouldn't be as averse to torture this time around.

"And what was the King's response to these events?"

The ugly expression that appeared on Christophe's face was one Ezra had never seen from the prince before.

"My father 'expresses his heartfelt sympathies to the families of those affected by this tragedy'. Or at least, that's what his chamberlain claims he said. No one has seen him in the past couple of days. He may be dead already as far as I know."

"I need you to question the prisoners," Christophe continued. "I know you aren't well, but if you could stand to be moved, we could transport you in a wheelchair tomorrow. I don't want to leave this any longer than I have to."

Ezra stiffened at the suggestion of being treated like an invalid.

"Until the day I am dead, I will walk wherever I may go. Forgive me for asking, but if you would permit me the rest of the day for bed rest, I will be better tomorrow."

"Your pride may be the death of you, but so be it. Rest now, I'll have some food sent up and see you tomorrow," the prince said, making for the door.

"See you tomorrow? Where do you think you're going?" Ezra asked, trying and failing to sit up.

With a look of trepidation, Christophe returned to his seat.

"I was going to go prepare the councilors for the formal reading of the charges that I plan to make against my father."

"Well, that's stupid."

"I beg your pardon—"

"First off, Your Highness, we can't tell anyone about this. At all. Not until you are in the throne room with Sir Adam and his knights backing you up and the two assassins ready to testify. Going to the councilors now will only tip off your father and put you in danger." Ezra could see that Christophe was finally listening to him, and continued on before he tried to interrupt.

"Despite my weakened state, Your Highness, I am still your best chance of staying alive until this matter is resolved. My inability to get out of bed is only for the sake of my recovery. Should someone attack you, I am able to push down my pain and defend you and Marya."

A scoffing sound from behind him showed just how much faith Marya had in his ability to back such a claim.

"I have to agree with Marya, Ezra," Christophe said, almost sympathetically. "While I agree with your suggestion not to notify the councilors, I believe the knights outside my door are better equipped to handle any threat that I may face."

"That may be true, Your Highness. But do you really want to put it to the test?" Ezra asked simply.

After a few moments of consideration, Christophe pulled his book back out.

"Good. Now go sit next to Marya."

"Why?" Christophe asked, frustration leaking into his voice.

"Because apparently, you've learned nothing in the months that I've been here. Look at her. Her back isn't to the door, no one can see her from the castle outside your window, she can use my bed a shield should someone enter, and she's armed," Ezra said, giving a nod of approval to Marya who sat a little straighter, a small smile on her face.

Grumbling something unintelligible, Christophe got up and dragged his chair around the bed to sit next to Marya. He sat and held the book in front of his face so he wouldn't have to look at Ezra.

"Good. Now I'm just going to close my eyes for a little bit. Let me know if you sense anything suspicious."

"Yes, Ezra, we will," Marya said patiently, pulling the covers up to his neck.

And, without meaning to, he fell into one of the deepest nights of sleep in recent memory.

27

THE THREE TRUTHS

Joe had kept detailed records, all of the evidence against the king, compiled in a portfolio in his room. Ezra hesitated at the door, remembering the last and only time he had been in Joe's room. They had carried the knight in, Christophe and Ezra, and had laid Joe on the bed. He had been covered in blood but still in good spirits at the time.

With Joe's smile in mind, Ezra pushed open the door.

Waiting just on the other side was Ferdinand, tail wagging. Upon seeing Ezra, Ferdinand drooped slightly, his tail stilling. The dog whined a bit, peeking around Ezra's legs into the empty hallway, then he returned to his place by the fire and lay down, ears drooped sadly on the floor.

Ezra sat on the floor next to Ferdinand and scratched his ears. As he did so, the letter in his breast pocket crinkled.

Before the ceremony, Joe had brushed by Ezra, slipping a letter into his hand while Christophe wasn't watching. The message had been clear. He was to find a way to read it without the prince finding out. Now, sitting in Joe's room, Ezra could not find an excuse to put it off any longer. He unfolded the letter and read.

Ezra,

Soon I will be gone. I can feel death around my heart like a vice. Do not mourn for me, as these past months have been full of suffering that will soon come to an end. I welcome it. However, I am leaving things unfinished. Christophe needs someone by his side who he can trust. He has friends. People like Adam, who he can count on. But all of them have more than one agenda, and life has a funny way of twisting allegiances. There is only one person that, after months of watching, I believe is suited to take my place.

That person is you, Ezra.

Ezra took a deep breath, not liking the direction this was going in, and kept reading.

I know this was only supposed to be temporary for you, and you have no obligation to do this. Don't let my request bind you, unwillingly to this mission. I ask that, only if it is something you desire, that you stay by Christophe's side. I will be able to rest easier, knowing that he is taken care of. Give it some thought. There's no rush for an answer. I'm not dying for a while, yet.

For now, enjoy my wedding and tell Marya that Lissa loved the handkerchief.

Best regards,

JOSEPH

Ezra was stunned. He looked to Ferdinand for answers, for an explanation, for anything. But he had fallen asleep by the fire, absolutely no help at all.

Truth be told, over the past few months, Ezra had found himself feeling more and more at home in the castle. His thoughts drifted to his apartment with increasingly less frequency. More than once, he felt sad that his post by the prince's side would end. He'd even given extensive thought to what it would mean for him to remain at the palace. But it was crazy even to consider. Wasn't it?

Folding the letter and putting it in his coat, Ezra got to his feet, groaning in pain, and stretched, his injuries leaving him in a state of almost constant agony.

He couldn't take the time to rest, though.

Ezra had work to do.

•　　•　　•　　•　　•

The throne room was dead silent. No one moved, save some nervous fidgeting or pointed glances. To the right of the throne stood Ezra, by Christophe's side despite the prince's protestations. His only concession was the cane he leaned on with a sword concealed inside. The King was meant to arrive nearly an hour ago. Ezra didn't know if this was meant to be a power play to show everyone he still set the agenda or whether he was using the time to make his escape.

Daniel, who stood waiting on the left of the throne, received the most stares. For once, he appeared his age. Fear had taken away all the king's bravado that Daniel was so good at mimicking, leaving a pale, frightened boy.

Ezra was considering whether or not the prince would let him collect the king when the great doors were thrown open. A man he recognized as one of the royal healers stumbled into the chamber, gasping for breath. Upon seeing the crowd he froze, quite possibly taken aback by the audience. He took a moment to steady himself, cleared his throat, and spoke.

"His Majesty King Lionel is in the royal chambers. He collapsed on the way here. It is the collective opinion of his personal physicians that he is not long for this world. Prince Daniel has been summoned." Having finished, the healer took one last stabilizing breath before flinging himself back out of the throne room to return to the king's side.

Were he not present at this moment, Ezra would not have believed a room could get quieter. Even the birds took a moment of silence for the soon to be late King Lionel. The silence broke fantastically when Daniel sprinted out of the room.

The lords, however, remained silent, now looking to their future king. Christophe waited a moment, his face guarded, then followed at a dignified, yet rushed pace. At the door he stopped, nearly causing Ezra to run into him, and he turned to face the court.

"I would have the heads of their houses join me."

The words were barely out of his mouth before twelve men hurried to fall in line behind Christophe. They set off again, parade in tow.

Unease was palpable in the air. Servants could be seen scattered throughout the castle, but their work was left untouched. Those servants they passed down the hall were huddled together, pausing only to bow to the crown prince before resuming their gossip with renewed fervor. The kitchen, when they passed it carried with it none of it's usual, frenetic energy.

The entire castle held its breath, waiting.

When they arrived at the King's chambers the doors were open and Daniel knelt by the bedside, gripping his father's hand tightly. The healer's stood by the wall while a priest walked around the bed, swinging copious amounts of incense from an ornate thurible, because the king didn't have a hard enough time breathing before.

Everyone crowded into the – now even more so – suffocating space. Daniel stood and backed up until he hit the wall and, by the expression on King Lionel's face, he would have liked to do the same, were he able to stand.

"Get out of my chambers!" he managed to rattle, collapsing onto his pillows in a fit of coughing.

"I would, Father, but I wanted to see you and discuss some things before we go. If you'll only pardon me this childish whim, I would be most grateful." Christophe's voice sounded odd. Happy and angry. Ezra had never heard him speak like that before. It sent actual goosebumps up his arms.

"You serve me!" the King shouted, whether, at the guards or the lords, no one was sure. "Get him out!"

No one moved, save for Christophe, who approached his father and sat in a chair at his bedside.

"They serve the Kingdom father, and it is their right to hear the truth before you pass on. Do you remember what you told me when I was a child?" Christophe asked, his voice softening slightly. "You told me that there were three truths to everything. 'My truth, your truth, and the truth.' I think we all deserve to hear that truth, father."

"Do you hear how he's talking to me? Is this the man you would have as your King? I bet you're happy I'm dying!" Too weak to lift his head, he was now ranting at the ceiling.

"I can't say that I am happy to be an orphan, no. And I'm certainly not as happy as you would have been were our roles reversed. I just want to know why father. I've made some educated guesses, but I want to hear it from you. Why have you been trying to kill me?"

The Lords started muttering but a glare from Ezra silenced them.

"You never honestly believed I was going to let a mutt like you succeed me! A byproduct of a loveless, arranged marriage that my tyrant of a father arranged. I have only one son, and he is at my side where he belongs. Not standing accusingly over my deathbed!"

Lionel's words hung in the silence that followed. Taking a quick glance at the lords, Ezra saw their once sympathetic faces hardening. Squabbling within the royal family was one thing, but attempted infanticide was another matter altogether.

"And you couldn't risk disowning me because I gave you no cause and, without that, you'd invite war with the Zouszian Empire," Christophe punctuated, more for the benefit of driving it home for the lords than to further inform his father of why he was a scumbag.

"What proof do you even have? All I hear are empty accusations! Yes, I wanted you dead, but you can't prove I tried to have you killed!"

This was the part where Joe was supposed to come in leading all the witnesses and carrying the more than damning evidence. Instead, Ezra opened the door, and a few terrified servants, some guard-escorted knights, and the two assassins filed in. The King clearly recognized them because his face temporarily shifted from pale to purple before settling on a splotchy feverish pink.

He then turned on his favored son.

"You stupid, idiot boy. What part of 'Take care of them!' didn't you understand?"

Daniel muttered something at the floor.

"Speak up, boy, I'm dying!" the king managed to yell, hoarsely.

"I said," Daniel shouted, eyes watery, "that I didn't think anyone else needed to die!"

The stunned silence that followed was shattered by the king's raspy cough that shook the bed.

"Then—Prince Daniel—are you confirming your brother's claims?" one of the Lords spoke up. "Is it true that you and His Majesty orchestrated a plot to kill Crown Prince Christophe?"

The king took a deep breath to yell something, but he was deflated by Daniel's simple, quiet, "Yes."

The prince looked devastated. But his grief was nowhere near that worn on Christophe's face. Ezra thought that maybe, despite everything, he had been holding out hope his brother wasn't really involved.

"You!" the king raged, pointing wildly at Daniel. "*You little*—" He clutched his arm and fell back in bed. The healer's rushed to his side, fussing over him for several minutes before stepping away solemnly.

"The King is dead. Long live the King!"

And the healers knelt. Then the lords, then Daniel and finally, for the first time since they met, Ezra knelt before him.

Since he was a child, forced to pay respect to the lords of the fighting pits, Ezra had knelt to no one. It wasn't until that moment that he knew what he wanted to do for the rest of his days. Ezra gave no thought to whether or not he wanted to; it simply felt right to pay respect to his king. Christophe had earned that tenfold.

When everyone stood, it was to find Christophe standing a little straighter. His face, a little more solemn. It betrayed none of the jumping and cheering that Ezra would undoubtedly have done in the event of his own father's death. Ezra could see the wheels spinning in the new king's head, no doubt overthinking what he should say. His first words as king. In the end, he found what was right.

"Well," King Christophe said, taking a deep breath. "We've got some work to do."

E

EPILOGUE

After weeks cooped up in the castle, healing and helping Christophe, a hunt was exactly what Ezra needed. He'd been tracking his prey for three days. In an effort to remain unseen, he could only move at night. The path was widely traveled, which made specific footprints nearly impossible to find. But he found them. The hoof prints of a galloping horse stood out on the muddy road.

He stood and looked ahead at the dirt road, where the signs of a single rider hurrying east were obvious. The marks were free of the morning dew that coated everything in a crystalline blanket. They couldn't be more than fifteen minutes old.

Daniel was close.

Ezra mounted up and pushed his horse to a gallop. He had already been away too long, and only hard riding on the return journey would allay any suspicions as to his absence. Should anyone ask, Marya was to confirm he had left the country to close out some old, standing contracts. Thankfully, that was unnecessary. Ezra had cut ties with his foreign clientele years ago.

"We are letting him go, Ezra," Christophe had told him. And as far as Ezra was concerned, he'd followed his King's orders to the letter. He'd let Daniel go. Christophe had, in no way at all, clarified that Ezra couldn't then go after and squash the little bug. However, just in case

the king was not as willing to accept this loophole, Ezra was determined that he never find out. That no one ever find out.

The sun still rested just below the horizon, but it was light enough for Ezra to see the rider up ahead. As far away as he was, he could still see that the horse was about to collapse. The rider, hopefully, Daniel, wielded his riding crop with an ever-increasing ferocity. Ezra could hear the slap of leather against flesh over their combined galloping.

"Hyah! Hah!"

Ezra knew without a doubt that it was the prince he was chasing. He easily recognized Daniel's weak, fearful cries.

The prince then took the only path open to him. He yanked hard on his horse's reigns and they disappeared into the woods. Perhaps he thought to get lost in the gloom of the forest. It was a smart idea and would have worked on anyone else. Ezra stopped at the edge of the brush and dismounted.

The thicket was two if not three feet tall. He could see the bristle bushes and could only imagine what kind of thorny plants hid in wait. Unless the thicket cleared up, this would likely be an arduous journey on foot, but it would definitely be a painful one for his horse, Clio.

Ezra tied Clio up just within the shelter of the trees, not so far in that she would injure herself, but enough to obscure her from passersby. He slipped on his gloves, retrieved the machete from his saddlebags, and resumed his pursuit.

The cold he'd cursed during the greater part of this hunt was now his friend. It meant that the buds had yet to bloom, giving him far more light than he would have had, come spring. It also meant an easier time wading through the bristly, thorny plant life. His horse would have cut herself to ribbons.

He began to sweat from the effort, despite the cold and took a rest. The sun had risen, so he had his bearings, and he knew he was on the right path due to the trail of destruction Daniel's steed had left in its wake. He'd only managed a few sips from his waterskin before a great crash shook the forest, sending birds into the sky.

Ezra heard the screams of the horse and Daniel's cursing and sensed the hunt was finally over. Silence was impossible with all the underbrush, so he went for speed. His feet carefully picked over roots and jumped thickets where they could. Now, so close to the end, was not the time to trip up or twist an ankle.

Ironically, when he caught up to Daniel, Ezra almost tripped over him. Daniel knelt in a clearing, at the edge of a small cliff. He did not react when Ezra approached, nor did he attempt to run when the assassin joined him at the cliff's edge and peeked over. Some ten feet down, his horse lay in a shallow riverbed. At least one leg was obviously broken, and it lay there, breathing heavily. In too much pain to move. Or to scream. Just waiting for the end. Much like Daniel, who sat at Ezra's feet, staring blankly at his horse.

"Are you here to kill me, Ezra?"

Daniel had never sounded older than he did right then. His voice bore the weary quality of those who had lived too much. The old men Ezra had come for in the dead of night, all had that quiet, wistful tone. And in many of them, as he heard in Daniel, there was a sound of relief. The struggle had come to an end. The pressure to live on, to meet expectations, and to fight when they'd rather rest, all of that would finally be over. When he did not respond Daniel glanced up, and Ezra saw hope.

"I used to be a good brother, you know," Daniel continued, filling the silence. "But I could not be both loyal brother and filial son in that household. I had to choose. My father was almost benevolent in his negligence towards Christophe. I was the one who took on all our father's expectations." Ezra sat on the edge, next to the prince. He bore the last words of so many. Etched into his soul forever. He would let Daniel speak until the end.

"Christophe was borne of an arranged marriage. Everyone assumes that's why my father hated him. I know that's what he said, in the end, at least. And for all I know it may have been true. But I think father hated him because he's a good person. Christophe has this sense of justice that stands strong, but not so strong that he is inflexible. And he is always willing to see the other side of things, his morals can bend enough to be a ruler, but not so much that they will break. Father knew he could never mold Christophe as grandfather molded him, and so he resented my brother. Luckily, he had a second, weaker, more malleable son in me."

Ezra did not need to look to see the tears on Daniel's face. He heard them in the prince's voice.

"The King nurtured darkness within me until I couldn't see Christophe's light. Or my mother's. Mother's love for a son who wasn't even hers just became a source of resentment within me."

Daniel turned to Ezra, and he met the prince's hollow, red-eyed gaze.

"I've made so many mistakes." Daniel's statement reminded Ezra that the prince was only eighteen years old. Eighteen years old and already the leader of a failed uprising.

"Are you telling me all this so I won't kill you?" Ezra asked. He thumbed the blade of his sword thoughtfully, waiting for the prince to beg.

"That was not my intent, no," Daniel replied, contradicting Ezra's expectations.

"Then why?" Ezra asked, barely suppressing a yawn. The high from the chase was wearing off fast.

"I've never told anyone the things I just told you. I don't think I even said them out loud. I just wanted someone to—someone to know. You know?" Daniel was on the edge of panic. The shock-borne numbness that had kept him calm up until this point was starting to fade.

"I do understand." And Ezra did. "But everyone has pain. Most of us don't attempt fratricide."

Ezra couldn't help but think back to the day the two of them had first met. An arrogant, apathetic child, he had just killed a great Ruskin white bear. To many Ruskyans, the killing of such a creature was evil. They considered the bear to be the soul of their country and to kill one was to bring a curse down upon yourself.

Maybe they were right. Maybe Daniel was cursed by some bear god. A good deal of unfortunate things had happened in his life since that event. The first and foremost being Ezra's entry into the castle.

"I love my brother. Even in the end, when he banished me, I could see he still loved me. I don't know how I lost sight of that." Daniel sighed deeply and reached inside his jacket. Ezra tensed, but Daniel only pulled out a letter.

"Give this to my mother. It says I've sailed south and not to worry about me and that I'm happy. Please, do this for me, won't you?"

Ezra nodded, taking the letter and stuffing it in his bag.

The young prince looked up towards the sunrise. It was beautiful. The sun, a deep orange, was accentuated by purples and pinks.

A new day.

"One last sunrise," Daniel said dreamily. "A perfect send-off. Isn't it beautiful Ezra?"

Ezra stood behind Daniel, sword at the ready.

"It really is." Ezra agreed.

And he swung.

•　　•　　•　　•　　•

He buried the prince in a grave deep enough to protect him from the animals. The ground was so hard that digging took a good part of the morning. He marked it with Daniel's sword and the sunstone the prince had kept in his pocket. Ezra hoped, not for the first time, that there was an afterlife. For Daniel had not had enough living in this one.

Filthy, tired, and in considerable pain, Ezra returned to his horse and made for the capital and his new home.

ABOUT THE AUTHOR

Writing since she was twelve years old, Emma has pursued many original stories as she honed her gift. She is an avid reader, having recently purchased her fifth bookcase. Emma lives in Michigan with her two cats, Echo and Kira, who were the inspiration for *The Sword and Shield*.

Learn more about Emma by visiting her blog at www.emmakhoury.com

ACKNOWLEDGEMENTS

This book would not have been possible without the involvement of a great many people. I will always be eternally grateful to my agent Alyssa for seeing something in this book and taking a chance on a new author, as well as my many beta readers who helped in building my confidence that this was actually a decent book and not a load of garbage. I want to thank my family and friends for supporting me and encouraging me to follow my dreams and for making sure I always know that I am loved. Most of all, I want to thank my Dad, whose unflinching faith in my abilities pushed me to be the best writer, and person that I could be.

I also want to thank my cats, Echo and Kira, for maiming me to the point that it took way too long for the scratches to heal. Without their loving abuse, I would never have had the idea about an assassin with an immune disorder.

NOTE FROM THE AUTHOR

Word-of-mouth is crucial for any author to succeed. If you enjoyed the book, please leave a review online—anywhere you are able. Even if it's just a sentence or two. It would make all the difference and would be very much appreciated.

Thanks!
Emma